Praise for Christian Baines

For *The Arcadia Trust* series

"Baines' brave new underworld is well devised, multi-layered, and dense with political and personal agendas—and it's frightening: so much so that I found myself looking over my shoulder more than once at night." FELICE PICANO, author of *Like People in History*

"Baines has a gift for twisted psyches, playing the supernatural to expose the human evils at play, and a talent for turns of phrases that leave you shuddering even as you turn the page." 'NATHAN BURGOINE, author of *Light*

"I love the world created here. It has the same feel as Laurel K. Hamilton's Anita Blake Series, with a little more grit, and of course, the added m/m element. There is plenty of paranormal elements involved, some more gruesome than others, but it is a very colorful and interesting story." JUSTJEN, *The Blogger Girls*

"Just fantastic! I'm just amazed by the imagination the author put into this, from the culprit to the resolution I just couldn't put it down." SARINA, *Love Bytes Reviews*

"A wickedly subversive wit." JEFFERY ROUND, author of *The Dan Sharp Mysteries*

"I really enjoyed this book and have great admiration for Baines' literary skill. My reaction to *The Orchard of Flesh* is that it's something of a mashup of Clive Barker and Noel Coward." ULYSSES, *Prism Book Alliance*

For other works

"Christian Baines is a writer with a bold, original vision, a vision not beholden to the limits of conventional genre tropes. This is a writer who knows his own voice, and a writer to watch." MICHAEL ROWE, author of *Enter, Night*

BY CHRISTIAN BAINES

THE ARCADIA TRUST *series:*
The Beast Without
The Orchard of Flesh
Sins of the Son
Tears in Time

Other books:
My Cat's Guide to Online Dating
Skin
Puppet Boy

CHRISTIAN BAINES

TEARS IN TIME

Christian Baines is an awkward nerd turned slightly less awkward author. Raised on dark humour and powered by New Zealand wine, he is the author of six novels including gay paranormal series The Arcadia Trust, Puppet Boy, Skin, and My Cat's Guide to Online Dating.

Born in Australia, he now travels the world whenever possible, living and writing in Toronto, Canada between trips.

TEARS IN TIME

ISBN 13: 978-1-9995708-5-9

FIRST EDITION: MAY 2024

EDITOR: L E DANIELS
COVER DESIGN BY JEANINE HENNING

Acknowledgements

First off, ***grazie mille*** to Elisa Rolle, who despite keeping my Italian phrases honest and accurate, was egregiously omitted from acknowledgements in *Sins of the Son*. On top of that, she's way too classy to say anything about it. Elisa, please accept my profound apologies and thanks!

Thanks again to editor extraordinaire and real-life Morticia Addams L.E. Daniels for all your patience, flexibility, hard work, and friendship since the beginning, and to my amazing cover artist Jeanine Henning for keeping the boys pretty.

Writing community is everything in this vocation, so thank you to author colleagues and friends, Kevin Klehr, J.P. Jackson, Jeffrey Round, A.J. Dolman, James K. Moran, David S. Pederson, 'Nathan Burgoine, Jerry L. Wheeler, Barbara Ann Wright, Nicole Disney, Felice Picano, Eric Andrews-Katz, Rob Byrnes and many others who've supported, signal-boosted, organized events and readings, and helped me in ways big and small.

Thanks to friends and family in Canada and Australia for accepting, encouraging and supporting me. Your love, signal-boosting, and patience when I'm all but ready to quit never cease to amaze and humble me.

Finally, thank you Dean, for your boundless patience and support as a creative mind and ego that has to live with mine.

TEARS IN TIME

By Christian Baines

CHAPTER ONE

Michel Beauvrie had learned early in life how to satisfy both a greedy landlord and a rapidly emerging appetite for human blood. With mesmerising beauty and supernatural guile, he'd walked the docks of eighteenth-century Marseille, inviting sailors with coin and well-to-do widows alike into his bed. Such prostitution has seen many of us Blood Shades through lean times. Such are the blessings of unageing flesh.

Nature, however, had rubbed a fly into Beauvrie's supernatural ointment. He'd been gifted immortality, but not agelessness. As the renowned allure of his twenty-something body gave way to thirty, then forty, his feeding became less transactional and more predatory. Tales of the beautiful youth with strong yet delicate hands that would attend a seafarer or sea-widow's every desire faded from the port. In their place emerged tales of a curse on the docks, disappearing those who might once have sought decadence in Beauvrie's bed. The mortals conjured several explanations for these vanishings, from divine punishment to a secretive drinking game with unimagined riches for the winner and dire consequences for the loser.

Some forty years passed before one witness, albeit after a night's drinking that put his tale under heavy scrutiny, claimed to have seen a corpse-like visage bent over a woman's throat, blood dripping on the cobblestones as sure as the contents of the witness' bladder as he stood there, aghast at the yellow-grey skin, stretched like parchment over sharp, angular bones. When Beauvrie looked up at him, bloody fangs bared, hissing with naked rage and barely sated hunger, the drunkard fled, barely making it back to the tavern where, pants soaked with piss, he had attempted in broken French to tell of what he'd seen. He'd been laughed out, despite recounting the particularly unnerving detail that the monster's face had been that of a young man, smooth and alluring as Beauvrie had ever been, framed in stitches. In the middle of this unbroken visage of youth, sunken, dark eyes as dead as the rest of the creature's body had fixed on him.

The drunkard had been found two days later, hanging by his wrists from a gangway, partly flayed and eviscerated from neck to groin, his remaining skin pierced with fishhooks. Attempts to find the perpetrator yielded nothing, even after several weeks.

One story claimed Beauvrie had fled to Scotland to live among the Kelpies, seducing and dragging wayward hikers to a bloody, watery end. Besides the improbability that a ravenous Blood Shade could pass among such secretive members of the House of Magick, this optimistic interpretation had failed to account for one insurmountable factor. Once venerated for his beauty, now trapped in a rapidly decaying corpse that would not die, Beauvrie had gone quite insane.

Among humans, the once golden boy of Marseille had become the nightmarish antagonist of tavern gossip. But for all its posturing as a self-appointed ruling authority over Blood Shades, the House of Blood took such a liability more seriously. With the Scotland theory debunked, they cast their net across Europe and captured Beauvrie within the year. His sentencing coincided with a short-lived idea that instead of final execution, offenders should instead be offered a chance at redemption, as far from home as possible. This was, after all, what the mortals of the time were doing.

They transported Beauvrie in a sealed coffin with a stake through his blackened heart. This had proved necessary after the first such transport had ended in a slaughter that years later worked its way through rumour to the pen of one drunken yet industriously creative Irishman. Such a mistake was not made twice. Beauvrie's immediate fate upon reaching Australia can only be guessed at, beyond the fate of the poor mortal fool who removed the stake. Beauvrie soon vanished into myth, until a bloody slaughter at a cattle station in south-east Queensland, along with tales of a pale, corpselike figure with sharp fangs and wispy white blond hair, had left little doubt of his survival.

Had the station's owners not been implicated in acts of murder, rape, and kidnapping against the local Aboriginal nation, this crime might have been punished more severely. But the House, whether for appearances, or as a political manoeuvre to smooth relations with the New World's immortals, had by this time condemned the colonial treatment of indigenous peoples. This change in policy earned Beauvrie another reprieve in the form of further banishment, this time from all inhabited dry land.

"You mean he couldn't set foot on land at all?" Giorgios asked me, eyes wide with wonder as the tiny Blood Shade sat upright in bed, his prematurely changed body quivering. "That he was to swim in the ocean forever?"

"Was to swim?" I asked, giving the childlike immortal a wicked fanged grin in the dark. "Dear child, he plagues the waters still. Some say he circles the Australian coast, picking off surfers and divers while the riptides take the blame."

Giorgios shook his head, a stubborn frown frozen on his little face as he threw back the blankets and got out of bed. "It sounds perfectly horrid. Why doesn't he go into the sun? I wouldn't want to live like that."

I'd not expected sympathy for Beauvrie's plight to be his takeaway from my story. But then, the Premature, though he'd come into this existence as a tender preteen, was at least as old as I. Such a mind was nothing if not agile with empathy and nuance.

"Where are you going?" I asked, following him up the torchlit hallway, where the polished wood floor gave way to bare sandstone. I couldn't remember coming this way. Come to that, I wasn't at all sure where we were.

"I'm thirsty." He led me around the corner without another word.

"You've just fed." Admittedly, I couldn't remember where or on whom. An immortal trapped in the body of a child, a Premature's appetite was as unpredictable as their early deliverance into nocturnal life itself. Fate was fickle, and so was feeding time. "I think you should go back to bed."

"Just a little further. I can smell them."

Smell whom, exactly? "Did I mention Michel Beauvrie's favourite delicacy is little boys who don't stick to their bedtime?"

"Hush! I won't be a minute."

I rounded one more corner to humour him, but enough was enough. I'd obliged the child with the scariest true story I knew. At no point had I agreed to babysit. I placed my fingertips on the stone wall and dragged them along with the satisfying sound of scraping stone. "Giorgios," I whispered between metallic squeals. "Giorgios."

He turned with an annoyance that poorly masked fear. He opened his mouth to protest, but only yielded a repetitive breathy chant.

Nephthys. Nephthys. Nephthys. Nephthys…

The voice wasn't his. Other words from an otherworldly tongue snaked into the mantra before a tall shadow blocked the torchlight behind Giorgios. By the time I shouted a warning, the sweet, coppery scent of his blood had already filled the air. He mewled a silent plea to the man towering above him in the shadows, then collapsed.

I couldn't move. I'd gone to rush the figure or snatch the boy away, only to be frozen in place, an unwilling witness to the silent cruelty not of some ocean-dwelling Blood Shade monster, but a man who now retreated to the shadows as if nothing had happened.

When I could move again, it hit me like a punch to the gut. But Giorgios couldn't be dead yet. We were immortal, damn it! With enough blood, he could be restored.

The only blood I could smell was already flowing from the boy into the furrows of an eight-pointed star—a symbol of the Shapers and their arcane ways—cut into the sandstone. Its potency pricked at my appetite like dozens of small pins as the breathy chant invoking Nephthys caressed me, sliding over my arms, back, chest, and legs. The combination of scent and words intoxicated me with pure, selfish want.

The unknown language sharpened, insistent. I wanted to help the boy. I'd seen his sister murdered in a cruel illustration of power, and I would be damned if I stood by and watched Giorgios share her fate. But desire had already overwhelmed both my conscience and good judgement.

I lowered myself to the carving and drank, allowing the sweet taste of the Giorgios' immortal blood to warm my ageless heart. Instead of satisfying my hunger, the taste only made me more ravenous. I licked the stones clean as fresh blood trickled its way down the troughs that formed the star. As it slowed, my heart quickened, unwilling to be denied more, determined to finish this wicked deed no matter the cost to my sanity or soul. I could not feed from the dead, but… Giorgios was not dead! The child gave a few futile quivers as I bit hard into his throat, drawing what fresh blood remained. His tender whimpers gave way to the moans of a grown man.

I didn't recognise Jorgas until it was too late to stop.

*　*　*

While humans are prone to talking through their dreams, awakening with a startled cry, or drenched in cold sweat, we immortal and ageless creatures are not so delicate. As a rule, we don't 'dream' at all, at least not in the way humans do. Yet, I had. My heart thumped as if it could break through my chest. Drenched with pink sweat, I could still feel the harsh stone on my fingertips and taste the Premature's sweet blood on the back of my throat.

But from recounting the legend of Beauvrie to draining Jorgas, the whole encounter had been as harmless and false as any human nightmare.

The familiar scent of the—very much alive—young man who lay beside me sweetened the room, calming me as I drew it in with each breath. Undisturbed, Jorgas lay on his back, one muscular arm flopped above his head, showing off a thatch of dark hair that thinned to almost nothing before fading into the soft down that covered his solid chest. The snarling tiger tattoo that decorated his pectoral seemed humorously at odds with such a vulnerable position.

As a man of surprising wisdom had reminded me, we all had our guardians.

I remembered putting Jorgas to bed as soon as we'd arrived home. Without a stitch of clothing on his back, much less the energy to fight me, the werewolf had accepted my help with uncharacteristic grace. I'd like to think I'd earned that trust as his sometime lover, but did I flatter myself? Would he have fallen as eagerly into the arms of the Shaper who'd helped me? Maybe. But if Jorgas and Iain had a past, I would not allow it to ruin the gift of the present. He could rest in my bed as long as rest would take.

I could also not accept that Iain was dead. Surely, I would have felt it, after all he'd shared? As a warlock—or Mentalist, as he preferred, he'd shared his knowledge of the realm to which his colleagues had banished Jorgas. He'd led me there himself, at great personal risk. Perhaps Iain had even shared his heart, in so far as he had one. Oh, yes, we'd shared perhaps too much for a Blood Shade and a Shaper. I could not accept his loss any more than I could reconcile my guilt at having left him behind. Of course, I'd had no choice. As I'd watched Iain be swallowed into a sea of snarling abominations, our sole gateway out of that infernal place had begun to close.

And what of the others I'd left behind? Had they seen us? It seemed unlikely that they'd shared even our perception of the place, which for me had manifested as Berlin, where I'd made my home just before the Nazi ascension. This made for a second time I'd escaped it, and the survivor's guilt had sucked on both occasions.

But I had rescued Jorgas. Selfishly, I accepted our losses. Not that my mentor, Colin, or Luca, the son of my dearest late friend had agreed to that trade-off. But I would get them back too, somehow.

Jorgas turned on his side. Never mind my own nightmares. How restless was sleep after what he'd endured? When had he last eaten? I got up and wobbled my way to the kitchen. There was no telling the realm's effects on my physiology, but we'd both need sustenance soon. I flipped on the kitchen light and pulled out the espresso maker.

Demetrius would need feeding as well. I tutted a few times, lifted the bag of treats from under the sink and called my cat's name. It was unusual not to have him pawing my chest or weaving around my ankles first thing in the evening. Such silence usually meant he'd ventured upstairs to enjoy the off-cuts of my neighbour's kitchen. Dorotha, my faithful tenant for longer than Demetrius had been alive, made no secret of her affection for 'Pooska,' and spoiled him rotten at every opportunity.

I opened the fridge only to find a bottle of poppers and a reminder that I never bloody learn. I remembered a gag gift, a lewd magnet with the words 'fill me' that now languished somewhere in the bottom of a drawer. Fortunately, my freezer still contained several of Dorotha's specialties. For all his loyalty, Brett, my Mannequin, could scarcely burn a pot of boiling water if asked to cook.

Where was Brett?

I slid the brick of paprika-rich frozen stew into a saucepan and set it to heat before retrieving my phone. No messages. No calls. No power. Really? I checked to see the charger was properly connected. It was. One more casualty of our trip through Hell. Brett would know what model replacement to buy.

As Jorgas' food warmed, I turned the vision over in my head. Michel Beauvrie? Hardly a story for children! But then, as the execution of Giorgios had confirmed, I wasn't much of a babysitter. The faceless figure, the taste of… Eesh! Yet, what stood out most in memory was the engraving. The Shapers could explain it, but with Iain, I'd lost my most reliable, if not entirely forthcoming expert on Shaper lore.

I snapped off the stove, poured a cup of steaming hot coffee and spooned the stew into a bowl. Not the most romantic of breakfasts in bed, but it would have to do. I returned to the bedroom to find Jorgas propped up against the pillows, arms flopped to either side, his solid, athletic body stretched out for my inspection. The sheet that covered his lower half barely concealed a telltale bump.

"What's up?"

Taking his offhand flippancy as a good sign, I passed him the coffee and stew.

"Thanks. Lifesav—Ow!"

"Are you all right?

"Yeah." He winced, setting the bowl and cup on the bedside table. "Except for everything hurting."

"Take it easy," I said, sliding in beside him. "I have no idea what you've been through."

This was no hyperbole. It was a rare human that returned from the Patrons' realm unchanged. We called those that did 'the Mutilated' for a reason. I had no clue what being used to prop open a doorway into that realm, or at least, the thin layer that separated our reality from theirs would do to a werewolf body.

"I'm just grateful you're still here."

"Yeah, yeah. Feelings don't suit you." He grinned, picking up the coffee and taking a sip before making a disgusted face.

"What's wrong?" I asked.

"I think that's yours." He passed the mug to me.

"I don't drink—"

"Blood?"

I sniffed the mug. Sure enough, Type O. I took a sip and spat it out immediately, trying not to spill the rest of the foul liquid.

"No good?" Jorgas asked.

"No good? It's petrol!"

"Petrol?" He leaned in and sniffed the mug. "It's not."

"Do you want to taste it again?" I set the mug on my bedside table. Maybe the Wound had messed with our taste buds. Whatever. I could always make more coffee. "How are you feeling?"

"Besides fuckin' hungry?" He reached for the stew with another wince.

"Let me." I reached over him and picked up the bowl, almost dropping it when he licked my chest, his mouth lingering on my nipple before he shovelled a spoonful of stew into it. He'd be all right. "Is it okay?"

He moaned, downing another spoonful. "Heaven!"

Assured he wasn't in for another rude shock, I watched him eat, comforted by the messy human-ness of it. Questions could wait, though I had dozens. Jorgas would need to know what had happened at the Arcadia Trust, about what the House of Magick had done to the Scimitar of Light, and about the friends we'd lost in the crossfire. And Iain. I wouldn't hide my relationship with Iain from him, even if he was reluctant to talk about his.

Jorgas put the empty bowl aside. A good sign. "So, what's been going on?"

I couldn't help it. I laughed, damn near dropping my human veneer as the sound bounced around the room. Perhaps I should have been angry. Furious that he'd abandoned me and embroiled himself in a Shaper plot that had put him in so much danger. But hadn't we all?

"Actually, where's my phone?"

Priorities?

"I pulled you out of that place naked. You don't remember?"

Jorgas shook his head.

"The machine you were in? Berlin?"

"Berlin?" His eyes widened. "No."

"The Nazi creatures?"

"Nazi…? I don't remember any of that."

Maybe this lapse of short-term memory was another side effect. Maybe he was repressing, or maybe Iain, in one last act of kindness, had worked some sort of erasure. None of these options made explaining our escape any easier. I doubted

Jorgas had forgotten Iain, but worrying him with the man's fate, without knowing exactly what it had been, seemed cruel.

"You've been missing." It was the simplest distillation of his ordeal.

"For how long?"

"Honestly? I don't know." Come to think of it, his phone would have been useful, right now. "Do you remember anything?"

Shame haunted his eyes. "I remember leaving you."

I reached around his shoulders, letting him rest his head against my neck while he hooked an arm and a leg around me. The movement had probably hurt, but in that moment, with his thick, brown hair tickling my chin, his body rising and falling with each breath, he wasn't showing it. He was simply there, grateful to be safe, as was I.

I stroked his back with my fingertips. It was warm, a stark contrast to my own underfed body. Had I been thinking clearly, I would have seized one of the Scimitars we'd defeated at the Arcadia Trust and drained them dry. Perhaps it would have made no difference. Who could say how our trip into the Wound had exhausted me? It had certainly exhausted Jorgas. Unfortunately, I couldn't join him in the demolition of reheated leftovers.

His hair tickled my chin as he shifted position, seemingly unbothered by the cold. Ordinarily, I could have reached for my phone and ordered in, loathe as I was to rely on such networks. Humans tended to forget their manners on them and most overestimated my interest in what was in their pants. To be fair, I was less than frank about my own intentions. In the end, the forum did the job in a pinch, but with my phone out of commission, I'd need to feed elsewhere, and soon.

The sound and vibration of Jorgas' heart tormented me, its temptation compounded when he lifted his head and kissed me, arching his neck.

"No," I said, flatly.

"For real? I know that look. You're starving." At least he was still the Jorgas I knew.

"You're not strong enough for me to drink from you. I'll hit one of the clubs later."

He frowned, squeezing me in his arms. "Will you, though?"

"I don't have much choice. My phone's emptier than I am, and it's not charging."

"Weird." He rubbed his face against me like a cat, his hand on my thigh. "Though, you do have a choice. Food or cuddles? There's only one way you're getting both."

I snorted a laugh. "Hey!"

He'd straddled me before I could react, though the pain that seared through him was evident.

"See? What did I say?" I stroked the length of his strong thighs as he eased himself back, the heat of his body teasing my crotch. Blood Shades, by our immortal nature, are not sexual beings, responding only to the blood in its endless variety. But Jorgas' blood awakened something in me. Some desire rendered dormant by centuries of evolution. Whether this effect was particular to Jorgas, or to the blood of werewolves in human form, I couldn't say. But at almost twenty-three, at the height of his physical prowess and sexual appetite, Jorgas relished this power, even now, rocking his hips back and forth over my waist.

I smiled as he ran his hands over my chest, shivering as his fingertips skimmed my flanks. When he dove in to kiss my neck, I felt no desire to stop him, enjoying having his body against my own again. No matter how hungry I was, it felt almost as wonderful as seeing his wolfish grin above me.

"Go on," he said. "A little bit won't hurt me."

A 'little bit' wasn't what I was afraid of. That blissful bite was the one act during which my inner monster and human affect merged. Once his blood awakened something primal, I couldn't promise I'd stop.

I playfully slapped Jorgas' hand away as he put it over my face, only to have him dive on me once more and start kissing my neck.

If provocation became tonight's game, he'd lose.

I put my lips against his throat, raking it with my fangs. My frozen fingers slid down his flanks to skim the fur of his behind. The smell of him sent a rumble through my stomach. I knew werewolves ran hotter than most species, much warmer than either ourselves or a typical human. But to have his pulse so close to my ear, his erection so swollen with hunger, pushing its way along my cool skin, tantalised me.

That little bit of extra pressure, enough to puncture his skin and release the faintest trickle of blood, came all too easily. My grip tightened as the sweet sanguine juice spilled over my tongue to my throat. If he was exaggerating his moans for effect, he was playing with fire.

Starved by our time in the Wound, I could feel it, that urge to lose control and simply feed. The hunger of a predator, unburdened by love or… Oh, hell! Yes, I loved him. I cursed each night I'd refused to admit it, and I'd be damned if I wasted another minute pretending otherwise. Yet, even so, the words seemed tawdry. He would know as I bit harder into his flesh, earning a small yelp that quickly succumbed to an enraptured moan.

He would know.

His renewed pleasure swept away any pain a sudden change in position might have caused as I licked closed the wound on his throat and flipped him on his back. His eyes rolled with the sweet rush of endorphins, enough to distract him while I slid down the length of his body and raked my fangs over the tip of his cock before fixing my lips to the inside of his thigh. Barely broken from the euphoria, he had no time to react.

I gave one of his nipples a hard squeeze, distracting him while I bared my fangs again and bit into his flesh. His entire body shuddered, going almost as rigid as his cock. My hands slid along the hardened muscles of his stomach, until, with a final gasp, he relaxed.

Lie back, wolf man. Just lie back.

I playfully slapped him as my other hand set to work teasing the space beneath his balls, tugging on his skin, animating his erection with an odd twitching that amused me, even as I drank. I slipped my hand lower, wetting his opening and gently plying its flesh, relishing his faint gasps and growls as the dual sensations of feeding and fondling gripped his nerves.

He yelped as I bit deeper, the sound a jolting reminder of the deadly powers we balanced against each other. Mine, the ability to draw every last drop of blood from his body to sate an immortal hunger. His, a wolfen creature that if I pushed my luck, might just as easily leave me in bloodied chunks, the collateral damage of its perpetual bad mood, even if Jorgas, the man, returned my love.

I released his leg, licking closed the wound as I withdrew. Again, his eyes rolled. Another gasp brought a short intake of breath as my sex, swollen to the peculiar chemistry of his blood, pushed its potent heat where my hand had been seconds before.

"Do it," he snarled.

I smiled. Didn't he know how foolish it was to reveal one's impatience to an immortal being? I pulled my hips back, withdrawing the lurid promise of my erection long enough to bring his legs up onto my shoulders. Hovering low, I silenced his imminent protest with a deep, lingering kiss, followed by several more down his neck, chest, and stomach. A long lick along the length of his cock set him shivering. I then righted myself and raked my sharp fangs along his muscular calf.

He let go his frustration with a small roar. And I let go mine, sliding inside him. The look of sudden shock that seized his face melted into one of raw pleasure as he welcomed me inside. I leaned in to kiss him once more, only to have his legs escape my shoulders and tighten around my waist as he brought me deeper. He brought his thick, solid arms up over his head. I pinned them there, enjoying his shivers as my fangs pricked the flesh of his chest up to his armpits.

All the while, I fucked him. All the while, he surrendered, catching himself with quick, horny gasps. I'd no doubt he was in pain, but if he cared, he wasn't showing it. I shifted my mouth to the other side of his chest, the one guarded by the tattooed tiger, which stalked the faux silver ring on his nipple. I gave the beast a long lick, savouring Jorgas' taste as he pushed himself deeper onto my cock. He brought a hand down toward his own.

I caught his wrist and pinned it beside the other above his head, giving one strong thrust to remind him who was in charge. His sudden gasp gave way to an ecstatic grin. He flinched as I teased his newly exposed underarm with my breath, running the tip of my fangs along his collarbone. The boom of his pulse maddened me. I was still hungry, and if his lust would be sated, so would mine.

I pushed inside and bit him once more. His cry told me I'd not been so careful this time, but he didn't fight me. On the contrary, he struggled one arm free and wrapped it around me, pinning my body to his. The heat of him melted the last trace of cold from my now far from malnourished body. I had to stop soon. I couldn't risk weakening him so quickly after his ordeal. But his grip would not yield.

"Oh fuck," he sighed. "Oh my god, I'm going to…"

He released one final bellow before the heat of his seed erupted between our bodies. I covered his mouth and let him release the full force of his cry into my hand, then quickly withdrew my bite, sealing his throat with one final, loving lick. I released his mouth, then sealed my lips over it in a deep kiss, allowing him to hold my body against his.

I don't know how long we stayed like that before finally letting go.

*   *   *

A row of neatly folded t-shirts in various colours—albeit mostly ranging from blue to grey to black—greeted me as I opened the dresser drawer. I pulled out one of the black ones, allowing myself a moment to sit and listen to the sound of Jorgas' shower. It was probably his first since he'd entered the Wound.

The sound reminded me of the first night he'd spent at my home, one every bit as soaked with blood, sweat, and sex as our last hour. He'd tried to continue our encounter while I'd showered, only for me to throw him out on his backside, naked and humiliated while I prepared to take him to the Arcadia Trust like nothing had happened. As if I'd felt nothing, either from feeding on him or from the then unnerving sensation of genuine arousal.

Seduction has been my primary and preferred form of feeding for much of my immortal life. But only Jorgas' blood, in human form, had ever aroused true lust. The ability to feel sexual pleasure and return the same in kind. I'd also suffered the taste of his blood in its toxic wolf form, and the unholy memory of it returned as I heard Jorgas retching in the bathroom.

"Are you okay?" I asked, just in time to find him doubled over the bowl, puking up a liquid stream.

He looked up at me, flushing away the bile and wiping his mouth before washing his hands. "What was in that stew?"

I winced a little, offering him a towel. So much for 'Heaven!' "You'd have to ask Dorotha. You didn't complain while you were eating it."

"It tasted fine! A bit bland? Watery, maybe? But fuck!"

That didn't sound like Dorotha's cooking. I thought again about the coffee, but this was different, wasn't it? This was nausea. The 'coffee' thing had been flat out impossible. Hell, I could speculate later. Perhaps we'd have better luck asking Deborah to pack him up something from Valia's. It seemed a good place to find Brett too, since he'd been spending so much time of late at Crown Street's last night-time café.

Then, there was the Trust. Even with the Scimitar of Light neutralised, the Arcadia Trust had been ground zero for the Wound's intrusion, where so many good people had been lost. I'd no specific reason to believe Brett, Isobel, Patricia, Kelvin, or even Giorgios, dreams notwithstanding, had come to any great harm, but I needed to be sure.

"Will you be all right if I go out for an hour?"

Jorgas finished rinsing his mouth and reached for his toothbrush. I'd not touched it since he'd disappeared on me. He brought his fingers up to his throat where I'd bitten him.

"Not to feed," I clarified. "I need to find Brett. Do you need anything besides more food?"

"Another coffee?" he said through a mash of toothpaste and bristles.

"If you want to try making more, it's in the second high cupboard."

He shook his head, continuing to brush his teeth while he clumsily dried himself.

I'd hoped for a request that would yield more clues as to his recent whereabouts. I knew from talking to his mother that Jorgas hadn't been home recently, so where had he gone? Where had he stayed?

"Hey." He rinsed his mouth and put the toothbrush away before drawing close and kissing my lips. "Thanks for coming to get me."

CHAPTER TWO

The evening air felt unusually thick and humid for September, but then, Australia's climate grew warmer and less predictable with each passing year. Even after decades, I'd not gotten used to it. A few dots of rain hit my face as I neared the top of the hill, crossed Oxford Street, passed the faux Mayan trimmings, Latin rhythms and cackling queens of Chicken Eatz'ya—home of Oxford Street's best drag shows and worst pun eight years running—and continued on Crown Street toward Valia's.

I'd called on Dorotha on my way out, but received no answer. Even pressing my preternaturally sensitive ears to the door, I'd heard no movement, not even the skittering of Demetrius' paws when I'd called him. Still, it wasn't the first time my cat had gone exploring and it wouldn't be the last.

A muscular youth in ripped blue jeans and a white muscle shirt caught my eye as I neared Campbell Street. Leaning back against the wall of Bone, the unsubtly named sex club that lured horny men numbed by the garish drag shows and dancefloors of Oxford Street, he stretched a muscular arm over his neatly trimmed blonde hair and exaggerated a deep yawn I guessed was meant to project cool, masculine indifference. Yours for the right price. He sneered as I passed him by.

I wondered in that moment what had become of Paul, the worker who'd helped me find Luca. Iain had claimed at least some of Oxford Street's rent boys as part of his outreach. In return, they provided a useful web of information. But even if I needed their help again, I doubted they'd be so forthcoming without the priest-come-Shaper at my side.

I reached the bright lights and catchy rhythms of Argon Records and stopped. I'd gone right past Valia's, and not until I doubled back to find its façade boarded up and tagged with spray paint, did I understand why. This didn't make any sense. The café had often struggled to keep its night-time hours, complicated by a heightened frequency of junkies and others who'd fallen through the cracks of Sydney's relentless march to the beat of 'me first' capitalism. But Deborah had said nothing about going out of business.

This was absurd.

Bright pop music from Argon coloured the street as a catchy tune overtook the somewhat mellow rhythms that had preceded it. The store was a relative newcomer to Crown Street, its walls lined with posters and t-shirts, mostly featuring bands and icons that long predated the customers who combed its racks in search of a retro thrill sealed in vinyl.

I peered inside the store, smiling at a clerk behind the register who looked a little too blissed out. Some singer named Marina peered at me from an album cover beneath a hastily cut sign that identified her as the voice coming through the store's speakers.

"Happy Mardi Gras," the clerk said without looking up.

"Same to…" I paused my browsing. "Mardi Gras is in March."

The man frowned at me, then resumed his work with a shrug.

I flipped through a row of LPs as a matter of course, though I recognised few of the artists. I've heard it said that one's musical taste is roughly defined by age twenty. If true, it made an immortal being's trip to the record store a somewhat hollow experience.

"Do you know what happened to Valia's?" I asked.

The man shrugged. "Closed up, months ago."

"That's impossible."

He shot me the same odd look, then went back to his phone.

I trudged up to Taylor Square, paying closer attention to the storefronts and bars. Many of their patrons wore shorts, t-shirts or less as they sat outside at tables, nursing cold drinks in the warm night. Plastic mannequins modelled garish underwear and tiny swimsuits in store windows dressed with rainbow flags and banners.

"You look lost, mate," said a small, earthy woman dressed in jeans and a navy-blue t-shirt, with a backpack slung over one arm. "Know who you're voting for?" She held out a pamphlet bearing the face of a grinning politician. "Adrian Tseng, a voice for today's Sydney."

I didn't care how stupid I sounded. "What's the date today?"

"Ah…" Her gaze cocked toward the rainbow flag flying over the square. "February twenty-eight. You from out of town? You should stick around for the parade next weekend."

I forced a smile, thanked her, and went on my way.

February? Five months? Five months?

I started walking up Oxford Street, avoiding passers-by, cringing as a display I might have once stopped to admire in the window of the local bookshop wished me a 'Happy Mardi Gras.' I narrowly avoided the path of an ambulance bound for Saint Vincent's as I crossed Dowling Street.

The walk should have settled my thoughts as I approached the Arcadia Trust. It did precisely the opposite, allowing me to ruminate the worst things that could have transpired in five months. Most of all, what had become of Brett?

No Mannequin could last that long without their master's blood.

I quickened my pace, if only to keep myself from the edge of panic. I knew too well the things that could happen to a Mannequin too long starved, not to mention anyone unfortunate enough to cross their path. Their mental disintegration wasn't as quick or violent as that of one who, say, had fed from two different Blood Shades, but it was equally unpleasant, and no less lethal.

I left the steady hum of Oxford and quickly ducked through the streets of Paddington to the Arcadia Trust. The jacaranda trees that dominated its front yard were all but bare as the last of their wilted violet petals dotted the ground. I cursed myself for not paying attention to such things. Then again, why would anyone suppose months had passed in the twenty odd minutes we'd spent in the Wound?

I bounded up the aged wooden stairs, stopping myself seconds before pounding on the imposing front door. Hopeful as I was of finding Patricia and others, it seemed foolish to announce myself so earnestly to a building I'd last seen overrun by religious zealots bent on our destruction. That arrogance had cost them their lives, or condemned them to fates I didn't care to imagine in the grip of the Patrons. The Scimitar of Light was dead. The very thought should have made me feel better, and probably would have, had the door not creaked open at my lightest touch.

The Patricia I knew would not have left her door ajar. Even if she had, the slow creak that announced my arrival would have brought Kelvin, her invisible Cloak Walker bodyguard and watchdog running with a disdainful comment at the ready, if not outright violence.

Most of the furnishings in the darkened hall were as I remembered them, albeit dusty and dishevelled. Paintings, side tables, one of which had collapsed, two ornate clocks, long decorative rugs that ran the length of the hall down to the ball room, where our encounter with the Wound and the Scimitars had happened. The last room I'd been in before losing five months.

Turning on the light seemed risky. My enhanced senses would guide me, and right now, they smelled an intruder. A man, though I couldn't place him. Probably some housebreaker who figured he'd hit the jackpot. Knowing the Arcadia Trust as I did, it wouldn't have surprised me if he'd run afoul of some trap installed by Kelvin.

The door to Patricia's office remained locked, despite my best efforts. The small parlour where Sophia had attempted to heal the dying Luca sat cold and empty, its fireplace barren, its books and jars of potent ingredients untouched. And yet each room possessed a strange, oppressive malevolence I couldn't place.

If Patricia Bakker, one of the smartest, most officious humans I'd even known had abandoned her home, she'd had good reason.

If the hall had hinted at neglect, the library looked like it had been ripped asunder to its last page. The floor lay strewn with upended books and pages torn loose. I recoiled as the powerful, acrid smell of ash hit my nostrils, though the fire that had caused it had plainly sputtered out months ago. In the darkness, I spotted a small door. The Prematures' private study. It too remained securely locked.

I'd seen Sophia die. As for her brother, Giorgios, the state of the library, their sanctuary within these walls, made me fear I'd witnessed more than a mere nightmare.

A loud creak above had me halfway up the stairs before the intruder opened a noisy door, betraying his whereabouts. I slowed near the top—fools rushed in, after all—but there was no need. In the dusty gloom of the landing stood Brett, as thin and pale as bone. His eyes glinted at me, obscured in shadow, but he was alive.

I wanted to snatch his frail form in my arms and assure him that whatever depravation he'd suffered in my absence was over. He took one tentative step forward, then another, passing a doorway that let the dim moonlight strike his face. His cheeks were sallow. Unkempt black hair hung lifelessly over his forehead, stopping just short of eyebrows too thick and mean for a slender face dotted with ill-groomed stubble. He reached out a bony hand, taking another step that bathed his emaciated body in moonlight. A grey tank top hung from his wasted shoulders.

Then, the creature opened its mouth, emitting a sound I'd not heard from man nor beast. A high-pitched, throaty whine that reached its crescendo as the glint of blackened eyes fixed on me. As the apparition staggered toward the stairs, I shrank away from this thing that now wore the face of my faithful servant and friend.

"Brett…"

Who knew if he could hear me? Or if any of Brett remained as he lumbered one foot at a time, staggering and catching himself on the balustrade until he stopped and looked at me, as though he had never seen my like before. He let out a sigh, dejection weighing down his face. It was a look I'd seen only when Brett had returned from an encounter with the Patron fragment known to us as Sklav. But it was enough for me to know he was there.

I raised my wrist to my mouth and bit into it, stopping as a sharp, breathy growl escaped my Mannequin. I could smell the anticipation on him, just as I could on any human seduced in prelude to feeding. Except the blood in such cases wasn't usually mine. Brett's eyes darted between my face and my wounded wrist as the scent spiced the air between us. I saw his tongue flick over thin lips as he inhaled sharply, then dived on me.

Immortal being or not, it hurt when his teeth bit into my flesh. Denied the blood for so long, did he even realise I was there? Brett was only the second Mannequin I'd taken on, and neither he, nor his predecessor had ever gone un-nourished. Instinctively, I pulled back, but the Mannequin, soiled fingertips digging into my forearm as he held fast, bit deeper.

I didn't want to hurt him, but my blood wasn't limitless, especially after taking so little from Jorgas. I'd known Blood Shades to tear a human apart after going barely a week without. What could a starved Mannequin do after five months?

I didn't want to find out.

Bracing myself, I wrenched Brett off my wrist, sending a shower of blood over both of us. Before he could leap on me again, I shoved him hard up the corridor. He sprawled and skidded into the darkness while I tended my brutalised wrist. The tender lick of a Blood Shade was meant to seal the tiny wounds left by our fangs, not the ravenous mauling I'd just received. In the meantime, I needed Brett to come to his senses.

An animalistic growl filled the darkness, then a high-pitched snarl as the thin, pale figure lurched away, taking refuge in the farthest room. Keeping my ears open for any hint of my servant, I drew nearer, until I rounded the dimly lit doorway.

Brett hunched in foetal position against the wooden footboard of a small, single bed, staring listlessly at some empty detail of the hardwood floor. His breath steadied with each inhale and exhale, even as traces of my blood trickled from his lips, soiling his chest and tank top.

I lingered in the doorway, watching as my blood returned colour to his skin. Though he still looked only a shadow of his former self, having lost by my estimate a good twenty or thirty pounds off his already slender frame, he was at least beginning to resemble the man I knew.

I swallowed, edging toward the head of the bed. I stripped a pillow of its case and tore the fabric into strips that I fastened around my forearm. I'd never pass for a medic, but I managed to fashion enough of a bandage before Brett looked up at me.

His confusion turned to astonishment, which turned to relief, which turned to tears, which turned to happy, laughing sobs until at last, he found words. "You? It's you!"

I dropped to my knees and held him. Minutes passed as we sat on the filthy floor together, Brett pulling himself tighter into my embrace as his strength gradually returned. So far, Brett was my only witness to all that had transpired. And if his condition, not to mention the condition of the Arcadia Trust was any indication, he'd been through his own hell since.

I kissed his forehead once more, pushing locks of long dark hair off his face and squeezing his shoulders. "Come on," I said. "It's time to go home."

The essence of a Blood Shade is remarkable medicine, but it doesn't work miracles. It took Brett more than one attempt to steady himself, descending the stairs with one arm clutching mine. Letting Brett set our pace, I at last eased open the front door. He was a mess, but without a phone, we'd have to make the trek back to Oxford Street to find a cab.

An elderly man watched us from across the street, where he leaned against a small car. His head was shaved to the scalp, and his mottled grey-white beard was neatly trimmed into a goatee. His firm, wiry frame almost obscured advanced years betrayed by the veins that snaked across his reddened head.

He averted his gaze, but not before his eyes caught mine. A human might not have seen it, but I knew that glint of recognition, and I didn't trust it one bit.

CHAPTER THREE

"Jesus!"

"A little help?"

Jorgas took Brett's weight from my shoulders and guided him into the living room.

"I'm okay, really," the Mannequin insisted, easing himself off Jorgas.

"You need solid food and rest," I said.

"And a shower," Jorgas added, screwing up his face. "Sorry, man. You reek."

I tossed Brett a sympathetic look. "Welcome home."

"Good to see you too." He tilted a smile at Jorgas. "I'll get a towel."

"Just be careful," I said. "Are you sure you're all right?"

"Thanks, Dad. I'm fine." He gave me one last smile before disappearing into the bathroom.

I dismissed his cheekiness with a light snort. Out of character as it seemed, it also comforted me to know he felt up to teasing and jokes.

Jorgas, meanwhile, frowned at me.

"What?" I asked.

"Are you going to tell me what happened to your arm?"

The damn thing had stopped bleeding, but it didn't look good, bandaged and soaked with my blood.

"The price of sating a Mannequin's starvation."

"Starvation?"

I sifted through a drawer of disused clothes, returning with a loose gym singlet left by some long-ago companion and a pair of elastic waisted shorts. They were the only clothes in my closet that would fit Jorgas. "Sorry, I didn't have a chance to pick up food. Are you feeling up to—"

"Don't worry, I'll go." He slipped into the clothes, which I had to admit, filled out nicely over his broad chest and thick legs. "Is Thai okay?"

"Thank you." I fished my credit card out of my wallet and handed it to him. "Whatever you'd like. Then we can all sit down and work out what's been going on these past five months—"

"Woah, wait a sec. Five months? What the fuck are you—"

I put my hands on his shoulders. "I'll talk to Brett first. Maybe we'll both get some answers."

Abandoning the questions I could see burning behind his eyes, Jorgas at last turned to leave.

"Go out the back."

"Huh?"

"We're being watched." I described the stranger who'd watched Brett and I leave the Arcadia Trust. I'd no evidence that he'd followed us here, but I wasn't about to ignore anyone with an interest in that house.

Jorgas disappeared through the small back gate. I hoped I was just being paranoid. The shower stopped and Brett returned, drying his long dark hair under a towel, another wrapped around his emaciated waist. Other than that, he seemed healthy once more.

"I needed that." He smiled at me.

"Your clothes should all be in your room. Assuming they don't drown you."

My Mannequin looked down at his body. "I haven't lost that much weight."

"You have. Now, get dressed."

I retreated to the couch until Brett emerged dressed in dark blue jeans and a black t-shirt, both of which hung loose on him.

"What do you think?" He leaned against the kitchen doorway with a smirk, pushing his hips forward with thumbs tucked into the belt loops of his now baggy jeans. "You'd still bite this."

I wanted to laugh, but the remark seemed awfully familiar. "Never you mind what I'd bite."

"Sorry, sorry." He raised his hands with a smile that belied his apology and sat opposite me. "What?"

I didn't break my stare. "You seem… comfortable."

"I guess I am."

"I mean for someone who showed symptoms of advanced blood starvation not an hour ago. Very, very comfortable. It's been five months, Brett. How did you survive?"

He stared out onto the street with a half-cocked smile.

"Hello?" I said, not sure whether to be concerned or annoyed.

"I heard you. I just… I don't know, exactly."

I eased back on the couch. "Have you seen the others?"

He sighed, as if the thought taxed him. "It depends who you mean."

"You were at the Trust. Patricia? Kelvin?"

He smirked at me. "Has anyone seen Kelvin?"

"Brett!" I snapped, making him jump. "This isn't a game!"

"Jesus," he raised his hands. "I'm sorry, I don't know! I don't remember seeing Patricia or anybody else there. It just… I didn't know where else to go."

"Go?" I asked. "Why not here? This is your home. You didn't think to check for me here? Where's Demetrius? Dorotha?"

He winced like the words hurt. "Ease up, will you?"

I tried to calm down, unhooking my fingertips from the edge of the couch. "What's the last thing you remember?"

He didn't answer at first. He couldn't have been at the Trust by chance. Couldn't have gone so long without seeing anyone. Yet, he had gone all that time without blood.

"At the risk of sounding banal," he said at last, "it's complicated."

"I'm worried, Brett. When I found you, you weren't exactly yourself."

He nodded, slowly. "That's truer than you know."

"And when did you start using words like 'banal'?"

He laughed, a sound that in the circumstances, should have been a balm for my soul. Instead, it sounded ironic, almost bitter, until he at last looked me straight in the eye. "You left me."

I tried to swallow; my mouth dry. I couldn't refute this. "I had to. Peter? Colin? I couldn't just abandon them. I didn't know we'd be gone five months."

"What about Jorgas?" He stared out the window. "You left everyone in the Wound, except Jorgas."

"There was no time," I protested. "The things we saw in there... Brett, I couldn't stay."

"You mean you couldn't leave him."

"Should I have?"

"No! I just don't think I understood what he meant to you until... you know."

"What are you talking about? And how do you know what happened in the Wound?"

Brett leaned forward in his seat, arched his fingers together and stared at me with those deep, expressive brown eyes that had captured my attention the night we'd met at the Black Soul. "Until you chose him over me. Like I said, you left me."

"Left you?" I caught my breath. Though the eyes were all Brett, staring at me from the centre of a drawn and pale face, the expression and the experience were unmistakeable. "Iain?"

One side of his mouth tilted upward. "As I said, it's complicated."

CHAPTER FOUR

"It's been five months." Iain relaxed into the couch beside me in his borrowed Brett body. "You can take your time."

"Sorry, I just… How?"

"Let's just say your blood helped. Up until tonight, it's been quite a challenge for both of us."

"Both of you?" I asked. "So, Brett's still alive?"

"Yes."

"Can I talk to him?"

"Ah, hello? I, Iain, am also alive and lucky to be so, thanks very much."

"I'm sorry. I just—"

"I know, it's—"

"—complicated," we finished together.

Another silence. I couldn't help looking him up and down again. The man sitting before me rested bony white hands on his knees, fingers curling and uncurling, betraying his nerves.

"You said it's been a challenge," I said. Whatever he'd done, he wasn't making it look easy now.

"Yes. In fact, we might need more of your blood soon."

"Mortal food's on its way. Can we see how that goes?"

He nodded. "It certainly won't hurt. To answer your question, I'm afraid Brett's…"

My shoulders tensed as I stared with anticipation at his dry lips. "Brett's what?"

"I barely recognised him when I found him. Skin, all sunken and yellow. Hair unwashed for… I don't know how long he'd gone without blood. This was several months before you and Jorgas came back."

Several months? It didn't make sense. We'd escaped the Wound right after losing Iain.

"I'll spare you the grislier details. Suffice to say, any semblance of sanity in the Brett you found at the Trust is only thanks to a concentrated effort on my part."

"A concentrated effort?" I asked. "As in warlo—Shaper magick?"

"The same magick that now allows us to sit and converse like civilised men, yes. Now, you ask if I can submerge myself, allowing you to talk to Brett directly? No. That would be like asking the driver and passenger to swap seats while the car is hurtling along a freeway and the passenger is in the harshest throws of heroin withdrawal. I could do it, but I doubt very much you'll like the Brett you meet, or that I could restore control. You'd lose us both."

"But…" The metaphor made sense, but it didn't satisfy me.

"He is here, and he is safe. He can hear you, see you, and taste whatever we eat. His senses are all functional. I'm not sure to what extent he can understand you, but the Joining puts us in constant communication. Anything you wish to say to him, you can say to me."

I disliked the resentment tinting that statement. "Iain?"

"Yes?"

"If Brett's here, where are you?"

He leaned back on the couch, spreading Brett's arms over the back of it as he shrugged. "You mean my body? I doubt it'll be a concern."

"Not a concern? Iain, if we get Brett back to any kind of normality—"

"Reylan, I take no pleasure in this, but understand, you may never get back the Brett you knew."

"Then he's as good as—"

"No," Iain raised an admonishing finger. "He's alive. I'm alive. That's as good as it gets for now."

"But your body—"

"If those creatures in the Wound left it alive, I doubt we'd recognise what's left."

My eyes went wide. "Then you have no intention of surrendering Brett's body?"

He slapped his fist down on the couch and groaned. "I did not say that!"

"So, what's the alternative?" I stood, every part of me quivering. "Do you have a plan for when Brett recovers? Will you move to another host like some psychic parasite?"

Iain too, got to his feet, drawing closer to me. "Before you get too high and mighty, he who feeds on the blood of companions before erasing their memory of it, know this. Without me, Brett would be dead. No argument. No question. Not sick. Dead. Now, could I have fought for my body in the Wound? Tried to hide from those things, with no escape plan? Probably. God knows if I would have succeeded, what condition I'd be in, or when I would have emerged, if at all. Ah, yes, the ever-unpredictable temporal mechanics of a Wound. Count yourself lucky to have returned to a world you recognise at all. Five months of immortal life, lost in exchange for coming home with Jorgas, safe and sound? I'd call that a bargain."

"Brett, on the other hand, is hardly safe, nor sound!"

"Really?" He grabbed hold of my arm, pressing my hand to his chest. Before I could resist, he pulled me closer, mapping my face, neck, and shoulders with his touch, pressing his forehead to mine. "This doesn't feel real to you? Solid? Human?"

"Stop it!" I pulled away.

He glared at me. "It was not a perfect solution, but it was the best one."

Again, I looked him over. The Mannequin seemed so unlike himself, it was impossible to see where he ended and his usurper began.

"My plan," he continued, "is to keep Brett alive until he can stand on his own again. We can worry about me when the time comes."

I'd not missed the tone beneath that last statement. "Iain, I was worried about you."

He swallowed, staring out the window.

"Oh, that's not fair! I will not choose—"

"I helped you free Jorgas. You chose, Reylan, before we even went into the Wound, you'd chosen him. I can't resent you for it, any more than I can resent you for leaving me behind."

"Iain—"

He faced me with arms crossed over his chest. "We can discuss this now, or later, as you wish."

"Should I also resent you for putting him in that machine? For using him?"

"Now who's being unfair? You know perfectly well he was crucial to the House of Magick's—"

"Iain, if your next words are about 'following orders,' I swear to every god that's out there—"

"Right," he muttered. "So, when I got you both out of there at the cost of my physical being, I was 'just following orders.' It might interest you to know that as a result, I have few friends left in the House of Magick who can verify that."

"I didn't…" Orders or not, he'd made a tremendous sacrifice to help me get Jorgas back. "I'm not ungrateful, Iain, for Jorgas or for Brett. I hope you know that."

He nodded, scratching at his bony elbow like a man trying to resist a cigarette. "Like I said, it was the best choice, in the circumstances."

The circumstances in which he'd found Brett, months ago? "How are you… Brett, I mean…"

"How did I keep him alive?" he asked. "Without your blood, it wasn't easy. His pain is my pain. Until you eased it tonight, I couldn't stay in his body for long."

"Where did you go?"

"Into dormancy. Like sheltering in place while the psychic house falls down around you. In short bursts, I could imbue Brett with just enough coherence to manage the essentials. Your neighbour, for example."

"Dorotha?" I asked. "You've seen Dorotha?"

"Yes. She wasn't in great shape when I returned. Blackouts. Falls. I can't be sure, but Shaper rituals can take a steep toll on uninitiated mundanes that participate. That said, she was almost ninety."

"Was?" Dread sickened my heart.

"When we performed the ritual. I arranged for a care home. Again, not an ideal solution, but I didn't know what else to do. I couldn't command Brett day and night. Last I heard, she was fine."

"Last you heard?"

"I haven't exactly been her primary carer," he muttered. "It was hard enough to keep Brett's mind together to make the arrangements. Everything's in your name, since Brett knows your codes. What you choose to do now is your business."

It seemed the first order of business would be changing my codes, though if Dorotha was taken care of, that left… "Patricia? Deborah? Isobel?"

"You have been careless with the women in your life."

"Iain, please?"

He rolled his eyes, though his smile was at last sympathetic. "Do you think I'd keep such things from you, if I knew? The café is boarded up. I stopped by Isobel's place only to find it empty."

"Empty?"

"And it's been cleaned. No supernal energies or residual signatures of any kind. I tried to find out if she'd sold it, but beyond confirmation of the building's existence, there's no reference to it, anywhere."

Discretion. No loose ends. That sounded like Isobel. Nobody would find her if she didn't want to be found.

"Deborah's disappeared, which is unfortunate. She had the beginnings of something great."

I remembered Iain cajoling Deborah into leading the ritual that had granted Isobel, Colin and myself temporary immunity to the sun's crisping effects. A Shaper? None of us had known, least of all Deborah herself.

"As for Patricia, the Trust has sat abandoned since the Wound opened there, as best I can tell," Iain continued. "If it makes you feel better, I can tell you they weren't pulled inside it. That sort of disruption leaves an energy signature. That suggests they left the Trust of their own accord. Nobody's been there in months."

"Except for you, in Brett's body? Why, if there's nothing there?"

His face darkened. "I said nobody's been there. I did not say 'nothing.'"

The slam of the back door broke my concentration. I overheard Jorgas swear under his breath, followed by the rustle of a paper bag. Iain and I exchanged obvious looks. Who was going to tell him? I knew precious little of Jorgas' relationship with Iain. I gathered they were intimate, but for how long, I couldn't say. Nor did I expect I'd ever know if Iain's affections had begun as something genuine. At any rate, he seemed to care for him now.

Our silent exchange didn't get by Jorgas as he entered the living room. "Okay, now what's happened?"

"Smells good." Iain smiled unhelpfully. He was right, however.

"Food first." I said, going to fetch plates. "Then, we have a lot to talk about."

*   *   *

"No fucking way," Jorgas at last managed to get out.

The wolf had sat in stunned silence, the fragment of basil stuck in his teeth driving me insane as Iain filled in details. He at one point asked how the Shaper had gotten his consciousness free of the Wound, but Iain's evasions were as skilful as they were maddening.

"As a master of the mind, a Mentalist's first duty is to safeguard their own," he said. "Take my word, this kind of astral projection requires great concentration and risk. Suffice to say there are cracks between the realms accessible only to a non-corporeal entity."

"So, how long can you go without your body?"

He cocked a half-smile I didn't much like. "As long as dear Brett can have me, now he's stable. But if you're asking how long I can spend in a non-corporeal state, we're talking hours. Sometimes less."

"Well," Jorgas shifted uncomfortably as he tried to reach the basil with his tongue. "How do we get you a new body?"

I glared at him.

"What? Can't we find someone who's brain dead or something? It's a win-win!"

"Medical and ethical complications aside," Iain said, pressing his fingers together, "your Mannequin's not strong enough to survive on his own. How long that strength will take to return or if it will ever return, I can't say."

Jorgas blanched. It seemed he only now understood the full nature of Brett's predicament.

"But you're sure it won't come to that," I said, "aren't you?"

Iain paused but played along. "Yes. I'm sure he'll be fine. We can worry about a more permanent solution later."

We stared at each other across the scattered plates Jorgas and Iain had emptied. The scent of Thai food did little to obscure the odour of raw anxiety exuding from both of them, and probably from me.

It was barely midnight, and I refused to waste the night worrying. Of the three missing women, Deborah worried me the least. She'd been a reluctant observer to the supernatural world and an even more reluctant participant. That left Isobel and Patricia, to whose whereabouts I'd no clue beyond an empty Arcadia Trust.

Isobel, on the other hand, I'd known for more than a century, and if anyone could help us with Brett and Iain's predicament…

Iain arched an eyebrow at me. "I told you her house has been cleaned."

"I know her better than you do," I muttered, beginning to clear plates. "And Iain? Stay out of my head."

"An unusually droll imperative just now." He got up to help me. "I don't have to read you to know what you're planning. Besides, it's taking everything I've got to stay in this head right now. Know that that means I can't come with you, or offer much in the way of magickal backup."

"Both of you are staying put," I said.

"Backup?" Jorgas asked. "Reylan, please don't do anything stupid."

I tossed him a look. "There's basil in your teeth."

CHAPTER FIVE

Taking my own advice, I slipped out the back gate before walking up to Oxford Street and hailing a cab to get to Balmain. I'd seldom been invited to Isobel's home. Like my own, it was a semi-detached row house, the kind hundreds of humans passed every day, not knowing the nature of its owner.

Leaving the cab half a block from my destination, I approached the darkened windows and clean, tan façade on foot. The small gate blocking the path running alongside of the house had been chained shut, a cursory gesture at best, since it was barely four feet high. I was preparing to leap over when I heard a low, hissing sound. I looked down, yanked my hand off the gate and backed away, just as the snake launched itself forward. It flicked its tongue at me with another sharp hiss before recoiling around the gate and resuming its appearances as a padlocked chain.

This at least suggested Isobel still owned the place. With a short run-up, I cleared the gate in one bound, landing as quietly as I could. I heard the accursed hissing and turned in time to catch the serpent's gaze as it reared, ready to strike again. I stilled my breath, staring at it until, satisfied I was no threat, it resumed its metallic form. I didn't know whether to be relieved or insulted.

A barking dog jolted me back to reality. I hid myself in the shadows beside the house. Surely, not all Isobel's home security would be as forgiving as the shape-shifting serpent. Perhaps the upstairs windows would be my best...

A light came on in the window above. If the house had been empty when Iain had stopped by, it wasn't now.

Gathering my strength, I bounded off the wall of the neighbouring house, then again, until I at last peered into the candlelit window and saw the shadow of a trim, suited figure scurry from view.

I tightened my grip on the ledge as it began to tax my strength. I'd not come prepared for intruders, human or otherwise. How had they gotten in? What did they want?

They also presented an opportunity. I needed to feed, after all.

The window was locked tight. Hearing the door at the back of the house, I stilled my breath, seeing a black-clad figure round the corner of the house and start down the path. I adjusted my position against the wall to strengthen my grip, waited until he was close, and dropped.

The man barely had time to look up, his sullen face frozen in astonishment and horror as I landed on him and muffled his scream. Pinning him down, I exposed his throat. The man's struggle subsided, becoming ecstasy as the bite's pleasures swept away fear. His pulse synced to mine until we at last reached that point of shared rapture. Strong, wiry arms that had tried to push me away now pulled me tighter, not wanting to lose a moment of my monstrous kiss. Then, as his heart began to slow, I released him, sealed his wound with a tender lick, then laid him out cold with a solid blow to the head.

I dragged the unconscious man into the shadows, frisking him for keys, a weapon, or anything else that could help me. I found a wallet with a driver's licence. Ken Donnelly. A fake, as if the absence of any bank or health cards left any doubt. Still, I pocketed it. My hand also closed around a smart phone. It was locked, of course, but I could fight with that later. I moved silently to the back door. My considerate, if unwitting donor had left it unlocked. Slipping inside, I found the place empty, just as Iain had promised.

Except 'empty' was not the right word. The lightless room had a presence all of its own.

I touched the phone to assure myself, though it seemed a poor idea to announce my arrival by using its flashlight. My Blood Shade vision should have discerned some detail, but it was like the walls themselves had absorbed and trapped any light from outside. I listened for movement, but the house was as silent as it was dark. I glanced back at the door through which I'd come, yet the light that illuminated its plain window failed to breach the void. I could see out, but there was no seeing in.

The intruder's blood coursed through my veins, conjuring paranoia in lieu of any tangible point of focus. I took the risk of pulling out Donnelly's phone, but its light offered nothing more than a glowing, locked screen. I turned it to where the wall ought to be, titled it upward, then swooped it down low near the floor. Nothing. I put the phone away, noting its camera was unsecured. At least I could take photos, assuming I found anything to see.

I couldn't be here alone! The man I'd jumped in the laneway couldn't have been here alone. Given Isobel's likely protections, perhaps this darkness included, the chances of any garden variety burglar surviving were slim. Yet 'Donnelly' had survived. And what kind of intruder snooped around by candlelight these days?

If candles had illuminated the upstairs room, then this accursed darkness had its limits. I'd get no answers fumbling around down here.

I stepped toward what I hoped were the stairs. I'd never set foot in such total darkness before. It felt like it should have resisted, somehow, like pushing through liquid. But there was nothing there. Only darkness until I connected with solid wooden floorboards. Panic seized me as my foot struck the bottom stair with a loud bump. When upstairs remained silent, I found the handrail and started my ascent.

Four stairs. Eight. Twelve. I wasn't sure what had possessed me to count the stairs in increments of four, but so it went, almost musical in its steady predictability.

Twenty-four.

Twenty-eight.

Thirty-two.

Thirty-six.

Isobel's staircase was not this high.

I froze, squeezing the handrail and listening. Nothing. Not even a creaking stair. Such silence couldn't exist in earthly nature. An absence of noise so deafening, my own breath unsettled me when I released it.

The only certainties around me were darkness, the wooden handrail, and the fortieth stair beneath my feet. That number, I could not trust. Had I gotten distracted? I reached for the wall on the other side of the staircase and grasped at emptiness. Leaning further proved equally fruitless, as if the wall simply weren't there. I climbed another four stairs. This was futile. Careful to put both hands on the rail before turning around, I began my descent.

Four.

Eight.

Someone was here. I could smell them.

I cursed myself for not taking the chance to ask Mister 'Donnelly' a few questions before knocking him out. He'd not been armed, but that didn't speak for his accomplice.

I felt a gentle sharpness behind my eyes, as if something were scratching behind them inside my head. I covered them with both hands as a great jolt of stabbing pain seized me. It was gone just as quickly, leaving me in the middle of the staircase in total darkness, the stairs beneath my feet the only solid sensation. I grasped for a handrail I could no longer find. I stepped forward, only to collide with a solid presence at a speed that might have killed any human. It pushed me into freefall, arms and legs flailing as I landed hard on my back.

At least I'd landed on a solid wood floor. Beyond the outline of an ajar door, flickering candlelight filled a room. Like the moonlight from the back window, it barely penetrated the darkness. I stumbled to my knees until my hand wrapped around the comforting familiarity of a wooden balustrade. I got to my feet, grasping the rail once more. I felt along its surface until it dipped to mark the beginning of the staircase.

I was upstairs. I'd fallen and landed on my back… upstairs.

Still sore, I felt my way along until I recognised the illuminated room that had once been Isobel's study. Yet instead of holding the veritable museum of arcane items as it once had, it was stripped bare.

Quelling the instinct to run, I eased the door open and surveyed the room. Empty, except for eight candles, each marking the point of a star, smeared in red on the floor. Hastily done, perhaps, but undeniable. I'd seen that shape. My footfalls barely made a sound as I approached it. Not even a creak from the wooden floor, as if the room itself had swallowed the sound.

With little to go on beyond the painted symbol and candles, I took out a clean pocket square—What? I'm old—and dabbed some of the blood onto it before carefully lifting it to my nose. Recognising the scent of lamb's blood should have made me feel better. It did not.

I noticed something odd. The candles seemed to burn brighter, their light filling the far corners of the room, illuminating a sarcophagus I was certain had not been there before. I use the term 'sarcophagus' loosely as it was little more than a plain black box, three feet tall and eight long, if my eyes weren't failing me, which I knew they weren't, regardless of the dark. If the damn box had been there before, it had been hidden by unnatural means. No light reflected off its smooth surface, as if the thing absorbed light as sure as the room absorbed sound.

It seemed cumbersome for Isobel's collection, but then, what did I really know of her dabbling in the arcane? She'd rarely seen fit to share and I was hesitant to ask.

Wetting my lips, I approached the sarcophagus, looking for any markings or identifiers. A cartouche, or even a warning. Anything I could photograph and take for study in a safe place where the laws of physics applied.

Nothing. I photographed the thing anyway.

The sound of the phone's camera broke the oppressive silence. So did footsteps on the wooden stairs.

I dove behind the only piece of cover in the room, the sarcophagus. Not thinking, I put a hand on the thing to steady myself. My gut turned instantly with dread and my skin tingled like pin pricks, as if my body knew that I was touching an object of immutable evil. I tried to shake the feeling as paranoia, but the sensations intensified. Whatever danger the box did or did not pose, my touch was not welcome.

I backed away into the wall beneath the window, even as the nausea refused to leave my stomach. I scarcely paid attention to the footsteps that thundered up the stairs. When they stopped, the only sound remaining was the heavy breathing of a man.

I took Donnelly's phone out again, reaching around the edge of the sarcophagus until I found the intruder in the view finder. He was a stocky, rough-looking man of about thirty, dressed in dirty jeans and a black t-shirt, with tightly cropped brown hair, a blunt nose, and a small beard. Donnelly's accomplice, I assumed. Yet, instead of looking around the room, piggish eyes darting around, looking for the intruder, he simply stood there, staring into space, as if standing on the precipice of something, my presence an afterthought.

I would have answers! Even if I startled him, he was only human, and I'd just fed. The phone wouldn't take video in its locked state, but it could capture stills. I positioned it again, ensuring I had a clean view of the brute's face, and took the photo.

His head tilted toward the sudden noise, as if the camera itself had yanked it down. I froze, unable to take my eyes off the screen as he gazed at it. But he didn't charge into the room, nor make any demand that I show myself. He simply stared at the camera, saying nothing, until he began taking off his shoes. I watched him put them aside, then pull the t-shirt up over his head, revealing a scarred, muscular body criss-crossed with what looked like prison tattoos. He finally unfastened his belt, lifting something from behind his back before sliding down his jeans and putting them with the rest of his clothes.

He was holding a knife. Not some cheap pocket knife either, but a vicious hunter's blade.

I tilted the phone to keep him in frame as he stepped toward the star on the floor. He paused momentarily at its edge, the illegible tattooed words on his stomach contracting with each breath. He stepped into the circle with renewed resolve until he reached its centre.

Two more figures joined us, each dressed in flowing white robes with hoods that obscured their faces. Neither said a word as they took up positions on either side behind the naked man. I wanted to laugh, the image the stuff of cheesy 70s films or juvenile frat initiations. But there was a precision to their formation, a perfect triangle formed between the two figures and the sarcophagus, with the apparent burglar at its centre.

I watched the screen, fascinated as the hooded figures took turns with a tiny blade, each cutting one of their fingers and smearing blood on the criminal's cheek before resuming their place. At no point did Donnelly's phone reveal their faces, but I didn't dare risk moving to get a better look. I doubted the hooded figures would be as passive as their compatriot. Or their vessel.

Had the man's icy stare into the camera been a plea for help? I was in every sense, a captive audience, and that idea, which only a second ago had seemed comical against a backdrop of humiliating nudity and theatrical robes, now filled me with dread.

At least they weren't chanting in Latin.

I squinted at the screen. No, I wasn't seeing things. The brute's feet were dangling several inches above the floor. Head bowed, he continued rising, until he hovered a good foot in the air. He lifted his head and glanced around the room, mouth uselessly mewling words without voice. At last, a cry escaped him, choked and empty, like… They'd cut out the bastard's tongue! Severed his vocal cords too, judging by the sounds he made. He flicked his head around, unable to see the figures behind him, or anything besides the sarcophagus and the phone. He choked out one final plea before his arm folded up behind him, snapping bone. One of his legs followed, then the other, one limb after another bending and reshaping itself, folding his body like a puzzle in cruel, unseen hands. Silent screams contorted his face each time his convulsions paused long enough for a look at Donnelly's phone.

He began cutting into his chest, arms and legs, deftly moving the knife between both hands. Perhaps it wielded him. The poor devil seemed awfully adept for someone whose limbs were now broken into so many pieces. Blood smeared across his body from head to toe, right to his fingertips, where it dripped to the floor, its source now little more than a writhing, twisting mass of bloody flesh and broken bone.

Heat radiated off the sarcophagus. I wiped my brow, leaving my fingers slick with the damp, pink sweat of a freshly fed Blood Shade.

What if this thing wanted my blood next?

I wet my lips and tried to keep the phone still. But my arm had begun to shake, until at last I felt something grab at it. My heart leapt and my breath caught as the device slipped from my grasp, hitting the floor with a loud bump. I stared at it, trying to ignore the slicing and rending I heard on the far side of the sarcophagus. I didn't dare retrieve the thing. I just sat there, knees drawn up to my body, a cowering ball behind a cursed box now eradiated with fresh blood.

Hearing a small choke above, I looked up to see what remained of the man. He was still alive, floating close to the ceiling, face down, looking straight at me. He reached out, the skin of his arm tattered and shredded, until at last his eyes disappeared within his head, as if what lay behind them had caved in. His body collapsed to the floor, and the room plunged into darkness.

I snatched up Donnelly's phone and drew closer to the wall, away from the sarcophagus as it grew hotter still. I couldn't stay here. There was no telling what the damn thing would do once it had its fill. I listened for any sign of the hooded intruders leaving. But who could know? I might have no choice but to push open the window.

The window…. Moonlight! This darkness was not so impenetrable after all.

I rose to my feet and reached for the latch, near yanking my fingers loose when it refused to budge. Of all the blasted… The two hoods were staring at me. The moonlight barely reached the bottom of their blood-spattered robes, though it showed up their sacrifice in his full, eviscerated glory. Still, the damned window latch refused to budge, burning my fingers as the sarcophagus grew hotter. I gasped as my hand brushed the glass and I had to let go. I looked up again, just as the figures turn to leave.

"Who are you?" I demanded, emboldened by the fact that they'd not yet tried to kill me.

The second figure turned to face me. As it drew nearer, I saw the jawline of a woman under the hood as she pulled it…

"Reylan?"

Deborah and I stared at one another, slack-jawed as the other figure returned to the room, grabbed my friend's arm, and pulled her back into darkness, slamming the door behind them.

The room grew hotter still, with a glow that now felt like cruel… sunlight.

Don't ask me why the light of the moon, itself no more than the reflection of the sun's rays does us no harm while the sun's full light will steadily burn us to a crisp. While we don't burst abruptly into flame or disintegrate like the 'vampires' of comic books or movies, we do burn, and I'd no desire to suffer such a fate.

I darted across the room, trying the door first, only to have it singe me. I snatched up the thug's t-shirt, looped it around my hand and tried again, but it wouldn't budge. Only one way out. I pulled the fellow's socks and one of his boots over my remaining hand and started punching the window with it. A few solid strikes broke the heated glass. I used the boot to clear the rest and launched myself out the window, gripping the wall of the house next door as I gasped for fresh night air. I slipped down the wall, taking care not to land on Mister Donnelly, whose image I quickly snapped with the phone before running for the gate. The 'snake' paid me no mind as I vaulted it in one swift leap, then froze.

The same man who'd watched me leave the Arcadia Trust leaned against the same car on the opposite side of the street. I recognised his bald head and mottled beard, along with his accusatory sneer, right before he turned to get back in the car.

I darted across just in time to stop the door being slammed in my face. I reached in, grabbed a fistful of the driver's shirt and pulled him out onto the street, pinning him down. "Who are—"

He twisted his entire body, sweeping my legs out from under me so fast, I'd no time to catch my balance. I landed hard, my forearm taking the brunt of the fall. Over my shoulder, I saw the man slide behind the wheel and shut the door behind him. I barely had time to get out of the car's way before it sped off. I took out the phone and snapped the number plate before he could round a corner and disappear into the night.

I looked back at Isobel's house, now silent and peaceful as I'd found it. No hooded figures. No thick-necked thugs, endless shadows or wayward sunlight. Just a house. I shook my head, putting distance between the accursed place and myself until I at last spied a cab.

CHAPTER SIX

All I could think about was Deborah, staring at me from under that white hood. Her voice calling my name before she was pulled into the shadows by her... accomplice? Captor? As long as Jorgas' larcenous skillset extended to the digital realm, I'd be able to identify the two men and the mysterious car at least.

That was, if Jorgas could tear himself away from making out with Brett/Iain on my couch.

I stood in the doorway of my living room, fingers tapping at the frame. At least they had the decency to look ashamed.

"I... we... ummm..." Jorgas stammered.

"Yes, I can see that," I said.

"Time and place, perhaps." Iain offered a smile I frankly resented seeing on Brett's face.

I dropped into the armchair facing them. I claimed no ownership of Jorgas, and the two of them 'remembering old times' on my couch was the least of my worries.

"You look like you've had a night," Iain said. "What did you find?"

I tossed Donnelly's phone to Jorgas. "I need the photos on that. Can you unlock it?"

"One sec'." He sniffed at the touch pad, then tilted it under the light before tapping out the six-digit code and bringing up Donnelly's photo. "This one?"

"There's three," I said, not disappointed. "Two men and a number plate. Feel free to explore. I got this one's ID but it's a fake."

"No kidding. The phone's a burner." He showed me the empty inbox. "Guy's not taking chances."

"Can you retrieve anything that's been deleted?"

"It's worth a try," Iain agreed. "Though I doubt he'd be careless enough to not disable the backups."

"He was careless enough for me to catch him off guard," I said. "And he was the lucky one."

"Lucky?" Jorgas asked, not looking up as he set to work on the phone.

I filled them in on all I'd seen at the house.

"So, which one was he?" Now, Jorgas looked up, squirming uncomfortably. "The… bendy-snappy, slicey-dicey guy?"

"No. Here." I took the phone and brought up… "That's not right."

"What's not?"

The 'photo' I'd taken of the victim was now as empty and black as the darkness I'd escaped.

"Seriously?" I muttered.

"A suppression field," Iain offered, solemn as a judge. "It's not unusual for Shapers to throw one over a spell site when they don't want to be seen, much less recorded."

"I could see them well enough through the view finder," I pointed out.

"Technology and magick, my friend. It's a strange dance. No Isobel, I take it?"

"If there's any trace of Isobel left in that place, I couldn't find it," I said. Not that I'd had much chance to find anything.

My best guess was that the inky void had meant to lead me to that room.

"But, Deborah?" Jorgas began. "What's she doing with—"

"I've no idea." I turned to Iain. "She'd begun manifesting Shaper powers shortly before we went into the Wound, right?"

"A few basic abilities, yes. But using them to protect you from the sun was a simple trick. The magicks you're describing are…" The way he shook his head only unnerved me further. "Forget the robes, the gore, and theatrics. Did you touch the box?"

"Yes, I touched it. Why?"

He avoided my gaze as he let out a breath, composing himself.

"Now what?" Jorgas asked, taking the phone back. "We're fucked?"

"Not 'fucked' exactly," Iain murmured. "But it knows."

"It's a box. How can it know anything?"

"A box that absorbed a man's blood and entrails right before your eyes."

Jorgas blanched. "Please tell me you touched it before it did that?"

"Before? After? During?" Iain asked. "The slightest touch is enough for it to know you."

"I was only curious," I muttered.

"So is the box," he answered. "And it can tell a lot about you from a simple touch."

"You're talking about this thing as if it were alive."

"Not exactly, but it is intelligent. The way you described the darkness…."

"There was nothing on the box, right?" Jorgas asked. "No hieroglyphs or anything? If we're gonna have Egyptian mummies and shit running around Sydney, I'm out. I mean it. I'm fucking done."

"A mercifully infrequent occurrence." Iain's voice was way too calm for my liking. "But a blood sacrifice suggests Necromancer magick."

"Great," Jorgas muttered.

"Is it a threat?" I asked. "How do we stop whatever it plans to do?"

"Listen to you," he laughed in a way that annoyed me. "Not back a day and eager to save the world?"

"No," I muttered. "Just Deborah."

"Ah, yes. I'm surprised she's involved. Her magick is Shamanistic in nature. That puts her in direct opposition to Necromancer magick, which—"

"In English?" I implored him.

"—means she has no aptitude for it, nor will she ever. Unless, of course, she's found a coven already."

Jorgas raised an eyebrow, crossing his arms. "A coven? Seriously?"

"What else would you have us call it?" Iain asked. "Ideally, there would be three of them, but never with more than three of magick's quarters present."

"Quarters?" I tried to remember. "The four primary schools of magick? Shamanism, Necromancy, Entropy…"

Iain nodded. "…and us, the Mentalists. I don't advise having more than one of our kind per coven. Egos like you've never seen."

I'd met millennia-old Blood Shades, but I didn't feel like pushing the point.

"Why not have all four?" Jorgas asked. "You'd be unstoppable."

"On the way to godhood, in fact. That can't be allowed for the same reason we can't allow a rogue Blood Shade or Flesh

Master to tear through the neighbourhood because they're having a bad night."

I stood up and went to the kitchen, noting Demetrius' empty bowl. The plastic container that had held Dorotha's stew dried on the dish rack.

"I can contact the hospice today if you'd like," said Iain, somewhere behind me. "You'll have them both back before you know it."

Without meaning to, I tensed. "What have I said about reading me?"

"Sorry," he said, lowering the hand. "I know this is still strange for you."

Strange? I had to laugh.

"What's funny?" Iain asked.

"Nothing," I said. "I'm gone just a few moments and now most of the people I know are missing. Two are fused together, perhaps irreversibly—"

"That's not what I said. I promise, I'll do everything—"

"It's possible, isn't it? The Arcadia Trust sits abandoned. Isobel's home is now a haven for, to use your term, Necromancer magick. I just saw a man turned inside out with the full participation of a human I thought I could trust. Meanwhile, another man appears to be tracking my every move. It's my first night back, Iain."

He nodded slowly, leaning against the doorframe. "So? What are we going to deal with first?"

"We?" I asked.

"Yeah, we." Jorgas said from somewhere behind me. He nodded at Iain. "You want another beer?"

"I'll get it," Iain picked up the bottle opener and snapped two bottles from the fridge open, passing one to Jorgas before giving me a look. "Feels odd, drinking without you."

"I don't think my beverage of choice would go down well in this company."

"Try making a coffee," Jorgas muttered.

"That's not funny."

"What now?" Iain listened intently as I recounted our breakfast misadventure. "It's probably just a side effect of the Wound."

"Probably?" I asked.

"Seems awfully petty for a coven hardened to human sacrifice. I wouldn't worry." Iain smiled at Jorgas, then at me. "So? What are we dealing with first?"

Good question. It wasn't like Isobel hadn't disappeared on me before. Patricia wasn't my responsibility, and even if she were, I didn't know where to look. But I had to know if Deborah's latest associations were by choice, and what threat they posed, to us or to anyone else.

On the other hand, fuck anyone else.

"Deborah," I said. "I have to know if she's been co-opted or manipulated by these Necromancers. Can you tell if a Mentalist has—"

"Taken control of her mind?" asked Iain. "Forced her to do things against her will? Not to dim your optimism, but you must be ready to find out that she knows full well what she's doing."

"She's a good person, Iain."

"I know that, or at least Brett does. But I remember that first taste of real power. How I saw the world in that moment. I'm just telling you to be prepared."

I nodded slowly. Still, I refused to accept Deborah's complicity in the evisceration I'd seen. "You said your powers are severely diminished in Brett's body, correct?" I asked Iain.

"You're looking for some magickal protection? Against what? Everything you described sounds like an effect cast on that house, not you. The man in the car notwithstanding, there's no reason to think this is about you."

"I'll settle for something general." I sounded like some human whining at their doctor for a prescription I couldn't name.

Iain grimaced. "You might find it a bit—"

"Can you do something to protect us, or not?" Jorgas asked.

Now, Iain looked downright offended, his scowl every bit the Brett I knew. "I suggest you think about this very carefully. When you both know what you want and are willing to do as I ask, then we'll talk." Without another word, he retreated to the living room. Jorgas opened his mouth, but I raised a hand to hush him.

"What?" Jorgas whispered to me. "We don't have time for this."

"No," I said. "He's right. What do you want?"

He sipped his beer without looking at me.

"Jorgas?"

"Is this about Iain and me?"

"I don't know. Is there an Iain and you?"

"Is there an Iain and you?" He posed no accusation, simply a confident question.

"There are things I need to tell you," I said. "Assuming Iain hasn't done so already."

"He told me enough. I thought Blood Shades couldn't—"

"We can't. You're the only one who's turned me on naturally, if that's what you mean."

"Until…?"

I shot a look at the wall separating us from Iain. "The tricks of a Mentalist? Brain sex, in the truest sense."

"Cute."

"I don't think you're one to be jealous."

"I'm not," he growled. "I don't care what you do."

"Oh, for God's sake, come here!" I closed the space between us and put my arms around his solid shoulders. He didn't resist. After a minute or so pressed against my shoulder, Jorgas looked up and kissed my cheek. "But you didn't answer me."

He shook off my grip just enough to take another drink. "I don't know. I've always thought Brett was hot, except it's Iain. You know we've got a history, right? We were there on the couch, talking, and I could see him. Iain, I mean. It doesn't make sense, but I had to."

"He has that effect on people. But for clarity, let's both refrain while Brett's body is on loan."

"Yeah," Jorgas admitted. "You're right. Do you really think you can separate them?"

I squeezed his shoulder. "I have to. I've lost enough people recently."

He smiled in agreement. Though Jorgas and Brett weren't close, they'd bonded well enough to become my family.

We returned to the living room to find Iain sitting in the centre of the couch, arms comfortably resting across the back of it, one leg crossed over the other. If he was still offended by our exchange, he didn't show it.

"What do you suggest?" I asked.

"A coven's assault can only be properly repelled with a coven's protection," he answered. "A magickal shielding created by two or more individuals."

"But Reylan and I aren't Shapers," Jorgas said.

"In that case, you're very fortunate to have me. But you are both supernaturals with advanced acuities. As a Mentalist, I can tap into those talents, provided we're sufficiently bonded in the traditional manner."

"Bonded?" I asked.

Iain's smile embraced its familiar mischief. "We need to have sex. All three of us, together. There's more to it than that, obviously, but I'll take care of the rest."

My lips pursed. "I'm sorry, come again?"

"Surely, you're not surprised?" he asked. "In order for me to imbue the two of you with the magicks I generate, we need to become part of each other. Absolute trust, kinship and vulnerability. Bonded in a celebration of life itself."

"But you've already fucked us both," Jorgas protested.

"Yes, and we had great fun, but in the Bonding, a power transference takes place. The two of you not only accept my protection, but are bound and sworn to protect one another."

"As you well know," I answered. "Jorgas and I have already 'bonded' on numerous occasions. I assure you, we're quite—"

"No three-way Bonding, no coven. It's that simple. I get it. You're not the first… initiates to feel squeamish about this. But a Shaper coven out in the world unbonded? Well, for a start, they're not a coven. Beyond that, they're vulnerable to a veritable horror show of hostile magicks, and if this particular coven has you in their sights, you won't stand a chance. I'm not asking for anything we haven't already done. One little threesome, that's all."

Jorgas looked from me, to Iain, and back again, letting out a thoughtful sigh. "I guess? It's not so different, is it?"

"There's one very significant difference," I said.

"Which is?" asked Iain.

I looked him up and down, from the dark, messy hair to the wiry frame and long, narrow legs. "That's not your body."

For the first time that evening, Iain looked surprised. "If this is a question of consent, I promise you, Brett is willing."

"Is he, indeed?"

"His thoughts are my thoughts. He knows you both. He trusts you. And it need only be once."

"So, I'm to understand my one hundred percent heterosexual Mannequin—"

"Let's say ninety percent. There's a rather fond high school memory tucked away back here, but go on."

"My predominantly heterosexual Mannequin, is suddenly down with the idea of…" I trailed off, raising my palms.

"Reylan's right," Jorgas chimed in. "Plus, our sex can get kind of wild. We could hurt you, badly."

"True, you'd both have to reign in your more animalistic urges. We can't have the two of you opening up gashes in Brett. But you've both managed it before, with me."

"How would it work?" Jorgas asked "You'd fuck us both?"

"In the case of an all-male Bonding, things must be mutually penetrative for all parties. An all-male coven is at an inherent disadvantage, so we need to get this right."

"Again," I said. "We're not a coven."

"Another point not in our favour. But we're defenceless without a proper Bonding, and we need all the help we can get."

"So, we'd both fuck Brett?" Jorgas asked.

"You'd fuck me, in his body, yes."

"And you'd fuck us?"

"Yes."

"And Brett's down with that?

"Nobody's fucking anyone," I said, "unless I talk to Brett first."

Iain shook his head. "You know that's not possible."

"The only time Brett ever expressed a sexual interest in me, he was out of his head with the confused lust of a Mannequin needing his master. If you don't mind, I'd prefer to hear verbal consent from him."

"I've told you what happens if I relinquish control. You're asking for the consent of a madman." Iain looked annoyed, thin, dexterous fingers drumming on the couch as though his patience were nearing its end. "You picked a hell of a time to flex your human ethics."

"What's that supposed to mean?"

He rolled his eyes. "As if tricks of the mind weren't standard kit on a Blood Shade's night out. Memory erasure? Hypnosis? Not to mention certain chemical influences, ideal for the impatient."

I could feel my own composure slipping. "How dare you?"

"Your species isn't known for gaining 'consent' before—"

"That is entirely different!" I barked.

"Reylan…" Jorgas was wise enough not to continue.

"Is it, though? Black them out? Take what you want from their bodies and send them off none the wiser?"

"For sustenance!" I hissed. "We need it to survive!"

"So, it's a matter of necessity?" Iain asked. "With no alternatives? No feeding off animals? No asking permission or seeking a willing human donor? Just skip through the night and take what you want, is that it?" He got to his feet and looked me square in the eye. I'd only ever met two humans able to do so without fear of my mental talents, Iain and Patricia Bakker. "What you need to survive right now, is a coven's protection."

"Iain, I will not do this to Brett."

He rounded the coffee table that was between us and grabbed my hand, pulling it to his thin chest. "You want to talk ethics versus necessity? Necessity, my friend, has arrived!"

Perhaps it was the fierceness in Brett's familiar eyes, or the memory of how we'd fought assassins and daemons together, or of how easily he'd assumed a false identity when it suited his fancy, or taken over Brett's body, or equipped us with the power to walk in daylight. Brett's body was in the possession of one of the smartest men I knew, and one of the most dangerous.

Jorgas touched my arm again, looking from Iain to myself, the muscles in his throat twitching.

Iain lifted his other hand and stroked Jorgas' cheek.

I caught his wrist. "This isn't settled."

"Brett's thoughts and mine are one and the same." Iain turned to Jorgas and smiled. "He knows you're attracted to him."

Jorgas flushed pink.

"That's enough," I said quietly. "Even if this were a democracy, and I'll remind you, you are in my house, there are four of us to consider. Since one currently has no voice, this… orgy of fortification, or whatever you wish to call it is off the table. I'm a Blood Shade, Jorgas is a werewolf, and you're… you, so don't tell me we don't have other options."

"What does that mean?" Iain said with a frown. "I'm me?"

"Yes, you! Moral compromise for the greater good doesn't usually extend to strapping people into infernal machines to facilitate a slaughter."

"A slaughter?" he scoffed. "The Scimitars? We're talking about removing the greatest organised threat to supernatural life on this planet, and all it took was the temporary detainment of one Flesh Master."

"Who's standing right here!" I reached for Jorgas' hand.

Jorgas looked from Iain, to me, then back. "Detainment? Iain, what's he talking about?"

"What?" Iain asked me. "You haven't told him?"

"He's been back all of a day!"

"Thanks to whom?"

"Stop fucking talking about me like I'm not here, both of you!" The power of Jorgas' beast rattled his words. "Iain, what is Reylan talking about?"

Iain pinched the bridge of Brett's nose. "This is not how I wanted to have this discussion."

"No?" I asked. "So, you were planning to have it, at some point? Perhaps in a few months, over a beer in a cosy pub somewhere, when we could all look back and have a laugh?"

"Reylan, will you shut up?" Jorgas hissed, turning back to Iain. "Tell me!"

"A doorstop between worlds," I resisted the urge to sneer. "Making it easier for the Shapers to corral their targets in one place."

Iain grimaced at me. "You're not going to make this easier, are you?"

"I just want Jorgas to have all the facts before he decides he wants to have sex with you again. Of course, if bygones are bygones, then all we need is Brett's permission and we can get down to it."

"Are you serious?" Jorgas' lips curled into a snarl. "Iain?"

"That's the problem with half-truths and omissions, isn't it?" I asked. "Even when they're for the 'greater good' they add up until—"

"Is it true?" Jorgas barked at him again.

"Yes. Just as it's true that I brought Reylan into the Wound to rescue you," Iain said, his voice flatter and calmer than either Jorgas or I could manage in that moment. "Just as it's true that you both left me there, which is why I stand before you in the body of your Mannequin, who by no fault of his own after being abandoned, now borders on insane."

In my bitterness and sarcasm, I'd forgotten the sacrifice Iain had made to set Jorgas free and let us escape. But it didn't justify using Brett now.

"Well?" Iain asked.

"What?" Jorgas shook his head at Iain. "We're just supposed to fuck like old times? Did you even like me? Fuck, man! I trusted you!"

"Billy, please?" Iain raised a hand. "I do like you. I'm sorry, truly sorry for what they did—"

"They?" Jorgas asked. "You mean you?"

"The House of Magick," I informed him.

"Shapers!" Jorgas snapped. "Fucking Shapers, like these freaks who've got Deborah."

Iain sighed. "I know this is—"

"*Fuck you!*"

"Hey!" I took Jorgas by the arm. "We still need him."

"Like hell we do! You fucking used me, Iain! Five months. Five months!"

Iain brought his fingers together under his nostrils as they flared. He was choosing his words carefully. "You're right. I owe you a proper explanation. Obviously, tonight's not the best time—"

"The best time?"

I caught Jorgas as he advanced on Iain with a roar that forced the Shaper to take several steps back.

"I think I should leave," Iain added, hastily. "You two take the day, sleep it off—"

"Don't talk to us like we're bloody children," I answered. "You betrayed us both, and now you have the gall to want sex?"

"Sex?" Iain spat the word out with disgust. "Is that all you think this is? Haven't you listened to a word I've said?"

"Every fucking word," Jorgas muttered.

"And it won't be happening until we hear from Brett," I said again. "End of discussion. End of debate. Another day won't make much difference. I'll give you one of my cards for a hotel."

"If we survive that long. I suggest you two find other accommodations as well." Iain's voice had taken on a distinct sneer. "And you? I know everything about you, William."

"Leave him alone," I growled.

"Alone?" Iain laughed. "He's been alone for the past twenty years! Playing the dutiful, conservative son. Forced to murder his first lover, even! That was nasty. No wonder you never mentioned it."

"Mentioned what?" Jorgas muttered. "Go on, say it."

"Then finally, you meet me," Iain continued, now speaking directly to Jorgas. "No more mumbling to musty old Father

O'Baer, pretending everything's fine. Suddenly, it's Father Grieg! Laid back, easy to talk to, kind of turned you on, too. I mean, be honest. You masturbated about me long before the first time we kissed, didn't you? It's nothing to be ashamed of."

"Iain," I growled. "We get it."

"And how could those feelings not get confused?" he kept on. "After all, it felt so good to have someone to hear all those painful secrets. Who'd never force you to look at the beast that killed those kids. You thought I was going to give you up for that, didn't you?"

"I didn't…" Jorgas stammered. "That wasn't…"

"Exactly! It wasn't you, but the beast you'd yet to tame. I know it. Reylan knows it. We're the only people you've got in the world who understand. But your dad?"

"Shut it!" Jorgas barked.

"When you killed him, that was a step too far, wasn't it? Not some stranger out in the forest. Not somebody they'd chalk up to an unknown killer because the wounds were just too horrific, but a man you had reason and desire to kill, who Reylan watched you kill."

"Iain," I said quietly. "Enough."

"That's why you left Reylan in the first place, isn't it? You couldn't stand that reminder, looking back at you in the eyes of the man you loved. You had to leave the whole, sordid truth of it behind. You couldn't even tell me, lying there, naked in my arms, no longer priest and confessor. But you can't lie to me, Jorgas. You don't think you're worthy of Reylan's forgiveness, or anyone else's. So, you ran."

"The point remains," I growled. "You and the House of Magick abused his trust. Abducted him."

"I'm not the House of Magick, Reylan."

"No," Jorgas said. "You were supposed to be my friend. You used me. You used Reylan. Now, you're using Brett."

"Iain," I said. "Go, now."

Iain turned to me, no longer hiding the annoyance in Brett's eyes. "You're sure that's what you want?"

"I don't want you in this house."

He shrugged. "So be it."

Works of popular culture have such curious notions of possession, full of tells such as the whitening of eyes, speaking in tongues, and other diabolic fictions. Brett simply stood there, his head bowed, his natural and extremely human brown eyes dull and lifeless.

True to his word—for once—Iain was gone. This was not at all what I'd meant.

"Brett?" I called.

My Mannequin at last lifted his head, looking not unlike he had when I'd found him at the Arcadia Trust. The spark of Iain's keen intelligence was gone from his eyes. In its place, I saw desperation and hunger. He cocked an eyebrow at me, then opened his mouth, his jaw hanging slack as he watched me come within reach.

I brought my wrist up to my mouth and punctured it, releasing the scent of sweet, fresh blood. Brett's eyes widened before he dove on it, slurping hungrily, mauling it, biting. His blunt Mannequin teeth bit into my flesh. "Easy… eas—"

The weight of his body hit with a force that sent me staggering backward until I tripped on the coffee table and landed hard with Brett on top of me. The glass table cracked and gave way. No longer satisfied with my wrist, Brett clawed at my chest. His nails tore my clothes. I screamed as his teeth tore out a chunk of flesh from my throat.

I felt Brett's weight vanish as Jorgas grabbed him and threw him across the room. I tried to get hold of my senses, but the burning pain was driving me to madness.

Jorgas screamed as Brett bit into him.

I rolled over and staggered to my feet in time to see Jorgas land a solid blow to Brett's cheek, where it left claw marks. Wide eyed, Brett turned to me and screamed, as if the pain had caught up to whatever adrenaline was driving him against us.

It took barely a glimpse of Jorgas' yellow wolfen eyes to know we were all in trouble.

Brett lunged for me again, determined to get at the bloody nectar his earlier bite had released from my throat. I fell to the floor and pushed myself out of his grasp, giving Jorgas enough time to sink rapidly extending claws into Brett's back and rip him away. My heart leapt as Brett's body dented the wall with a hard crack. Mannequin or not, he was human and fragile.

One look at Jorgas told me everything. Wolfen eyes aglow, thick hair shrouding his legs and arms, he was changing. He opened his mouth to protest but I shook my head, wincing as my neck continued to bleed. Jorgas ducked another swiping lunge from Brett, retreated up the hall and shut the door to the spare room behind him. I heard the lock turn, even as I collapsed to my knees. It wouldn't hold the wolf if it wanted out, but getting away from us might give Jorgas time to calm it down.

I could barely lift the hand I raised toward Brett, and there was no calming him. Not when the substance he craved soaked my clothes and spattered the room. He paused for a moment, head weaving from side to side like a snake, until he pounced.

With what little strength I had left, I gripped his shoulders, sank my fangs deep into his neck and drank, ignoring the coppery taste of blood spoiled by madness. My body rose to it, desire pushing through the bitterness, the ruined metallic taste of whatever it was I held in my grasp. Not Brett, but a blood-starved fiend barely aware of the man it possessed.

Hunger and rage had replaced my loyal boy, and I'd no idea how to bring him back.

His ragged fingernails lost their grip on my skin. His mouth froze in a silent scream of pain and hunger that quickly faded. Colour drained from his flesh, save the bloodstains through his shirt.

Dropping to the floor, I ran my hands helplessly over Brett's shoulders, lifting him to rest against my legs. Feeling for a heartbeat, I lifted my bleeding wrist to his mouth. Maybe. Just maybe… A line of my blood smeared his dead lips.

I held Brett's body, stroking his arm as if he were simply asleep. The gentle tap of rain on my windows drowned out any other sound in the house, save my own breath, fetid with blood.

The thing I held wasn't Brett, I told myself again. A tiny, pink spot splashed his forehead. Knowing it had run down my cheek, I wiped it away. I squeezed a dead hand.

"Reylan?"

I didn't answer Jorgas at first. I wondered how long he'd stood there. What he'd seen. How many times he'd called my name before I at last recognised his voice.

"Is…?" If he finished the question, I either didn't hear it, or refused to. Jorgas didn't insist. He waited a little longer before putting a hand on my shoulder.

"Don't," I said quickly, bringing my own hand up to it and realising as he shuddered that it was the one with which I'd held Brett's. "Please, just…"

He didn't need me to finish, instead squatting against the wall.

"We, umm…" I was supposed to be the one who helped others understand their place and feel safer in the supernatural world. My great fucking work and legacy. "We should bury him."

Jorgas swallowed. "Just like that?"

"Well, what would you suggest? An ambulance? A coroner? Maybe the police? Tell me, what procedure am I missing that would make this better because…" I caught hold of myself. How could I blame, or even focus on Jorgas? "I'm sorry."

"Hey, no, I'm not buying that. There's got to be someone! Iain talked about a Necromancer? They can bring him back, can't they?!"

"Bring him back?" I murmured. "Do you even know what you're saying?"

"No, I don't fucking know! Just… something! Otherwise, you wouldn't have… No, no, you…" He choked down whatever words he'd hoped would follow, buried his face in his fists, and screamed.

I eased myself out from under Brett and lowered his body to the floor. Then, I took Jorgas in my arms. I didn't know if he was crying, or how close he and Brett had really grown in their short time together. Was another death more than Jorgas could take? I waited for him to lift his head, then immediately wished he hadn't, since it forced me to face Brett's body.

"Why would Iain do that?" Jorgas asked, his voice surprising me with its sudden calm.

"Iain?"

"Why would he just leave, like that? He knew what would happen, didn't he?"

I didn't answer, mostly because I couldn't stand the truth. Iain had left because I'd told him to, and I could rationalise that or blame Iain all I wanted. The end result was this. I couldn't even be sure if Brett's mental state had allowed him the peaceful end my kiss usually granted. The terminal, blissful combination of arousal and renewed innocence. Was it true? Or a comforting lie Blood Shades told their clumsy protégés? For Brett's sake, I hoped it was true.

"Reylan?" Jorgas asked again. "Hello?"

I'd ignored his question for a good thirty seconds. "I… I don't think it's much use thinking about that right now."

Somehow, Jorgas understood. Or he knew I couldn't explain. We sat, holding each other, not looking at Brett's body, or anything in particular. We simply were, and to my astonishment, it felt like enough.

"I'll go get some ice," Jorgas said, at last getting up.

He was right. I wasn't sure what we'd eventually do with Brett, but digging some hole for the body of this man who'd never asked to cross my path, yet had honoured that service so faithfully? That, I would not do.

CHAPTER SEVEN

Brett stood at the foot of the bed, his bare skin bathed in the grey-green light of early evening. I gripped the sheet, bundling a fistful of it as I sat up with a start. The apparition watched me, his brown eyes wide, shoulders hunched forward and head tilted like a bird sizing up a strange beast in its territory. His hair was a dark, stringy mess, and his throat bore the tell-tale marks of my fatal attack. We'd cleaned him, of course. I couldn't cover him in ice without at least that dignity. But drained dry, Brett's body would wear what I'd done forever, assuming he was dead.

And he had been dead.

He stared at me as if Jorgas weren't there, even as the werewolf stirred, his face curling into a scowl before he relaxed once more. He flopped open an eye still heavy with sleep and smiled a moment before seeing that I was not smiling back.

Jorgas lifted his head and shook with a start, pushing himself back into the pillow just as I had a moment before. "Jesus!"

Not quite, but too damn close for my liking.

"Brett?" I called, not expecting a reply.

"What happened?" Jorgas whispered. "How—"

"I don't know," I said, not taking my eyes off the figure.

"What do you mean you don't know? He's like a fucking zombie now, or something?"

"Don't be ridiculous." In fairness, I'd never met an actual zombie, and had heard too many stories to dismiss the idea. "Wait here."

Jorgas sat perfectly still, face drained of its familiar, good-natured cockiness as I pulled back the sheet and got out of bed. Brett never took his eyes off me. Good. If he wasn't interested in Jorgas, that would probably make this easier.

On the other hand, I was the one who'd killed him.

"Brett," I said again, "can you hear me?"

All I got was another tilt of his head.

I came closer, raising my hands. "Do you understand me?"

I could hear Jorgas breathing. My breaths grew heavier too, and I certainly should not have been able to hear it over Brett's. Of course, now steps from his face, I realised he wasn't breathing at all.

"Is he… okay?" Jorgas asked, a note of hope in his voice.

To my best knowledge, living humans, including Mannequins, even possessed or reanimated, normally showed some sign of respiratory activity. Brett showed none.

"I'm not going to hurt you," I said, slowly reaching to feel for his pulse.

He batted my hand away with lighting speed.

"Woah!" Jorgas breathed.

I gave my heart a second to withdraw from my throat before trying again. This time, I reached for one of his wrists. Again, he swatted me away. Despite our mutual curiosity, I clearly wasn't welcome to touch.

"What the fuck's wrong with him?" Jorgas whispered.

I raised a hand again, shushing Jorgas behind me. The last thing I needed was to provoke some ghoul with lightning reflexes and who knew what kind of strength, no matter whose face it wore. Slowly and silently, I started backing up towards the doorway.

Brett tilted his head again, if one could call this thing Brett.

"Come on." The hallway's floorboards creaked under my bare feet. "Come with me."

The figure just stared.

I cast a glance into the bathroom. The presence of a bathtub full of crushed ice, conspicuously absent of my dead Mannequin and friend, proved that this was no mere apparition. I'd glanced away for only a second. Looking back to see Brett mere inches away, I cried out with a start.

"Everything okay?" Jorgas called.

"Yeah. He moved. Thanks for the warning." Calming my nerves a second time, I stepped around Brett and led him to the room that had been his. I looked around at the few possessions he'd been able to bring in his abrupt transition from human to Mannequin life. Signed posters of bands led by men in a close personal relationship with eye-liner. A bookshelf that had contained photos he'd eventually discarded because they reminded him of loved ones he'd never again see. All that remained was a shelf and a half of plays. From Wilde to August Wilson, Beckett to Mamet, even two dog-eared screenplays by some presumably Italian fellow named Tarantino. The few remnants of the actor Brett had hoped to be. I propped open his closet, pointed to his bed, and scanned his eyes for any flash of recognition. Any life at all. There came none. Those eyes never left me.

I pointed to the bed again. "Sit down?"

The invitation seemed to perplex him. That fucking head tilt…

"Sit down," I said, more forcefully this time. I led by example, sitting on the end of the bed, keeping my hands on my knees.

One step at a time, he advanced.

I patted the edge of the bed for emphasis. "That's it. Sit here. Sit down."

It was like talking to a frightened animal. Did Brett remember how he'd died? Nonetheless, he obeyed, watching me over his shoulder as his slouched body bent to take a seat. This creature, this newborn of sorts, imitated my moves like he was unsure how to operate the gangly, long limbs of a young man who in life had towered over me.

"That's it," I said, not knowing if I was trying to assure Brett or myself. "Do you understand?"

That stare, unyielding as stone, was his only reply.

I looked into the smooth, brown depths of his eyes, devoid of the life that had once filled my Mannequin, and had an idea. A bold and dangerous one, perhaps, but where had the life behind those eyes come from? I lifted my wrist and bit into it, releasing the sweet elixir that had sustained Brett as my faithful servant.

Brett frowned at the steady, gentle stream of blood flowing from the punctures. It seemed to confuse rather than entice him. He jerked his head back as I held the bleeding wrist up to his nose. Several drops splashed his bare leg, but he didn't drink, nor did he speak.

I licked closed the wound, then instinctively went to wipe the blood from his leg. Alarm filled his eyes and the muscles in his shoulders tensed. Right. No touching. Got it. I slowly rose from the bed, keeping one eye on Brett as I approached the door. Sure enough, he began to stand up.

"No." I raised a soft hand. "You stay here."

He paused, head tilting again at this instruction, before standing and taking a step forward.

"No," I said again.

He would not stop until he was halfway across the room, staring at me all the while. Great. The child was either a slow learner, or a brat with superhuman strength and reflexes. I closed the door behind me and locked it from the outside. It hadn't always been cosy quarters for my faithful manservant, after all.

Standing in our bedroom doorway, Jorgas' eyes were wide. "What the hell?"

"I know, I know. I…" What, exactly, was I supposed to tell him? I had no answers. There wasn't even an 'Arcadia Trust' to ask. "He's almost totally non-responsive."

"But he's alive," Jorgas added. "He is alive, isn't he? That's good, right?"

I shook my head. I'd brought Brett back from the brink of mortal injury to make him a Mannequin. Bringing him back from the dead was another thing entirely. My throat tightened, but as I braced for more questions I couldn't answer, strong arms took me in a hug. I held Jorgas against my chest for minutes that felt much longer, cherishing the safety of it.

I'd no idea if the being now occupying my guest room was more child or corpse, or if any trace of Brett remained. But I would find out. I'd been Brett's world, except for the one place where he'd spent quite a few of those last days before I'd disappeared. That, coupled with what I'd seen of Deborah since our return, made Valia's our next stop.

*   *   *

"Fuck me!" Jorgas took the words from my mouth.

He'd managed to break us in through the kitchen, but any trace of the Valia's I remembered had been stripped from the building. The service counter and fridge remained, though without any sign of commerce. No cash terminal, no platters that had once held the day's baked goods, no coffee machine, no beer taps, or even a menu. The place had been cleared of tables and chairs, while the imprint of torn away booths marked the floor and walls. Even the makeshift front door

Brett had helped Deborah put in place was gone. A plain wooden board had been nailed in its place, with another on every window, shutting out all light. Fortunately, the power still worked. Unfortunately, it also illuminated a carving on the floor.

I recognised the symbol's eight points. Not exactly the same as I'd seen in my dream or at Isobel's. Not hewn into rock or painted in blood, but undeniably the same symbol, into which I'd seen Giorgios bled.

"Hey," Jorgas took my hand. "Are you okay?"

I would have to tell him eventually, but it could wait until I had a better idea of what to say. "Search the kitchen. See if there's anything else left behind."

He frowned at first, but obeyed when I gave his hand a gentle squeeze.

I turned my attention to Brett, who in the meantime had fixed his on the star-shaped carving with chilling familiarity. I'd considered the timeline before bringing him here. Supervised by Iain, Deborah's first foray into magick proper had allowed myself, Isobel, and Colin to walk in sunlight. A simple, childish ritual of rhythm and chanting, but no mean feat for a first timer, surely? I remembered Iain being quite protective of Deborah as well, as if he'd a vested interest in her growing powers. But human sacrifice? How quickly or how far had Deborah's powers—and ethical flexibility—come along, and how involved was Brett? With my Mannequin still non-verbal, I had only his behaviour to go on.

"Do you recognise it?" I asked.

Brett turned his head, offering me a glint of comprehension before he stepped inside the carving.

The lights around us flickered silently before giving out altogether. I watched Brett's silhouette, lit only by a narrow beam of streetlight that shone through a broken corner in one of the boards. It illuminated his face, allowing me to see the fog of his breath.

Fog? On a muggy summer's night? Wait… He was breathing!

"What happened to the lights?" Jorgas asked, joining us.

I raised a hand, signalling him to keep his distance, then reached for Brett. It was like reaching through an unseen barrier into a freezer, but Brett showed no discomfort. He just stood there, head lolling, breath fogging the frigid air.

"Brett?" I reached further. "Brett, come on."

He dropped to his knees with surprising agility, then leaned back, pulling his shirt up over his long body and tossing it aside. His wiry arms reached to either side as if he were bathing in the cold, skin like grey parchment prickled with goosebumps.

I jumped, withdrawing my hand as he abruptly punched the floor, splintering one of the boards and pulling it up. He snapped a splinter off and pierced his chest with it.

"Jesus," Jorgas muttered coming up behind me.

Brett dipped his hand in the blood and smeared it along one of the grooves in one smooth motion, graceful as a dancer. He cupped his hand around the wound and repeated the motion on another part of the pattern. The blood smelled nothing like the man I knew. It was bitter, almost chemical. Far from being appetising, it turned my stomach.

Jorgas squeezed my arm. My better sense duelled with curiosity and trepidation, telling me we didn't want Brett to finish what he as 'painting.' If I could believe what I'd seen in the dream, then this room, once a refuge filled with comfort and laughter over blooded tea, had become a place of evil, like Isobel's. Like the Trust. Of course, if I couldn't believe the dream, interrupting Brett might cost us our only chance to learn what had happened to him. Might. If. Maybe. These were some of my least favourite words.

I called Brett's name again. Again, I was ignored.

Damn it! I couldn't allow my Mannequin to be used in a blood ritual I didn't understand. I turned to Jorgas, tilting my head toward the other side of the carving. Understanding me, he walked around it, his breath steady. When he'd taken up position directly opposite me, I summoned my courage and crossed the carving's border. The air wrapped around me with a chill I'd seldom felt since leaving Europe's harshest winters.

Brett's head snapped up to face me, his eyes bright. Ignoring the cold, I held out my hand again. His breath carried the same fetid stench as his blood, one of filth, rot, and falsehood. We had to get him away from this place.

"Brett?" I whispered.

In the dark, I heard him pick something up from the floor. Jorgas burst from the darkness and threw his arms around Brett's shoulders, dragging him back. I could just make out the shape of Brett raising the splinter and thrusting it backward before a deep scream told me the weapon had found its mark. I doubted it could kill Jorgas, but an injured werewolf acting on instinct was a danger to both of us. Brett was in no state to respect that danger, and right now, whatever controlled him was goading it in the most foolish way possible, straddling Jorgas and striking him with repeated punches.

I'd barely taken a step before Brett's body flew past me, and the unmistakeable musk of a changed werewolf filled the empty room. Jorgas' long, fully transformed snout crossed the narrow beam of light. He roared again and charged.

I ran for the back door. A sharp claw sliced into my jacket before I could reach it, cutting me. I ducked to avoid a worse fate, giving the mindless creature time to block my escape. I silently cursed, trying to make out detail in the pitch-black kitchen until I remembered the freezer. I fumbled for the latch, unhooked it, lifted the lid and climbed inside. I landed against something hard and lumpy, my breath catching as I heard the freezer's latch seal me inside. The wolf battered my shelter in its fit of rage. With one last roar, it finally gave up.

Okay. This was fine. I could survive at a temperature below zero with little oxygen, at least until Jorgas got a hold of himself and returned to human form. Hopefully, he wouldn't kill Brett in the meantime. Or re-kill… whatever the fuck were we dealing with, assuming death wasn't a better fate for him.

I shivered, repositioning myself against the frozen mound. My hand brushed away some of the frost that had gathered on… cloth? I wiped away more of the chilly crystals, feeling out the object until my hand brushed cool, frozen skin.

This was not fine. This was not okay.

I lurched within the confines of the freezer, swallowing the urge to cry out. Gathering myself, I felt out more of the clothed shape with which I'd entombed myself. I sniffed the air, not that I expected to sense much from a frozen cadaver, but there was something familiar here. The bitter copper of death mixed with the heady sweetness of… Blood Shade. A very small Blood Shade, no larger than a child. A Premature.

I couldn't say if I lay there next to Giorgios' body for more than an hour, or just a few minutes. Jorgas' mastery over his changes wasn't exactly predictable. But what I'd seen in my dream now felt all too real. Was he even dead? He was after all, as immortal as myself. How long had he been in here? Who was the figure I'd seen slit his throat? Perhaps it had happened here, but who knew? In my dream, the floor had been stone.

"Reylan? Reylan!"

"In here!" I hammered on the lid with my rapidly numbing hands, then kicked it for good measure.

Jorgas unlatched it with due haste and helped me climb out. "Are you crazy? What if I couldn't change back? You could've been stuc— Holy shit!"

"Yeah," I hauled myself up over the lip of the freezer and looked at Giorgios' frozen body. "That."

"Is that…?"

"One of Patricia's Prematures? Yes. His sister was murdered by a Shaper while you were… away."

"Looks like someone finished the job."

I couldn't answer him. Sophia's killing had been a cruel form of collateral damage. But if my dream held, the Shapers had killed Giorgios for altogether more ritualistic purposes, assuming of course, he was dead. It was remarkable what our kind could survive, including a slashed throat. For now, however, Giorgios wasn't going anywhere. "Where's Brett?"

Jorgas shook his head. "Also, that. I didn't see him go, but the back door's ajar."

Panic seized me. "You didn't follow?"

"In wolf form?"

I dashed outside, checking the laneway behind the café and the adjoining street before running out onto Crown Street proper. Sure enough, Brett was long gone, which left us royally fucked. But I did see a car I recognised.

Once was coincidence, twice was creepy. Now, the same balding figure stood across the street, photographing me. He pocketed his phone and immediately started toward his car.

Oh no, fucker, not this time!

With Blood Shade speed in my step, I crossed the street in a few short bounds to head him off. The man turned around, and started jogging toward busy Oxford Street. I followed, weaving around clusters of clubgoers, careful not to draw attention as I kept pace with my surprisingly swift prey. A gaggle of girls in tiaras briefly came between us, just as the lights of Oxford and Crown changed against me. I took my chances, darting around vehicles, ignoring curses from drivers as the bald head disappeared down the slope into the quieter streets of Darlinghurst. Seeing I was still in pursuit, he broke into a run.

Chasing him into a laneway between two townhouses, I heard the clattering of a wooden gate, then the barking of a large dog before I saw him. He made it to the top of the gate and balked, eyes darting between me and what I took to be the dog on the other side. Correctly deciding that I posed the greater threat, he leapt to the other side of the gate, sending the dog into a flurry of snarls and barks. Yet as I closed the space between us, I heard no tearing of fabric, no shouts, just footsteps getting away. I vaulted the gate after him, seeing the German shepherd locked behind a mesh door. Its owner yelled something as I passed through the beam of a security light my prey had activated. I slowed enough to try and get a whiff of him in the humidity. Not far, not far at… there!

I closed the gap between us and seized his leg. He tried to escape, but the movement only made him easier for me to pull to the ground. A solid fist belted my ribs, knocking the wind out of me, but I refused to yield now. I brought my own fist down across his face with a sharp crack that sent a spurt of blood across the pavement.

The man howled with pain, clutching his nose as he spat blood. "Fuckin' hell, pretty boy!"

I couldn't believe my ears, or my eyes as I looked at the extremely visible man I'd straddled. "Kelvin?"

He pushed me off him. As both of us sprang to our feet, I found myself staring down the pointed end of a sharp wooden stake. It wouldn't kill me if it caught me in the heart, but it would paralyse me, leaving me open to whatever else my assailant had in mind.

Kelvin was Patricia Bakker's most loyal aide, spy, and attack dog. I didn't understand how, or why the Cloak Walker, who typically couldn't be seen even if he wanted to, now appeared like any other man on the street, or why he was now threatening me with a weapon at all.

I tried to steady myself. "What the hell are you doing? Why are you spying on us? Where's Patricia? Why can—"

"You think this is fuckin' Twenty Questions?" His face still twinged where I'd hit him. "Mine first, pretty boy, if you're even him."

"If I'm me?" I asked, flabbergasted. "You're one to talk! I can see you!"

"No shit," he muttered. "And I see you, mate, going to some bloody interesting places since you showed up back in town. Do you want to tell me why?"

"Patricia," I repeated. "Do you know where she is?"

"My questions, remember? Who the fuck are you and what are you looking for? Answers. Now!"

Spiffy. Five months into the future and my relationship with Kelvin had gone right back to our first meeting. "Listen to me, you strangely under-concealed misanthrope! I have, in the last two days, returned to a city where, to put it mildly, everything is wrong. The Trust. Valia's… Damn it! How do I know *you're* who you say you are?"

Not that there was any mistaking that voice.

"Kelvin, it's me," I said, firmly. "Jorgas is at Valia's, and there's something there you need to see."

To my surprise, he relented. We ignored the various clubbers and queens we passed in the street, including the same muscular tough who leaned against the wall of Bone. Perhaps he'd become one of its attractions. I heard Kelvin gasp behind me, then turned to see him clutching his stomach.

"Are you all right, mate?" the hustler asked.

"You mind your business," he snapped. Then to me, quietly, "You too, pretty boy."

Yup. It was Kelvin. The hustler sneered and went back to his cigarette.

I called for Jorgas as we arrived, but got no response.

"What in the bloody Hail Satan happened in here?" Kelvin asked, staring at the broken carving that now dominated the café's shell.

"It can wait." I guessed Jorgas had gone to look for Brett, but I wasn't about to volunteer that information. "Here."

I opened the freezer, and for the first time saw what pure horror looked like on Kelvin's face.

CHAPTER EIGHT

Jorgas wisely returned to us after a search of the neighbouring streets turned up no sign of Brett. Kelvin's demand that we wear blindfolds while he drove us to Patricia's new lair seemed paranoid, but I was in no mood to argue as the first rays of dawn pricked my skin.

While I appreciated the windowless room, I wasn't so fussed on the ugly Formica desk almost half my age, the large filing cabinet with a bottom drawer that refused to close, the empty corkboard with a few stray pins in it, or a wooden chair I flatly refused to sit in for fear of tetanus.

If this was the Arcadia Trust's new secret digs, Patricia was certainly slumming it.

I could only speculate as to where Kelvin had taken us. His unexpected appearance—and unexpected *appearance*—left me with bigger questions. Always the charmer, he'd staked me on our first meeting before offering so much as an introduction. Since then, however, we'd fought side by side as allies, however grudgingly. This, of course, also didn't mean a damn thing. Did he plan to come back? They hadn't tied me up. Surely, that was a good sign.

I heard a door open behind me. By all means, come in.

An uncomfortable déjà vu came over me as the excommunicated Sister Patricia Bakker circled me with the kind of fascination usually reserved for a museum piece. I recognised that glint in her eye from our first encounter, now summing me up all over again, as if we'd never met at all. Most everything about her was the same. The trim, well-tailored cream suit. A short crop of blonde hair neatly styled into a no-nonsense cut. Her face seemed noticeably more drawn and tired. This expression too, I'd seen before, in her rare moments of vulnerability. But this former member of the Order of Saint Francis in Prague, and numerous appointments before that, so she'd claimed, was not accustomed to showing vulnerability.

"Do I get a hug?" I muttered.

She stared at me as if we were strangers. "Are you all right?"

I looked around the dingy room. "I might be doing better than you."

Patricia nodded. "You've seen what's become of my home."

"You also seem very aware of my recent movements. Tell me, did it not occur to Kelvin to… oh, I don't know… say hello instead of stalking me? I thought our relationship had moved past such games."

She refused my bait, instead raising an eyebrow in that familiar, oh so irritating fashion. "We recovered Giorgios."

I nodded, reining in my flippancy. "I'm sorry."

"Indeed. Did you kill him?"

"No! Why would you think that?"

"I don't know what to think, just now. The last time I saw the Reylan I knew, he disappeared into a Wound opened up inside the Trust's walls. So, no, I don't know what to think, and I'm not at all sure who, or what I'm talking to right now."

"I could well say the same, Patricia, and if you don't mind me saying, Kelvin seems to have changed a good deal more than I. Care to explain that?"

"I'll explain nothing until I'm sure you're who you seem."

"Oh, this is absurd!" I snarled, looking her in the eye. "What's your working theory, if I'm not who I say I am?"

"The proprietor of the café, what was her name?"

The sudden question threw me, if only for a second. "Deborah. What about her?"

"When did you last see her?"

I thought back to Isobel's house, to Deborah's face when she'd recognised me. And she had recognised me. "You know perfectly well when I last saw her. Kelvin was there."

"Was she the same person you remember?"

"This is ridiculous. She…" I trailed off. The face, the voice, the manner had all been Deborah, but… My stomach turned. "We didn't speak."

Patricia nodded. "So, you can appreciate my position. As for what would convince me—"

A sudden, all too familiar scream cut her off mid-sentence.

"What the hell?" Patricia muttered, leaving me in the room.

"Patricia? Patricia, we're not done here!" I barked, starting after her.

More shouts came before roughly two-hundred pounds of muscular werewolf landed in human form at my feet with a startled cry.

"Jorgas?" Smelling blood, I knelt at his side. "What have you done to him? Patricia? Answer me!"

"Calm your tits, bloodsucker. He'll be fine, for now, at least."

The vocabulary was certainly Kelvin's, but the female voice wasn't.

I advanced on the unkempt, pot-bellied woman who'd spoken. "Damn it, what did you do?"

She snapped her jaws at me with a loud hiss, while an unseen heat sent me flying back into the empty corkboard. Both it and I slid to the floor, where it bounced off my head with an unseemly bump.

"Jesus, Clay!" This time, the voice was Kelvin's. Sure enough, the same man I'd chased through the streets rushed to Jorgas' side. "What the fuck did you do? I said—"

"What?" answered the stranger. "You said bring him in. Tell your little wolf, if he tries to touch my knife again—"

"She was gonna cut me!" Jorgas barked.

"A little nick," the woman scoffed. "Then you decided to be a hero and got stabbed. You happy now?"

"What's going on in here?" Patricia demanded, re-entering the room and moving quickly to help Kelvin. She looked up at me. "Reylan, can you…?"

I was way ahead of her. The amount of blood told me this was no mere flesh wound, and I'd no idea what healing it would do to me in my present state. But this was Jorgas. I had no choice.

Returning to his side, I lifted my bruised wrist to my mouth and punctured it, allowing the life-giving juices to flow. The nausea hit me almost immediately. The room began to spin, and I felt the faint sting of Jorgas' nails pierce my skin as he grabbed my wrist and drank. I wrapped my free arm around his back and held him as his wound washed us both in blood. But he would not waste a drop of mine, as the euphoria of its power took over, enflaming his greedy hunger. The room spun around me again. I felt sick, at least in those seconds the world appeared to me, before the grey haze of fading consciousness obscured it. I tried to push Jorgas away, but fatigue shrouded me. My head lolled, my cheek resting against Jorgas' thick, dark hair. I thought I heard Patricia say Kelvin's name, but I couldn't be certain.

I lurched as the weight was pulled suddenly from my arms. The scent of Jorgas' blood soaked my clothes, mingled with the fresh scent of my own. I choked on emptiness, consciousness threatening to escape me at any second, until the sinewy flesh of a pale forearm appeared in front of my face.

I instinctively bit into it, ignoring the scream. A free hand clutched my shoulder as its owner braced against the pain. He relaxed as warm blood began to quell my hunger with its bitter, yet vibrant flavour. I'd never tasted blood quite like it, but the moment left me no time for scepticism. As our hearts slowed to beat in synch, my sense of the outside world returning with each sip of the life-giving blood, I recognised the scent of the man who'd offered it. He clung to me like a lover, lost to the sharp ecstasy of the feed. The last person I would have expected to volunteer himself.

I forced myself free of Kelvin's arm and lifted my head to catch my breath. He gasped, deprived suddenly of my kiss. I took his hand one last time and licked closed his wound. My own had already begun to seal with the fresh vigour of the feed. Peter to pay Paul, some would say. The spinning, hazy room sharpened into focus. I saw Jorgas, slumped against the wall, his shirt drenched in blood. Still, his breathing was steady. The woman in the tattered khaki jacket who'd struck me grinned, her scarred face smug with satisfaction.

I launched at her, ready to avenge the attack on Jorgas. But as I raised my hands to pull back her chin and grab her throat, a great chill struck me in the chest, just as the heat had before. Again, it knocked me flat on my backside.

"You'll want to stop that," the woman muttered as a strange black fog swept around her and slowly assumed humanoid form, all but scraping the ceiling. Its long, shadowy limbs connected a series of supple joints as it tilted its head, studying me until it turned to Patricia.

"Are you convinced they are who they appear to be?" the figure asked, its voice ethereal, neither male nor female.

"After that display?" Patricia looked at me with an air of apology. "I told you to let me—"

"And we would have been here all bloody night, waiting for you to make up your mind," said the woman, who I now took to be Clay. "The wolf's his boyfriend, right?"

"That's no business of yours!" I snapped.

"Yeah, that answers that. So, I reckon they're legit. We can always do another test if you want."

"You certainly will not!" Patricia barked.

"These men are here at your insistence." The shadow figure's voice embodied calm, in so far as it had a body. "We will remind you that it was you who suggested caution."

I waved my hand at them as if I were silencing children. "Patricia? You suggested this?"

"A lot has changed since you left," she answered.

"Yes, and one of you needs to bring us up to date." I glared at the tall, lanky shadow, then at the dark grinning face of Clay. "Perhaps with some introductions?"

The strangers looked us over, seemingly bemused.

Jorgas threw them a scowl. "Can we at least get off the fucking floor?"

*   *   *

"It began almost immediately after you went into the Wound." Patricia looked down at the long, heavily stained bar, where we now sat surrounded by the tattered remains of a Kings Cross night spot lost to gentrification, then left to rot.

Kelvin poured fingers of whiskey into four squat tumblers and passed one to each of us. "To the Arcadia fucking Trust," he muttered, raising his glass, "such as it is."

91

To my surprise, Patricia raised her glass to meet Kelvin's, their expressions sombre. Jorgas and I joined them. I watched Jorgas and Kelvin down their drinks in one swift movement, then pretended to sip my own. I hated whiskey.

"What do you mean, such as it is?" I asked.

"You're looking at it," Kelvin answered. "The two of us, and the two of you, if you want."

"But…" I trailed off. With Isobel missing and the Prematures dead, he was right.

Patricia took a sip. "Imagine a rip in the fabric of space, time, and the common-sense laws of physics. That's the Wound, in its simplest terms. A point at which the rules of one universe and the rules of another converge with chaotic results. You can traverse it, with risks and limitations. A skilled enough Shaper can even manipulate it. Closing it, however, proved more difficult than Isobel or I had hoped. Funny thing, once it starts growing. It's not like a black hole that absorbs anything within reach. Rather, it warps it. Not in so far as appearance, but inside, changing the very integrity of whatever the Wound touches as it gobbles up anything it can reach. Waiting for you, we watched it expand to fill the ball room, hoping, against probability that you might be able to recover those lost."

"And eventually you gave up?"

"We'd little choice. Brett pleaded with us to give you a few minutes more. To retreat and give the thing whatever space it required in the hope you'd find a way out before it got too big. We didn't realise that it was already too late. Then, Brett went to go after you."

"He what?" My fingers tightened around the glass.

"But the Wound wouldn't let him. It was like putting his hand through sticky toffee or tar of some sort. We'd no spell or power to throw at such a thing. We could only watch as it absorbed him."

My eyes widened. "Absorbed? You mean, Brett did follow us?"

"No, that's what was so odd."

I was in no mood for vague riddles.

"It was like the poor guy was pickled in jelly," Kelvin added. "Except, he wouldn't stop moving. The lines of his body just kept shifting somehow. Bending, unbending… then the thing started growing faster."

"That's when we had to leave Brett behind," Patricia finished. "I'm sorry, Reylan. When we were able to return, the Wound was gone."

"What do you mean, when you were able to return?"

"We couldn't stay in that house with the Wound expanding the way it was. Georgios had no protection against the sun, so Isobel took him away while Kelvin and I retreated to the back courtyard. We'd planned to hide in the wine cellar. It seemed the safest place, until we realised the Wound hadn't followed."

"Hadn't… what?"

"We saw no sign of anything outside the ordinary when we turned to look back at the house. The stonewashed wall, complete with ivy, looked just as it did every day. Whatever shape the Wound took, it didn't breach the Trust's walls. From the outside, it was like nothing had happened. I might have felt foolish had Kelvin not been there to corroborate what I'd seen."

"So…" I exchanged glances with Jorgas, who sat quietly, taking the story in. "What happened when you went back inside?"

"I realised the Wound had not been dispersed, but replaced."

"Replaced by what?" Jorgas asked, anticipating my question.

Kelvin snorted. "Fucked if we know. But I never want to feel that again."

"As I stepped across the threshold and approached the ball room, it was as if some sense of cold dread had filled every space, every nook and crevice within those walls. An evil I'd not felt since… Well, I'm sorry I can't be more specific."

"Since what?" Jorgas pressed, his interest now piqued for both of us. "You've felt this before?"

"A triviality. Paranoid déjà vu in the moment. In any case, I dismissed it and began searching for Isobel and Georgios, without success."

"Where had they gone, then?" I asked.

"Your guess is as good as ours, pretty boy," answered Kelvin. "That's the last we saw of either one of them, until today. Don't suppose you know how the poor kid ended up in the freezer?"

I bristled at the unsubtle implication. "Are you accusing Isobel—"

"We're not accusing her of anything," Patricia answered, coldly. "But I can't put any faith in her intentions or make finding her a priority based on what little we know."

"Where was Brett during all this?" Jorgas asked. "You said it was like he'd been stuck in jelly. He must have been there when you went back inside, no?"

Patricia shivered with discomfort. "I wasn't exaggerating when I described the feeling that enveloped both of us when we went back inside as an all-encompassing dread. We tried to find all of them, of course. Kelvin searched upstairs. We turned over every room between us. As I passed the foot of the stairs, however, I could have sworn I heard voices. Not clear speech, but a faint whisper, like an indistinct conversation heard from across the street. That's when I looked up at the stairs, and saw Kelvin."

"'Saw' being the operative word?" I asked.

"Not my finest hour," the Cloak Walker muttered. "Standing there on the landing, starkers, freshly inducted into the choir much too fucking visible."

"Isobel and Brett were nowhere to be found, and it was obvious we'd no control over whatever was going on inside the house. If it could render Kelvin visible…" Patricia paused, weighing her words. "Who knew what else we could expect? Kelvin quickly gathered up some clothes and we left."

"Yeah, on that note." The Cloak Walker pulled his t-shirt over his head and shucked it off behind the bar, before going to work on the belt that secured his trousers. "This stuff itches. I don't know how you lot stand it."

I caught myself staring at the wiry frame of the elderly but spry man whose birthday suit was now on full display and quickly looked away. "Don't you have company?"

"You really think they're bothered?" Kelvin asked.

"Look, who are *they*, exactly?"

"Yeah, you can start with the one that stabbed me," Jorgas added.

"That's a question best put to Joboram. They'll want to speak with you both, I expect."

"Joboram?" I asked. "They'll want to speak with us, will they?"

Patricia shook her head. "Joboram is one of a thousand names, but it's the one they gave us for simplicity. Clay, of course, you've met."

"Yeah," Jorgas muttered. "The crazy bitch."

"Yes, about her…" I said, not feeling up to defending Jorgas from a second stabbing.

Patricia let out a long sigh, as if reluctant to volunteer the information. "The common term is yowie, or yaroma. Joboram, specifically, is Quinkan."

"Quinkan?" I recognised the word, if only through hearsay. One of the native supernatural guardians of Australia's land.

But I'd never, to my knowledge, met one. "I thought they controlled Cape York. North Queensland? They're a long way from home."

"And you're a long way from Denmark," Patricia said, flatly.

"I just didn't expect a Quinkan to be part of your… whatever the Trust is now." My lack of experience was showing. From what little I did know, the Quinkans, Jimbra, and other supernaturals indigenous to Australia had mostly abandoned the major cities to foreign interlopers and transplants like myself. I'd heard tales of brutal conflicts with little substantiation, and I was not about to go prying when it came to powerful beings of which I knew so little. Yet, what was to prevent them from walking among us? We all had our veils. "Where does Clay come in?"

"Clay is Quinkan as well. Anurra, to be precise," Patricia explained.

"Yeah, she's… something," muttered Kelvin.

"So were most of you, as I recall." Patricia downed the last of her drink and tapped the edge of her glass.

Kelvin poured her another. "Anyway, they're all the help we've got right now. Not that much cooperation's happening unless it's on their terms."

That checked with what I'd heard of the Quinkans. A resentment of outside contact and a general disdain for supernatural politics and the hegemony of the Houses. The latter didn't bother me. On the contrary, it at least gave us something in common.

"Such as the cooperation of stabbing someone, before being introduced?" I asked.

"What?" I recognised the sneer behind the voice. "I didn't snap it off. That's how you know we're friends."

"Bloody hell, Clay," muttered Kelvin.

"Or how I know you're friends, at least. I was just gonna nick your hand, but no. You had to be a smart arse and fight me, didn't ya?" The woman straightened her jacket over a tight t-shirt that barely contained her squat, barrel-shaped belly. She pretended to wipe something from the corner of her mouth and suck it from her fingers. "You're all right though."

"Glad you approve," I muttered.

"Since you're unfamiliar with the Anurra," Patricia added, her face not without empathy, "you should know that an intruder's intentions are often gauged by the flavour of their blood."

"I reckon you'd understand that, Blood Shade." Clay looked far too pleased with herself.

True enough, I could tell a lot about a companion's emotional state by the flavour, heat, spice, and subtleties of their blood when I tasted it, but 'stab first, ask questions later' greetings rubbed me the wrong way.

"It won't happen again," I said.

"You're fucking right it won't," Jorgas muttered, downing another drink, which Kelvin refreshed. I never thought I'd be so grateful for the Cloak Walker's company, despite his current visage.

"Where is Joboram?" I asked.

"What? You thought we'd all just chill at the bar?" Clay asked. "Get to know one other? Small talk? Hey, I know. Once we're all bored with trying to impress each other with what we do for a living, how about we talk about which gym we go to, or bitch about how much we're paying in rent? That's what we do these days in Sydney town, right?"

I gritted my teeth, losing patience. "With all we've seen since returning, I'd rather be acquainted with any new allies."

"Allies?" Clay's laugh sounded like a frog being turned inside out. "You're killing me."

"Joboram speaks to us in their own time," Patricia said quickly. "As I understand, it takes a lot of effort for them to manifest in a way we can comprehend."

"I see," I said. "And Clay's what… the muscle?"

"Say that again," the Anurra muttered, baring a mouth full of needle-like teeth that stripped away any human visage as her eyes flashed red.

Oh honey, two could play that game.

"Enough!" Patricia snapped, silencing her. It was oddly comforting to see a little of her authority return.

"Whatever." Clay straightened her jacket again. "I've got better things to do."

I waited until the creaking steel door had slammed shut behind her before turning back to Patricia and Kelvin. "Charming."

"Like I said, pretty boy," muttered Kelvin. "The Trust these days is Patricia, me, and you two, if you want."

"In that case, why are they here? Why are you here?"

"One thing fundamental and sacred to the Quinkans is the protection of those who are lost. Children in particular, though when you're as old as Joboram, that's a relative concept." Patricia took a long sip of her drink.

"How old is Joboram, exactly?" I asked.

"A question best asked of them. Until they're ready to speak with you, you can enjoy safe harbour here."

"Safe harbour?" I asked, not at all liking the implication.

"We have strong reason to believe your home has been compromised."

"You can dispense with the black ops double speak. What do you mean?"

"Kelvin's been following you these past few days. He's not the only one."

"I see. And did you perhaps think that this other party might be following Kelvin or trying to find you?"

A dark look passed between them.

"No disrespect," I said. "But I've only just returned to my home. I'll not be forced out by some unseen voyeur who may or may not exist or pose a threat."

"Was what happened at Isobel's house enough of a threat for you?" Kelvin asked. "How about what happened at the Trust? Don't tell me you didn't feel it, pretty boy. I felt it across the fucking street. That place did not want us inside it."

"First of all, can we stop talking about that building like it's a self-aware thing?" I answered. "Secondly, I found Brett there, inside, which you two could not. He was in a state, to put it mildly."

"I know that," said Kelvin. "I saw him. How's that change—"

"I've given you my answer," I said, firmly. "What time is it?"

Patricia brought her pale fingers up beneath her chin. "Almost nine… in the morning."

I tilted the glass, examining my still ample finger of whiskey. "Crisis has bred healthy habits, I see. Look, you can tell Joboram they have until sunset to speak with me. The moment it's safe to leave, we go."

"I will tell Joboram no such thing," Patricia bristled. Fair. I had just treated her as a messenger. "They'll speak to you, and to us, when they're ready."

"Fine. Though I'm going home as soon as it's dark. If they choose to come and speak to me there, it'll be when *I* am quite good and ready."

Patricia nodded, that familiar arched eyebrow making it clear she saw through my bravado. Indeed, I doubted I could keep Joboram out of my house if I tried. Common folklore had it that it was our kind who could come and go by mist, but even if such legends had credibility, Joboram, from what

I'd seen, possessed abilities to shame the most protean of Blood Shades.

Hearing snoring, I looked to my left and saw Jorgas slumped into a chair, out cold, his glass resting precariously in his fingertips.

"Someone's wiped," said Kelvin. "And before you ask, no, I didn't put anything in his drink."

"I made no such…" I smiled. "Very funny."

"You'll both be safe here, for the day at least," Patricia said. "You have my word, and Clay's, I'll make sure of it."

I believed her. For all I could say about the Anurra, Clay had been nothing if not frank with us. "Thank you. Though we'll still be returning to my home come sundown."

Patricia nodded. "If I can't change your mind. Though, you may wish to make a small detour."

"May I, just?" I asked, suspicious again.

"To Balmoral Crown Hospice and Care Centre, where your tenant, Dorotha has been a patient for several weeks now."

I smiled at her with silent thanks. Another small win. How I needed them.

CHAPTER NINE

When Joboram failed to honour me with an audience, I called a cab to catch Rosewood Crown Hospice and Care Centre's visiting hours in the short window I had after sunset. I've grown fond of Sydney in the thirty odd years I've called it home; its extended bright summer days, less so. A slow, labyrinthian chase in a taxi through evening North Shore traffic followed, with an 8.30pm cut-off time, its Minotaur.

At last, I spied the sign for the hospice across the road, with three lanes of traffic between us. "Just here is fine."

"Sir, is no stop here. It's okay. I make roundabout."

I checked the time on the cab's dial. 8.17pm. Fuck that. I waited for traffic to stop again, then put a hand on the driver's leg.

"Sir?" The man glanced at me, his soft, dark eyes widening as they met mine. I had him.

"Here will be just fine," I said, my voice soft. "How does two hundred sound for your trouble?"

"I…" His pulse quickened as he looked at my hand again. "My wife—"

"Yes, won't she be happy you're home early?"

The tip of the driver's pink tongue broke through his lips. He didn't take his eyes off me as he released the locks. "Could we just… maybe…"

I put the money in his hand. "You have a wife."

Slamming the cab door shut, I darted across through the gelatinous traffic flow, just a little Blood Shade speed driving me on.

"Mister Raymond!!!" Dorotha spied me as soon as I entered the lobby, smiling with outstretched arms that wrapped me up in an enormous hug that cut me off mid 'hello.' "Where have you been? I was so worried!" Her smile fell as soon as she released me and saw my face. "Mister Raymond? All is well with you?"

"Yes," I took her hand and let her lead me up the hall, ignoring a scowl from the weaselly receptionist who'd demanded I sign in. "Everything is fine. I was called away on sudden business. Extremely sudden."

I'd been so eager to see her, I hadn't thought about a cover story. Even though Dorotha knew of my condition and the company I kept, I doubted 'stuck in a hell dimension with a skewed sense of time' would fly.

"Ah, your friend, she did mention something about that."

"Did… she?" I asked, daring to wonder if this mysterious benefactor might in fact be Isobel, or even Patricia. But it was Iain who'd organised Dorotha's care… or so he'd said.

"Yes," Dorotha continued, beaming as we rounded another corner. "Everyone has been so kind. Oh, but to see you, Mister Raymond? How I have needed this! And there is, I think, someone else who is happy to see you too?"

A familiar ginger face looked up at me from a chair as we entered the room. Demetrius sat with folded paws, his expression making it clear that my absence had been unauthorised. I was quickly forgiven, as the cat bounded off the chair and began weaving around my ankles. I bent down and scooped him into my arms, a stupid grin on my face.

"Hello! Hello, yes, there you are! Did you miss me?"

Dorotha shuffled past me and collapsed into a comfortable-looking armchair. She invited me to sit in the one Demetrius had vacated. "I did not know when you would be back, Mister Raymond. They want to put him in pet home, but I say no! Pooska must stay with me! In the end, a little paperwork and all was fine."

"Yes, but… are you okay?"

She waved away my concerns. "A little fall, Mister Raymond. One or two. A sprain in my wrist. It was so kind of you to arrange all this, but is not necessary."

I frowned, reminded that the arrangements for Dorotha's care had been made in my name, on my account. "Well, of course, when I heard about your injury…"

"How did you…?" she began, panicking me in my lack of an excuse. "But of course, your friend. I knew she was special as soon as I met her, Mister Raymond. When that fellow, Father Grieg was teaching her… the drumming we did? The magic, so you and your friends could walk in the sun. Deborah, I think is her name?"

Yes, it was, and given recent revelations, it chilled me. "Yes, Deborah…?"

"She took care of everything. The doctor says I should be back home in a week or perhaps less. Don't you worry, Mister Raymond. They are just being careful. I feel fit, healthy and happy. Deborah said just last week that I would hear from you soon, and here you are."

Last week? Curious…

"Do you know how to contact her?" This must have seemed an absurd request to Dorotha. In fact, I risked worrying her by undoing the whole lie, but… "My phone died and I lost her number."

This was technically true.

Dorotha shook her head. "She never gave me that, Mister Raymond. There was no need. Every few days, she comes to see me and check that everything is fine. She and the nurses take care of everything. Next time, will I tell her you need to speak with her?"

"No," I said quickly. "I'll see her soon, I'm sure."

If Deborah had been Iain's proxy for dealing with the care home, and he'd used Brett's knowledge to speak for me, it meant one of two things. Either Deborah had acted out of loyalty to Brett, not realising he was Iain, or she'd accepted Iain as an ally, knowing full well what was going on.

A darker interpretation painted this as the work of Shapers who thought nothing of embracing dark magicks. That meant they knew exactly who and where Dorotha was. They controlled her care, and I could no longer take Iain's motivations for granted, assuming I ever could.

"I think," I said, petting Demetrius, "we should ask the doctors about taking you home. You did say you've been feeling better?"

"Oh, yes," she beamed. "Mister Raymond, that would be so wonderful."

I couldn't guarantee Dorotha would be any safer, but she would at least be under my roof, where we could reach her quickly if there was trouble. What anyone had to gain by hurting an elderly Polish widow with the most tenuous of links to the supernatural world, I'd no idea. But I'd seen enough death and disaster recently.

I put a hand on hers and squeezed. "I'll make the arrangements."

"Do you want to take Pooksa, now?" She ran a hand over Demetrius' furry head as he ran up to her. "He's no trouble, mind you. I simply ask. They feed him. Clean his kitty box. Like royalty! Such a cat."

I considered the ease with which my cat arched into Dorotha's plump hand, and what the companionship was likely doing for both of them. "If he's no trouble, he can stay with you for now."

"No trouble at all, Mister Raymond." She lifted the cat into her lap, smooshing his tolerant face as she stroked his head. "None at all."

I had to admit, as I bid Dorotha farewell and returned to reception, the sight of them both safe and sound relieved some of my apprehension.

"Reylan?" Deborah sat in a far chair, dressed in a plain blue tank top and jeans, her once neatly maintained bob chaotic and choppy. Yet her face and complexion, as I saw it, seemed healthy, save the distraught expression. "I heard you were here."

Hello to you too, I thought. "Are you all right?"

"You have questions, I know."

I lowered my voice to a whisper. "I'm very worried about you! What I saw…"

She brought up her hands, a futile gesture of apology. "I'm not the person to explain it. I'm glad you're okay."

"Not the person…" I remembered her face at the house, and the fate of the unfortunate thug. "What are you involved in?"

"Come with me, quickly."

I couldn't say no to Deborah, especially not now. I followed her out to the small carpark spread out behind a grove of trees at one side of the building. She led me to a white car parked beside an oleander tree, where I could just make out the features of a slender Asian man behind the wheel. He didn't look at us, even as Deborah opened the back door.

"It's okay," Deborah said. "He's a friend."

"Hello," I said to the man.

His lack of acknowledgement didn't convince me. But to what would I be abandoning Deborah if I left now? I got in the car before I could second-guess it further. Perhaps something in my manner, an agitation so slight I couldn't see it myself, caught her eye.

She put a hand on mine, her voice soft as down when she spoke. "Don't worry, it's me."

The North Shore wasn't exactly my home turf. After dark, I recognised even less. I could however make out the shape of a dozen luxurious vessels berthed at the dock, where we arrived after just a few minutes driving in silence.

Offering me one final smile, Deborah got out of the car.

"Where are we?" I asked, following. "Why are we here?"

"You want answers, right?"

Hell yes, I wanted answers. To what, was open for debate.

*   *   *

I looked around the clean polished fixtures dotting the deck of the boat where Deborah had directed me to wait. Five minutes passed. Ten…

My stomach lurched as the engine revved and the boat eased out of dock. I was tempted to leap off the back of the boat to dry land. But that would leave me right back where I started. Fine. It couldn't be later than nine-thirty. I had a good six or seven hours before sunrise, even if my host failed to emerge. The door leading below deck was locked tight. I couldn't even see who was controlling the boat!

Okay. Less fine.

I eased into one of the chairs on deck and watched the lights of the North Shore pull further away, while those of the city drew nearer. As we rounded the peninsula that held Taronga Zoo, I tried not to take the roars of unseen lions as an omen. Answers, Deborah had promised. Answers, I would have.

The engine at last stilled and we dropped anchor. Moments later, a small, far-too-cheerful-looking man emerged from below, carrying two tall red cocktails.

"Good evening," he said with an inflection that irritated me. "Sorry to keep you waiting. Bloody Mary? Let me know if it's not to your taste. Not so experienced with the blood cocktails, unfortunately."

"Wrong time of day, isn't it?"

"We shall see," he said, sipping his own.

I took the drink from him and sniffed at it. The bitter copper of animal blood hit my nostrils like noxious fumes. I carefully set the drink down.

"That bad? Sorry, like I said…" The man tilted his head at me, brow furrowing above his handsome features. The sunglasses were a little facetious, given the hour, though taking them off gave away his identity at once. I'd seen it on posters and fliers.

"Adrian Tseng," I said. "You're Deborah's friend."

He nodded, sipping his drink.

This explained a lot, including this little pleasure cruise. Much as I tried to avoid human politics, I knew something of the man's rise to political stardom. Courting both the Chinese community of Haymarket and the rainbow vote, Tseng had risen from student politics to serious contender for city council in just a few years. Talks of an ascension to the Lord Mayor's office within a decade were no longer laughed off. Not bad for the Trans child of conservative migrants, or so he'd claimed in numerous interviews and debates. Of course, it was easy to claim what one wanted in the absence of any real opposition. More than one of Tseng's opponents had fallen ill or mysteriously no-showed on debate night and Tseng, seemingly a natural-born politician, had seized every such moment.

"Deborah," I began, not really sure what or how much to tell this man. His silence invited me to continue. "She needs help."

"Don't worry. We've always looked out for each other."

I glanced southward again, trying to get my bearings.

Tseng grinned, pointing to a sandy cove that lined a gap in the rocks. "It's said the first Shapers to settle in Sydney practiced their rituals at Lady Bay Beach. Supposedly, there wasn't a wealthy lady of fashion in Eastern Sydney who didn't have her 'guide' to the spirit world, a keeper of good fortune, or a mystical healer. This was a very lucrative city for Shapers at one time."

I was already growing tired of his blasé attitude. "I didn't come for a history lesson, Mister Tseng."

"Oh, but they kept it discreet. First of all, no proper Christian lady of any social standing would admit to having sought the aid of witchcraft. Secondly, it was the fad of the time, mostly fulfilled by charlatans of questionable skill. Why should those with a genuine connection to the arts not take advantage?" He waved his hand in the air with surprising delicacy. "Try your drink again."

"No thanks."

"I insist. Allow me to save some face as a host, at least."

I brought it to my lips again. Much better. "Cute."

"You as well, though that's not why we're here."

"I mean the… It was you!"

His grin showed up flawless teeth in the moonlight. "How did Jorgas like his coffee? Just a small test, to make sure we could reach you. No harm meant."

"No harm?" I challenged. "Who are you, really?"

He smiled, swirling the red liquid in his glass. I wondered if he was about to frustrate me further by playing obtuse. "I am… in practice, you might say. Not quite as good as the Shapers Patricia Bakker had working with her, but I'm on my way." He tipped his drink toward me and took another sip.

"Can I say the same of Deborah?" I asked.

"Deborah? Yes, I suppose you can. She hid her powers remarkably well. I'm surprised at your friend… she did tell me his name… Owen?"

"Iain," I corrected him.

"Yes, Iain. Abandoning her after helping activate her powers? Talk about kicking baby bird out of the nest."

"He didn't…" I stopped, knowing I was being goaded. "What is it you want, Tseng?"

He tossed me another faint smirk and drained the last of his Bloody Mary. "You're very curious, for a man who just returned from a hell dimension with a traumatised boyfriend. Much less one who just lost another."

"Another?"

"Iain."

I leaned forward, my ears pricking at a subtle implication. "Do you know where he is?"

Tseng shrugged, lounging back further in his seat. "I can tell you he's alive. Beyond that, it gets fuzzy."

"Fuzzy? If you can't be more straightforward, I swear—"

"He's more alive than my husband, who you murdered in cold blood. Is that straightforward enough for you, Reylan?"

The accusation, coupled with my host's sudden stone-faced expression, sent a lurch of bile up my throat.

"Not even a denial? Wow. They said you were something, but wow."

"I cannot deny a crime whose victim I don't know," I pointed out.

"That many, eh?"

"Your husband?" As much as he annoyed me, I wasn't completely without empathy. "My condolences, but I'm not in the habit of harming my companions. I don't know who you mean or what you're talking about."

Tseng tutted his tongue several times and folded his arms. The gesture only emphasised the muscles that filled out his white shirt and short sleeves. "Companions, yes! That great affirming word for victims of your nightly lust."

"That's hardly fair," I said. "Unless you've the same low regard for promiscuous mortals?"

"I've a low regard for them when it's an act of rape, yes."

"Okay, that's it!" If his goal was to see me angry, he'd accomplished it. Despite my height when I stood to face him, the man was unperturbed. "Whatever high horse you think you rode in on, either get to the point or take us back to the dock. What do you want, Tseng?"

"Remember, for a start."

"Remember what?"

The image of a tall, muscular blond man on Tseng's phone jogged my memory. Rory. I'd euthanised him after he'd come face to face with an unhinged werewolf. The night we'd both met Jorgas. "I… I'm sorry, but you've been misinformed."

"Have I?" Tseng asked. "So, you do remember him? You did kill him?"

"To end his suffering!"

Tseng laughed bitterly in my face.

"So, is that it?" I asked. "You plan to kill me? Alone, on a boat with a being who's physically far superior—"

"Lest you think you're punching below your weight, I'll remind you, we can convince you the room you're in is stretching endlessly in darkness, or closing in around you."

"I see," I murmured. "So, you were at that house." My neck had started to itch.

"We're explorers, by nature," Tseng said, getting up and strutting around the deck like he was enjoying the night air. "Who knows what else we might unlock within ourselves?"

"At the cost of a man's life? And you lecture me about murder?"

"Oh, him? A kidnapper and torturer of little girls? Pardon me for not sparing any tears."

"And the boy?" I asked, scratching at my skin as the itch grew worse. "The Premature?"

Tseng seemed surprised by the question. Perhaps I'd found his ethical compass, after all.

"Was his life worth it too? A child?"

"I really don't know what you're talking about." He checked his expensive-looking watch. "Oh my, is that the time? Where does it go?"

Dread hit me as I followed the direction of his gaze. East. Dawn. The first light, creeping over the cliffs of Watsons Bay. This was impossible. We'd spent only a few minutes talking . . .

"What have you done?" I demanded. "Tseng, this isn't funny!"

"Funny?" he asked, returning to his seat and crossing an ankle over one knee. "We were discussing murder, alleged in my case, but very real in yours. I don't find that funny."

I didn't know how, but he'd sped up time, or more likely, slowed it down within the confines of the boat.

"Tseng, if I don't get below deck in the next few minutes—"

"What? You think I'm going to spend the day watching over some sleeping Blood Shade who slit Rory's throat?"

"That did not happen!"

He glared at me, unconvinced.

"Take us below and I'll tell you exactly what happened. No lies. No tricks. Deborah will vouch for me."

"Deborah?" he laughed. "She doesn't want anything to do with you."

"She… But we just—"

"She brought you here because you need to hear this, Reylan. I can forgive. I can give someone the benefit of the doubt and perhaps put aside… revenge? Oof, that word. That's if I think my point is clear. Is it? Because if you and your friends don't stop prying, all you've experienced so far will seem like a cosy bedtime story."

"Now, you listen here!"

"Please! You're inherently selfish, and that's how you like it. While I don't share such detachment, I can appreciate it. So, I'm giving you one chance, either prove you've moved beyond your little world of clubs and… 'companions' as you call them—"

"Prove what? What the hell are you talking about?"

"—or take that wolfish boyfriend of yours and leave Sydney for good. Now, swim."

"Excuse me?"

"I'm being more than reasonable. Prove to me you're not monsters, or make sure we never cross paths again. You won't like the third alternative."

Another ferry blasted its horn as it approached. With Blood Shade speed, I could rush below deck before Tseng even realised what had happened. But what then? I'd be pinned down in hostile territory. Even if I managed to kill him—a big if, against a Shaper who could alter time itself—I'd be foolish to assume he didn't have friends backing him up.

"Here. A little something to improve your odds." He extended a silver coin I first took to be a fifty-cent piece, with the familiar sharpened edges of its twelve sides. A closer examination, however, showed this one had only eight. Both sides were perfectly smooth to the touch.

"My odds?"

He gave me a knowing grin. "A gesture of good faith. I'm sure you won't need it, being so physically superior and all."

There would be no convincing him before the sun's rays charred my flesh, and I had nothing to gain by begging. Not giving him the satisfaction of another look, I held my breath and rolled overboard.

CHAPTER TEN

Parched skin, blackened with age and tinged with the green of the sea, covered the figure standing naked over a wooden table stacked with grimy papers and foul-looking potions. Wisps of white hair hung from a mottled scalp, and an unmistakeable smell spoke of what might be the slowest death in the history of creation. My heart thumped faster, a lump rising in my throat. I tried to sit up, only to strain against tight bonds. I resisted the urge to cry out, instead letting my eyes adjust to the darkness of… I was in a fucking cave, stripped of my clothing, strapped to a wooden table by strong ropes.

Over the faint crashing of waves against rocks somewhere nearby, I heard the distinct clink of metal tapping metal, overlaid by mutterings of old French. Fluent though I was, the words were archaic and incoherent. But they erased any last doubts about the identity of my captor.

Jesus. Fucking. Christ. The tale my subconscious had told little Giorgios in his bed, embodied before me. Coincidence? More like fate itself had farmed my memories for a suitable nightmare, now made flesh.

"Michel?"

He ignored me, continuing the flurry of clinks and inaudible utterances.

"Michel?" I'd no idea what to say, much less how he'd receive it. How he'd even been allowed to live baffled me. I could scarcely imagine the torture of such a rotting, miserable existence. Yet, he'd also not chosen to end it himself by greeting the sun. "Michel Beauvrie!"

"To the brine and down again, he enters my domain. What curious immortal be who longs to know such pain?"

Of all the horrors against which I'd steeled myself… anything but rhyming verse!

"Michel?" Every word hurt. He'd hit me underwater with the force of a torpedo. I'd no way of knowing what other side effects might stem from the man's bite, which I now saw was oozing blood, blackened with gaping injury. Still, I felt no pain. Perhaps I had bigger problems than the poetry.

"A name beloved, a name now lost, bereaved and gone away. The waves still bring them to me. Waves of salt. Waves of blood. Nourish mine with supple flesh."

There was a tone to this freestyling I did not like.

"Michel Beauvrie!" I said again, a command this time, hoping my powers might compel his cooperation. They did not.

"Most beautiful of landers? That was me, once. So long ago, and only yesterday. Yet soon, soooooon my beautiful walker of streets and fields and forests."

So much for mental manipulation. He simply had too little mind left.

"No more stitching, no more sorrow, no more stitching, no more sorrow," he sang.

"Michel!" I barked. "Look at me!"

"Look at you?" The words echoed around the cave like a howl as he turned to face me.

For all the terrors I'd seen, none prepared me for the sight of that face, clinging to cheekbones that had once made Beauvrie such an enviable prize. Yet the skin, tinged though it

115

was with the green sea, could not have been more than a few weeks old. I was sure, if I looked, I'd find reports of some youth who'd disappeared in the waters of Sydney Harbour, or off one of its beaches, or perhaps not even from Sydney. Beauvrie was rumoured to have made the entire East Coast his oceanic domain, and over a century, could have accounted for any number of disappearances, some more notable than others. Had they all wound up stitched to the creature's rotting face, victims of a vain attempt to recapture an eternal youth stolen by ill luck? Still, there was no hiding those eyes, black as squid ink, the last kiss of life long subsumed by a triple curse of genetics, vanity, and hate.

"Ah, yes. Look at you, such beautiful death. They all love to look at you, lander."

I tried to flinch as a skeletal fingertip brushed my flank, but my reflexes refused. Even when his nails scraped my flesh, and I realised they were not fingernails at all but the points of fish-hooks, weaved into his fingers, I felt nothing. Why hadn't I healed? Would I still feel nothing when they dug into me?

"They all love to watch, to see who next has the honour of courting the fair prince, all while asking 'who is that beautiful boy?'"

Hell, Beauvrie wasn't talking about me. He was mourning himself. I glimpsed a trio of candles on the table where he'd been working. Their flickering lights reflected off a sharpened blade.

"Such beautiful flesh," he whined in that same sing-song voice.

I choked as a wave of putrid fish and death wafted over me from the creature's breath. I had to get off this table. But then what? I couldn't move. I could only stare as Beauvrie sank one of his hooks into the inside of my thigh, then out again, pierced through, tugging at the skin to pull it tight. He ran the back of his other hand along it, muttering some more.

"Michel," I whispered. "Whatever you're about to do…"

A trail of blood gushed from the fresh wound as he pulled the hook from my skin with surprising elegance. I winced as he ran the back of another down my cheek. My face wasn't numb.

"They used to scoff at me," he said, voice high-pitched over the sound of waves. "Laughed about the boy whore of the port. Yet at night, they came. One, then two… They'd peel off from their friends and look for the boy whore and he would answer. Soon, they stopped laughing. Soon, they understood. Beauty… beauty must be shared, not kept to a few selfish men. And if it's eternal…"

The implication took on a horrifying clarity as that face turned away. The face he'd stolen from his last victim. A face that would fade like all the others. Now, he wanted mine.

"Michel," I choked again. "You can't—"

"Beautiful forever! In darkness long enough, the fair prince shall walk again among men. The selfish defiler, alone. To know himself, as the prince now does."

"It won't work, Michel!" I couldn't tell if he would even understand my pleas, but I had to try. "You can't just… slice me up and wear my face forever. It'll rot, like all the others."

"He lies now, desperate to return me to the waves where I have too long obeyed the will of landers. Been a good boy!" He stood up, stroking the inside of my thigh with his hooks. "No more."

I tried to steady my breath as he returned to his work bench. Truthfully, I'd no idea what would happen if Beauvrie succeeded in flaying me alive. Even if my skin did regrow, I didn't fancy the idea of a bloodthirsty monster roaming the streets wearing my face. I closed my eyes and tried to settle my mind enough to connect with Beauvrie's. Either his madness would open enough cracks for me to slip through and find some shred of reason, or—

With another shriek, Beauvrie was upon me, hooks spearing into the flesh of my shoulders, the peeling, rotted skin of his legs pressing between my own. I gagged as rancid seawater breath broke over my face, turning away as Beauvrie pushed out a long black tongue and licked me from forehead to throat. I tried bucking against the ropes again, but it was useless. His eyes possessed nothing but the inky blackness of death. His mouth spread open to reveal sharp teeth that pointed every direction but straight. I cried out as they bit into my throat, then released a great scream as pain spasmed through my body, merciful numbness giving way to agony.

Then, just as quickly, it was gone, along with the apparition Beauvrie had realised with such horrific detail in my mind.

"He plays a game mastered by his betters," Beauvrie murmured, still hovering over his work bench, his back turned to me. "Quaint and foolish."

I looked down the length of my body just to make sure it was still intact. My own fault for opening a mental corridor for Beauvrie to exploit. The older Blood Shade's powers far exceeded my own. Yet, so did his weaknesses. Think! At least I could stall for time. "Michel, please! I'm begging you to not do this. It won't work!"

"Begging? Go to the distant world, Michel. Leave our shores and retreat to the sea, Michel. But I've been such a good boy. Done all they asked and more."

"Have you? You murdered the humans you fed from, and you didn't stop after you were banished. How many have you 'disappeared' offshore?"

"Is it me, or is it the sea? Nature's hunger, a natural predator's alibi, yet they call me indiscreet?"

"You killed and ate a sitting prime minister!"

He hissed, turning to face me, one hooked hand curved around the hilt of a sharp, serrated blade whose shine belied the rest of Beavrie's mangled, deathly appearance. "No more shall the landers stand in judgement, clucking their fat tongues, sucking down their sweet indulgence."

A shudder went through me as he reached out again and stroked my cheek with the curve of his hooks. I coughed as another wave of fetid breath broke over my face, then cried out as Beauvrie's free hand shot out and seized hold of my jaw, jamming it open as he held me firm.

"No more fat tongues…" The high-pitched sing-song of a child humming a nursery rhyme was back as he brought the blade toward my face.

Every muscle I could still feel tightened, braced for pain. Then, just as fast as he'd been upon me, Beauvrie withdrew. I coughed again, spitting out what I could of the rancid taste to no avail.

"Oh," Beauvrie murmured, shaking his head as if he'd just taken a blow to it and was trying to remember where he was. "Oh my, it is… really quite toxic in here, isn't it?"

I tried to breathe, to slow my heart to some kind of normality. What was wrong with him now?

"Okay… okay, I think… I think I'm going to be sick." Beauvrie's entire manner had changed, now awkward and clumsy. He grimaced, lips peeling back to show rotting, blackened teeth as he stared at the hooks in his fingertips. "What the hell?"

"Iain?" I'm not sure how I knew. Every new mannerism in this ghastly figure just felt familiar.

"Oh good! Right first time." His gentle sarcasm removed my last doubts. "I was worried I'd have to convince… No, I am going to be sick."

"How are you…" I trailed off as he turned away from me and vomited a great stream of bloody sea water, guts, and bile over the cave floor. To say it smelled like the runoff of an abattoir, only fishier, would have been a gross understatement. "Are you okay?"

"Not really," he answered, coughing out the last of it. "But if we don't get you out of here, you're dead, so… perspective, right?"

"How did you find me?"

"He launched a psychic attack on you, didn't he? I've spent enough time in your mind to know when it's in trouble."

"To know when it's… Wait a minute!"

"Look, a minute we do not have! His mind is sick, sicker than Brett ever was. Staying in it will destroy me. I'd say we've got about twenty seconds to get you out of here."

Twenty seconds? I turned to the cave entrance. "It's daylight out!"

"You'll have to risk it," he said, using Beauvrie's knife to cut my bonds.

"Please, just do what I say."

"I can't move!"

"As soon as I leave Beauvrie's body, I'll flood your mind with a force that'll hit like raw adrenaline. You'll feel like hell, but you'll be able to get out of here. Unfortunately, hiding from the sun is up to you."

"Wait! Adrien Tseng…"

"The politician?" A note of caution replaced the urgency in Iain's voice. "Yes?"

"He's behind all of… whatever this is. What happened at Isobel's. The Trust. I'm sure of it."

Iain stared at me through Beauvrie's dead eyes. "You really ought to leave them alone."

I frowned, my blood suddenly cooling. "What do you mean? Iain!"

Without warning, Beauvrie launched himself at me, howling with rage, any shred of humanity gone as his hooks dug into my flesh. Using his momentum and the strength Iain had granted me, I toppled us both over the table before wrenching myself free and darting for the stream of sunlight.

I braced myself for the searing pain it would bring, still unprepared for the pain of Beauvrie latching onto my back, hooks breaking my skin once more. I tucked myself into a tight ball, keeping as much of Beauvrie's body as I could between mine and the sun. Then, I hurled myself into the light, spasming in its awful warmth, light scorching and curling my skin as I launched myself over the edge and plummeted toward the waters below. I heard Beauvrie shrieking, felt wretched heat as he exploded into a ball of flame. I felt myself getting lighter as the sun burned up Beauvrie's older, less resistant body. But it would afford mine a little more mercy, so long as I hit the ocean before burning up.

My fall broke with a sudden jolt. Cool shadow wrapped itself around me, snuffing out the embers of Beauvrie that had caught fire against my own skin. I focused on the strange voice whispering to me in a language I didn't understand. Somehow, I recognised the blissful coolness of being shrouded in the Quinkan's form as they drew me into their long shadow.

"It's all right." The voice, now speaking English, was like balm on my tortured skin. The pain of the sun and Beauvrie's attack again gave way to sweet numbness. "Sleep."

I didn't need to be told twice.

CHAPTER ELEVEN

Crisp, clean sheets brushed my skin as I stirred against the gentle firmness of a comfortable bed. Soft moonlight illuminated the body of a handsome, olive-skinned youth lying next to me, his chest rising and falling as he slept, powerful arms flopped lazily over the top sheet.

I pulled back the sheet and sat up, examining my freshy healed torso before looking around the plain but functional room. My reflection stared back at me, surrounded by the gold-painted frame of a mirror overlooking a desk strewn with a red t-shirt and pale blue jeans. I looked normal. No scarring or damage that I could see. My eyes glinted with a vigour that only came from having freshly fed. I looked down at my presumed donor and stroked his chest with the tip of my finger.

He opened his eyes and smiled at me. "Hey."

"Hey," I answered, not sure if introductions were in order.

His kiss, however skilful, did little to clarify matters. But the warmth of his healthy body next to mine, and the familiarity of his flavour, though I didn't remember drinking from him, gave me a sense of safety.

"Where are we?" I asked. "Who—"

"Shhhhhh, hah." He kept on kissing me along my cheek, then down my neck and chest. "You like me?"

Realising English was not his first language and doubting I would get reliable answers, I let the boy explore me as he wished, not having the heart to tell him any sexual arousal on my part would be performative. But perform I did, swelling myself to distract him as his mouth went to work.

I remembered the Quinkan, Beauvrie, Iain telling me to leave Tseng alone. No, he'd told me to leave *them* alone. Who in the hell were 'they?' Deborah? I'd have happily complied, except…

"You okay, baby?" my companion asked, looking up at me with earnest eyes, eager to please.

I nodded, slowly. "Perhaps we can just relax for a while?"

He grinned, showing a mouth full of healthy human teeth as he wrapped himself around my body and kissed my neck again.

I tried to get comfortable with the mortal as my mind raced. This could well be a trap, but why would Iain free me only to trap me? And the Quinkan had no reason to keep me captive.

My companion nuzzled my chest. Even if I was a prisoner, I could hardly complain about the room service. I could feel his blood pumping through me.

A sharp knock at the door was a good sign. Jailers weren't usually known for such courtesies.

"Enter," I called.

I hadn't expected to see Kelvin's face. But then, I wasn't accustomed to seeing Kelvin at all.

"You feeling all right?" he asked, ignoring the man draped around me.

"No complaints," I said. "Except where the hell am I?"

"Above the bar. Joboram brought you back here and did most of the work patching you up."

"And um…" I tapped the boy's muscular shoulder.

Kelvin shrugged. "Figured you'd be hungry, and I was right. Poor Leo barely got his gear off before you latched on. Thought we'd have to tear you off him."

"Satisfaction guaranteed," added Leo, putting an arm around the back of my neck and nuzzling my shoulder.

"Does he remember?" I mouthed silently at Kelvin.

He shook his head. "Don't think so. You were pretty out of it. Do you remember?"

I shook my head.

"Weird. There's a lot about the Quinkans we don't understand. Joboram's not exactly giving up their secrets."

Speaking of secrets… I kissed Leo's cheek, giving his shoulders a final squeeze. "Thank you."

"Mmmm, you're welcome, baby," he caught my mouth in another deep, open kiss before sliding his athletic body from the bed and collecting his clothes.

"Thanks mate." Kelvin took out a tightly rolled wad of cash and passed it to the boy as he got dressed.

Leo slipped into his sneakers and returned to my side for one last kiss. "Bye, sexy."

Kelvin closed the door behind him. "Good bloke. Doesn't ask questions."

Perhaps not, but I had a few. "Where's Jorgas?"

"With Patricia. Just some damage control, don't worry."

"Damage control?"

"Look, it's mostly formality with the Quinkans. Nothing she can't handle. You focus on you. Sounds like you were a fucking mess when Joboram found you. Michel Beauvrie? I've only heard stories. That's rotten luck."

"Yes, luck," I muttered, replaying my meeting with Tseng. The coin. A little something to help your odds? A gift from a wielder of fate… Motherfucker! "How did Joboram find me?"

Kelvin shook his head. "I don't know the how, or the why. Some Quinkan code about helping people in trouble."

"They seem awfully selective about applying it." Perhaps a certain disembodied Mentalist had called in a favour. Damn it, why had he helped me? "I've never heard of this."

"It usually applies to children. Relax, it's not worth working yourself up."

I heard a heavy sliding door downstairs, then footsteps getting louder. The look on Patricia's face as she entered the room troubled me far more than Kelvin's vague assurances.

"How are you feeling?" she asked me.

I considered some smart remark about 'better than you look' but resisted. "I'll live. I appreciate the nourishment, though I thought you weren't big on—"

"Human donors?" she asked. "Only for trusted friends."

Kelvin snorted.

"Where's Jorgas?" I asked.

"Resting. Don't worry, this shouldn't take long."

"Patricia?" Something in her tone pricked the back of my neck. "What, exactly, should not take long?"

She leaned against the wall, sighing deeply as she folded her arms. "We need help, Reylan. We cannot leave the Trust as it is. Even if we can't regain control of the building, something malevolent has taken root there, and it can't be allowed to fester, grow, or be discovered by some idiot developer out to turn a profit."

I nodded. "Still not seeing where an answer to my question falls into this."

"Patience, pretty boy," muttered Kelvin. "Bottom line, we need the Quinkans."

"Quinkans, like most indigenous Australian supernaturals, are part of the land. Their connection and sensitivity to it and its ley lines will give us a much better idea what we're dealing with, and hopefully, how to defeat or at least contain it."

"Though of course," I said, beginning to understand. "They want something in exchange."

"No more than our cooperation. The killings I asked you to investigate for us. The teenagers, found near Macquarie University?"

My heart sank into my stomach, leaving my blood to chill. "The ones you accused Jorgas of—"

"The killings Jorgas' friend Simon committed in his wolfen state, yes."

I wouldn't have called them friends. "I thought this was settled. Simon's dead. I killed him. We even went to the funeral. I assume that was his body that we watched go into the ground. Case closed, yes?"

Patricia nodded. "Yes, he's dead. But the Quinkans have their own laws and traditions. These demand satisfaction when children are harmed by a supernatural being on their land."

I stared at her, the implications of this landing as I tried to breathe. "I... wasn't aware of these traditions."

"It's just politics, pretty boy. All Jorgas has to do is tell them what you told us and we're golden."

"Since both Houses have strict rules about harming children that run close to the land's own laws, these matters rarely come into arbitration. Since Simon's already dead, their code is already satisfied. It's just the formality of declaring Jorgas innocent. All he has to give them is that the truth."

"Patricia," I murmured. "There may be a complication."

The confidence had drained from her face as her mouth flattened out, her voice barely a whisper. "Un-fucking-believable."

*　　*　　*

"I still don't understand why you want to tell them a truth that could get Jorgas… what? Killed?"

"Technically, the Colonial Restitution Treaty allows them to remove his supernatural abilities. Both Houses signed it." Bitterness punctuated Patricia's words.

"Remove the wolf? How, exactly, will they do that? Don't try and tell me this is some gentle, humane or enlightened process!" I remembered the agony of my own maturing and transformation, as every blood vessel rewired itself of my digestive system. "It likely amounts to the same thing!"

"Most probably."

"Well, that's fuckin' brilliant," Kelvin muttered. "The one time the Houses decide to pretend they're woke and it's gonna get that kid killed."

"So, in that case, we lie!" I hissed. "Don't look at me like you're too righteous."

"I might be prepared to do that," Patricia answered, hands on hips betraying her impatience. "But it won't do any good. This isn't some human court where we argue our case. What happens is Joboram reaches into Jorgas—"

"They what?"

"—and once they do, they'll know everything. It's a ritual of total transparency and candour."

"So? Refuse it!"

"Even if that didn't make Jorgas look guilty as sin, I can't go against the treaty. If Jorgas did kill those teenagers, his life belongs to the Quinkans to do with as they wish in accordance with their traditions."

"Damn it, Patricia! I doubt very much he even knew Quinkans existed at the time, much less to whose laws he was beholden."

"And if you had been honest with me from the get go, or indeed told me the truth at any subsequent point in our relationship, I could have prepared… What the hell did you think I was going to do?"

"I don't know, kill him yourself?" I snapped. "I'll remind you that at the time, you and I were not friends."

"So, you didn't trust me?"

"No, I did not!"

"Yet, you expect me to trust you now, after this revelation?" Her eyes burrowed into me with furious indignation. "Do you think so little of us? That I'd judge the stupid actions of a lost young man in such one-eyed terms? That I'm that simple-minded?"

"Yet you were, and are still willing to let Joboram enforce this barbaric treaty?"

"I didn't know the two of you had anything to hide! An agreement with the Quinkans can't be revoked, Reylan. I'm sorry. If we do, they could rightfully force us out of the country, and we'd lose the Trust forever."

"The Trust? Oh, well, good heavens, we can't have that! Gods forbid we save Jorgas' life by surrendering a building! I say, let them have it! Let whatever's taken its crumbling walls over tear it apart. If the Quinkans want us to leave, so what? We go to New Zealand? Back to Europe? You're honestly telling me the Trust can't continue without—"

"A rousing sentiment, but here are some facts. We have no idea what could happen to the city if whatever currently festers in that 'bloody building' is allowed to grow. And there's one more significant problem." Patricia cast her gaze toward Kelvin. At least he'd compromised on his preference for nudity.

"You're worried there might be side effects?" I asked. "To your visibility?"

"We're a bit past 'worried,' now," Kelvin answered. "Weakness and fatigue, stomach cramps, constant headaches, nausea… As of last night, I'm having cold sweats and this morning I spewed up blood like one of your lot after a bender."

"Jesus," I remembered him clutching his stomach outside Bone. But pity was the last thing he wanted.

"So," Patricia said, cutting the diagnosis short. "I'm afraid accepting exile in humility and starting over isn't an option."

"Then, there's your mate, Brett," Kelvin added, "or did you forget about him?"

"I didn't forget!" When did my list of troubles get so crowded? "I'm sorry. A lot on my mind."

Patricia nodded, her shoulders relaxing as she exhaled. "Which is why I don't want to waste energy fighting. What's done is done. I can't go back on the agreement."

"Tell them it wasn't yours to make."

"Just as Jorgas' guilt wasn't your secret to keep."

"Fine!" I barked again. "Let's all be nice and sorry! Will that help us move on? Because this is Jorgas' life!"

"So, how do we save it?" Kelvin growled.

I stared at Patricia long enough to know she was lost for answers.

"No, no, no, don't give me that," Kelvin continued. "Look, he pisses me off, but if that kid deserved death, I would have done it myself. I know we're still half a team down and not prepared for a… legal fight or whatever you want to call this, but it's where we fuckin' are, so how do we do it?"

"I can buy us time. Ask Joboram to delay," said Patricia. "Then, I'll have to contact the Houses."

"Yeah, because they bloody love you," Kelvin muttered.

"One of them is bound to know someone with a better understanding of the treaty. There has to be a loophole or…"

Colin would have known. Of course, Colin was no longer here.

"I'll do it," I said, hoping someone in Europe or America still owed me a favour. "No offence, but a request from me will carry more weight than from either of you."

A glance between them made it clear they couldn't argue.

CHAPTER TWELVE

"Loïc."

"Reylan." Loïc's pale, angular face peered at me from the screen, his eyebrows slightly asymmetrical, a twitch that suggested either mirth or madness tugging at the corners of his mouth. Irritation? Bemusement? Blind rage? It was impossible to tell with Loïc. "We tried to reach you weeks ago."

"I'm afraid I don't have time for a catch-up."

"Then you can tell me in person, after you've explained what happened to the Scimitars, and to Colin and Isobel, who we've also been unable to reach."

"Isobel hasn't been in cont—"

"The House passed its directive three months ago. All Blood Shades and others subject to House protection are to leave Sydney as soon as they're able. We're consolidating essential resources in Hobart, but most Australian members of the House are relocating to other countries."

Other countries? "Loïc, if we can slow down for a moment—"

"You, specifically are needed in Europe. We'll arrange transport to Stockholm for you and your Mannequin, Brett… Fuller, I believe. Most of your Sydney compatriots have relocated already, but if you know the whereabouts of Colin, or Isobel, you're to—"

"Will you please shut up and let me finish a sentence?"

The Belgian Blood Shade glared at me as if I'd just burnt him through the screen. "I beg your—"

"Stop. Talking. Now." I enunciated each syllable as if he needed to read my lips. "I am not in contact with Isobel or Colin, nor do I possess any knowledge as to their whereabouts." This was technically true, though admitting to misplacing both one's protégé and one's mentor was a poor look. "I need legal help."

His lopsided smirk finally bloomed as if the sudden change of topic amused him. "Go on."

"How familiar are you with the Colonial Restitution Treaty?"

"Is that a joke? I was there when we cleaned up after Leopold. Why are you interested in—"

"My…" Boyfriend? Partner? Consort? "A close friend and ally may be on trial for… a youthful accident."

"You're telling me someone drained a child on Quinkan territory?"

I was about to confirm this misapprehension, but hesitated a second too long.

"Oh, I see." Loïc's smirk reminded me I was talking to a glorified lawyer with more than a century of experience cutting through bullshit of every shade. "We're talking about your other friend."

I nodded.

"In that case, I can't help you."

"You can," I challenged. "But you won't?"

"As you well know, a Flesh Master falls under the House of Magick's jurisdiction. It's nothing personal. But it opens us up to allegations of interference—"

"Since when has interfering with House of Magick affairs bothered you?"

"Spoken like someone who's never had to clean up a diplomatic shitstorm."

"You'd be surprised," I muttered.

"Look, this isn't just bureaucrats screaming at each other. We're talking blood feuds, oaths of fealty, centuries-old codes of honour that demand satisfaction and can easily escalate—"

"All from helping one Flesh Master boy who made a horrible mistake before he could be found and mentored? Whose assistance to our community has earned him sight from the House of Blood?"

"If word got out, as it inevitably would, that we interfered… What do you mean, sight? You can't just see a werewolf on the House's behalf because you're involved."

"I didn't," I said quietly. "Colin saw him, for his role in containing a Patron incursion."

I fairly thought Loïc was going to burst an immortal blood vessel before his face relaxed. At least that insufferable smirk was gone. "That's convenient, given Colin's absence."

"Convenient or not, a boy's life is at stake."

"Your 'boy,' Reylan, yours. Listen, unlike some in the House, I could care less the company you keep in your bed, but let's be open with each other. We're talking about your boy, which gives you an immediate conflict of interest."

"The Quinkans don't need to know about Jorgas and myself."

"You've really no idea how Quinkan trials work, do you? They see everything. Total candour and transparency are at the heart of Quinkan jurisprudence. Tell me, has the skinny, shadowy one touched you yet? Maybe healed an injury of some sort?"

I nodded, not liking his general direction.

"Then you already have no secrets from them." A hint of sympathy seemed to cross this phrase. Sympathy, from Loïc, I did not need. "Look, if you have something to hide, and you're willing to risk the fallout, bring Jorgas with you to Sweden. Just don't ask us for protection if the House of Magick winds up hunting you. I'll make preparations for your arrival and explain further when you get here. You have three days to make your arrangements."

"There won't be any arrangements, Loïc." Anger swelled in my chest at his dismissive suggestion. Never mind that such 'preparations' would reveal I'd lost Brett as well. "I'll tell you everything I know about what happened to the Scimitars, the Patron incursion and the Arcadia Trust. But until Jorgas is safe, I remain here."

"Be reasonable, old friend."

I snorted at the sudden promotion. "Such as the reason of granting a second chance to someone who needs only a little guidance to find a better path?" I lowered my gaze. "Old friend?"

"Not now!" he snapped at someone off-screen. I heard a door closing. Loïc then glared at me, reminded of the mercy I'd shown him one night in Montmartre when I'd found him panicking helplessly over the body of a freshly exsanguinated cabaret dancer, his face and evening clothes wet with blood. Oh, how quickly some of us forget.

"Loïc, I need options. Then, I'll do whatever you need me to do."

He sighed, leaning back in his chair with one leg crossed over his knee, against which he tapped a pen incessantly. "There is a provision, in the CRT."

"CRT?"

"Colonial Restitution Treaty. Pay attention!"

"Of course. Go on."

"The Quinkans can't just put someone on trial, mortal or otherwise, they need to be invoked, and in the trial of a supernatural being, that invocation must come from one of—"

"The Houses," I muttered. "Christ."

"Not quite. Any individual supernatural of the 'invading clans' as we're called can call for a Quinkan trial. But it's almost never done without authorisation from the relevant House, in this case, the House of Magick. Are we clear so far?"

I nodded. "So, the House of Magick authorised this?"

"One of their rank had to call for it in the first place. It can't be someone from the rival House. Can you imagine centuries-old feuds being played out over Quinkan show trials?"

"But Patricia's not part of the House of Magi…" I trailed off. Oh, damned fool.

Loïc tilted his head. "Upset any Shapers, lately? One that might have raked through your friend's past?"

Tseng's blood was looking tastier by the minute. "So, how do we win?"

"There is one way to dramatically improve his odds, though it also raises the stakes, should you fail. Plead guilty, and request a shared binding."

"A what?"

"Instead of the Quinkan simply reaching inside him for an account of the incident, your friend is allowed two advocates, whose knowledge is added to the arbitration."

"Like lawyers?"

Loïc squirmed as if the term made him uncomfortable. "More like character witnesses. This is about proving your friend deserves a second chance. That he's evolved, and won't put anyone else at risk. The defendant and his two advocates share the experience in full, and I should warn you, what results is often a rat's nest of memories that muddy the facts as much as clarify them. I'm not surprised the Quinkans will only indulge it under sufferance. But, if you request it, they will honour that request."

"You mentioned higher stakes?" I asked.

"Yes. Should you fail, the advocates will share in the defendant's punishment."

"I beg your pardon?"

"Your friend will be stripped of his powers as a Flesh Master, and any advocates will lose their powers as well."

"What if the advocates are human? Or have already lost their powers for reasons unknown?"

It could work. Patricia would surely advocate for him, and as much as I hated handing Jorgas' fate to Kelvin, at least he was on our side.

"What makes them human, exactly? A soul? An identity? Self-awareness? You can be sure the Quinkans will exact a price they feel is fair."

Right. As if I could ever let Jorgas go through this without me. "And the judge?"

"Will be the Quinkan."

"Oh, bloody hell, Loïc!"

"That is the treaty. Do with it as you will." A deep breath betrayed his exasperation. "If you reach Colin or Isobel, have them contact me as soon as possible."

He ended the call before I could reply. Old friend, indeed.

I sighed, leaning back in my chair. Jorgas' advocates would have to be Patricia and myself. She had opened us up to this mess by betting on Jorgas' innocence as much as I had by obscuring his guilt. We both owed him.

The ceiling creaked quietly above my head. At last, I had reason to smile.

*　*　*

"Ah, Mister Raymond, good! I was just coming to see you!"

The comforting brush of fur against my trousers distracted me. "Hello, you," I swooped Demetrius into my arms and chuckled at his tiny snarl as I cuddled him into a ball.

Dorotha quickly returned with a sizeable container. "For you. Well, for your friends. They eat, yes? They would like babka? Father Grieg, perhaps? His grandfather was Polish, I think."

I lifted one corner of the lid, allowing the sweet smell of fresh pastry and chocolate to hit my nose. "You've had time to make bread already?" Perhaps 'thank you' would have been more appropriate, but I was a little taken aback. There was no sign anywhere in the apartment that my tenant had ever left. Nothing had been moved, broken, or vandalised. I wasn't sure what I'd expected.

"You think I am away for so long I forget how?" She flapped a playful hand at me and went to settle in a plump green armchair. She put her feet up on a tan ottoman and raised a half-finished glass of some spirit I didn't recognise. "Please, sit, sit! You want, I get you—"

"I'm perfectly fine," I said, stopping her in mid-rise from her seat before taking my own. "I'm just happy to see you home, safe and sound."

She smiled, spreading a blanket over her knees as Demetrius jumped into her lap. The cat settled in with a purr after an obligatory rotation. "Thank you again, Mister Raymond. The hospital? They were very kind but oh, such awful places. You promise me, if it is my time, you leave me. I die here, on the floor, right there."

"I'm not sure I can promise that."

A knowing smile passed between us. As good as it had been to see her at the hospice, this was her home. Our home. Her entire life surrounded us, with mine just below. For all I'd recently lost, perhaps that's why I'd traipsed up here the moment I'd heard her.

"You have a good friend in Deborah," she said. "She is a good woman. Perhaps a good woman for you, if you were not ah… Oh, but that is just silly interfering. Forgive me, Mister Raymond."

"I think she'd prefer Brett, which is probably best," I said without thinking. Shit.

"That skinny boy? Perhaps. I was surprised I did not see him. I thought he worked with you?"

"He's been very busy." I considered compounding this lie with some story about Deborah or Iain having a contact at the hospital, but hadn't lies led me to my current predicament?

"You know, I think of you like my son. Isn't that silly? You are older than me, I think?"

I raised a smile, unable to deny this.

"My strange son and his fascinating friends. When I was little, my parents took me to visit my grandfather's village. I never met my great grandparents, but we visited their grave. I will never forget, on the way back, walking from that cemetery, it was November, freezing cold, and seeing the four graves. One was small, for a little child, but each was covered in a steel cage. To prevent the dead from digging their way up and living again."

Or just as likely, grave robbers, I kept to myself.

"It is so curious to me, Mister Raymond. How one could look at a man like you and see a corpse? A daemonic spirit in flesh and blood, in a man who has brought so much life?"

"I have no children, Dorotha."

"No, no, I mean to my life! And to your friends? And… perhaps some of those boys you bring home have fond memories of you too?"

"Dorotha!"

She giggled, raising her glass high and finishing it as Demetrius tried to reposition himself on the blanket she now agitated with small kicks of glee. "Oh, but I am glad you found Father Grieg, Mister Raymond. He is a good man, like you."

I didn't realise how I had ached to hear those last five words until she said them out loud. It's not in a Blood Shade's nature to cry, but in that moment… perhaps it was simply exhaustion. Perhaps it was worry over Jorgas. But Iain? Since arriving back at Patricia's makeshift lair, I'd barely thought about the man who'd rescued me from a fate more final than a caged grave.

'A good man, like you.'

Words that had warmed me just seconds ago, sent a chill through me now.

CHAPTER THIRTEEN

"The Quinkans have agreed to a shared binding." Patricia stated this as if laying out the rules of some game. "It took some persuasion, but since neither Jorgas, nor any of the victims are of the People—Aboriginal, that is—it is our right."

"You're sure you're willing to do this?" I asked. "You understand the risks?"

Patricia sighed, looking away as if having second thoughts. "Those are two very different questions. At least we can trust the Quinkans to be impartial arbiters."

"And his executioners? Sounds very impartial."

"Let's not anticipate the worst."

"I intend to be ready for it, all the same."

Her look darkened. "I hope you're not planning to do something foolish if we lose."

"If we lose," I said, biting my tongue, "there'll be nothing left to stop me."

The sound of a door closing ended our discussion. It seemed so odd to see Jorgas standing there, so casual as his life hung in the balance. As for Kelvin, I guessed a t-shirt and track pants were formalwear for a man accustomed to full-time nudity.

"What's going on?" Jorgas asked, still wearing the clothes he'd put on at my house.

I pushed the container forward on the bar and opened it, allowing the smell of fresh babka to fill the bar.

"Aww, sweet!"

"I'll get a knife," said Kelvin, as Jorgas reached in, tore off a hunk of sweet bread covered in chocolatey sauce and stuffed it in his mouth. "…or not."

"How's Dorotha?" Jorgas asked through a mash of babka. "Did you find Brett?"

I gave Patricia another look. "He doesn't know?"

Calm, Reylan. Calm…

"We should discuss this all together."

"Discuss what?" Jorgas asked, finally swallowing. "What's going on?"

I put my hand over his and squeezed, resisting the urge to break into a screaming rant.

*　　*　　*

"They want to what?"

"It's called a shared binding," said Patricia, "and we're going to win it."

"Are you sure about that?" Jorgas demanded. "I don't even hear about this for almost a year and you're telling me now, it's death penalty shit? Fuck! I didn't even kill… I didn't—"

"Jorgas," I said, not letting go of his hand. "They know."

He stared from one of them to the other, helpless, face quivering. "I… I… fuck! I… I'm sorry!"

"No, you listen to me." Patricia fixed him with that familiar, all-business expression. "You're not the first supernatural to have done terrible things before coming to peace with what you are. By going through this ritual, we have a chance to prove you're more than that. What you mean to

141

Reylan. What you've done for us. People of your nature are often forced to prove themselves through deeds. To my mind, you've done so, several times over."

Kelvin nodded. "We've all fucked up, mate. You're more than that."

I frowned. Something about the Cloak Walker sounded awfully subdued, though it could have just been a side effect of his visibility.

"Thanks," Jorgas said quietly. "That… that means a lot. So, what do we do? Lie?"

Patricia was doing her best to look confident, but her fidgeting hands told another story. "That's the one thing we don't do. The ritual will render truths about you that may affect Joboram's decision, but under no circumstance, at all, should any of us attempt to distort or change those truths."

"And if we did?" I asked.

Patricia shook her head. "Clay isn't here for decoration."

"Right," I muttered.

"There's no version of this that doesn't end with Joboram knowing the entire truth," she continued. "They didn't call for this trial, but according to the treaty, their traditions and final judgements stand. Technically, our job is not to prove your innocence, but your worth as a Flesh Master."

Jorgas blanched. "What does that mean?"

"If they find you wanting, the penalty isn't death. It's the removal of your wolf, which you might survive."

"That's all I fucking wanted in the first place," he said. "Wait, might?"

"That's if we can't prove your worth as a Flesh Master and a man." Patricia put a hand on his arm. "But I have no doubt we will succeed."

Unlike the lie I'd spun for Jorgas, nobody was buying this one, but it comforted us in our denial. The only one who didn't benefit was Jorgas, who sat in abject self-loathing, his face a map of worry I'd not seen since the night he'd shown up at my doorstep, fresh from having brought Patricia Simon's corpse.

"So," I said. "Patricia and I will join you in this as your advocates, during which Joboram—"

"—will be able to read all three of you like a book, so no funny business," Kelvin finished. "You'll be all right, mate. We've got you."

"So, you're like… my lawyers?"

I nodded. "Except if we lose, or lie, we go down with you."

"You… you'd both do that for me?"

"Seriously?" I asked.

"Jorgas," Patricia's face was earnest, with no cynicism or hidden agenda. "Remember, you're not on trial for the killings, you're on trial for your character. In that, I have absolute confidence. The prosecutor—"

"Yes, about that…" I muttered.

She silenced me with a look, trying not to get chocolate on her fingers as she tore off a piece of pastry for herself. "They can enter each of our testimonies as they see fit, and I have no doubt they'll try to manipulate the guilt you feel. You can't rise to it. The facts are on your side. Be confident and know who you are."

"The facts?" The first traces of tears pricked his eyes. "The fact is I killed those kids."

"The wolf killed those kids."

"Yeah, and that's what they want to pull out of me, but it's one and the same!" He sounded now like the frightened Jorgas who'd begged me in a back alley to kill him and spare him this lifetime balancing morals and monster. "You're telling me this is all down to how I feel? Controlling my emotions? Isn't that what dropped me in this shit in the first place?" Without another word, Jorgas left the bar. I heard a heavy fire door slam. Emotional control? I doubted even I could manage it in his place.

"Not an exact science, is it?" I asked. "How long do we have to prepare?"

"On the contrary, the Quinkans will know every facet of his being." Patricia sighed. "Truthfully, I'm not sure how long we have. Not that it would make any difference if we had months."

Perhaps we were going about this the wrong way. Perhaps if Jorgas were overwhelmed with guilt, the Quinkans might deem it punishment enough. Or was it a simple balance sheet? The thoughts and deeds of an entire life weighed like some celestial ledger? Heart? Feather? Anubis could go fuck himself.

Patricia squared her shoulders. "Just do what you can with him."

"What I can?" I asked.

"As I understand it, he's never been more at peace than when he's been with you." She popped the piece of babka into her mouth, opened the file in front of her, and began to read.

Kelvin shrugged.

Knowing I'd get no further help, I followed Jorgas. He sat outside, slumped against the wall with a lit cigarette in hand and something of the homeless chic returned to his manner.

"You want one?" he asked, raising the pack in my direction.

"I'll pass, thanks," I said, spotting the cheap brand. I had standards for ingesting poison.

"A little present from Clay. Wish she'd told me there were strings attached."

"Somehow, I don't think cigarettes will factor into the Quinkans' decision." They seemed more like a cynical favour to a condemned man. I sat down next to him, trying to ignore the acrid smell as I stroked the inside of his thigh, saying nothing. I didn't need Iain's abilities to tell that my presence had infinitely more value than words.

It was Jorgas who finally spoke. "I'm gonna guess there's a reason we're not just jetting off into the sunset… or sunrise, or whatever? I mean, they want me gone, right? Reckon they'd go for exile instead?"

"As a matter of fact, the House of Blood would prefer I did just that. They want me in Europe as soon as possible. Sweden, specifically."

"Oh, great. I like Loreen."

"I could even risk bringing you with me. Unfortunately, Patricia and Kelvin need the Quinkans' help to recover the Trust's building."

"The building? They're risking my life for a fucking—"

"Something in there turned Kelvin visible, and it's killing him."

Jorgas stared at me, momentarily dumbstruck. "No shit? He did seem kind of off."

"As in, not constantly insulting us and unusually concerned about your welfare? Yes."

"So, if we leave?"

"Kelvin dies."

Jorgas shook his head, taking one last drag of the cigarette then putting it out on the street. "I guess it had to happen, right?"

"What had to happen?"

"Did you think we'd just be able to sweep it all under the rug? I mean, I managed to put it behind me, mostly. Father Grieg… Iain helped."

My eyes went wide. "You told Iain?"

"Fuck, no! He just helped me sort out a lot of shit, both before and after things got complicated."

"Complicated," I murmured, resenting the taste of the word in my mouth. Jorgas may not have told Iain about the deaths, but there was nothing to stop the Shaper reaching in and plucking the knowledge from his mind. "I'm just curious, when exactly did you start sleeping with him?"

"When did you start sleeping with him?"

Fair.

"Did he really save your life?" Jorgas asked. "From that French monster?"

"Michel Beauvrie," I muttered. "Yes, he did. How did you know about that?

"Kelvin told me."

Intrigued as I was, I didn't cross-examine this either. "We're not going to let them kill you. Even if it's your life or Kelvin's."

"Don't promise me that. You can't just trade Kelvin's life for mine."

"There might be another way to save Kelvin. We don't know."

"Exactly! We don't fucking know. No way. The guy's a prick, but I won't let you do that." Jorgas looked at me, his face tired. "What about Brett? What happened to him? What happens to him?"

"Hey," I said, putting a hand on his cheek. "Give yourself a chance to matter, will you?"

"You're talking to me in self-help memes now?"

"In what?"

"Fuck, you're old." He broke into a grin, stifling a laugh as I squeezed his leg. "That's gonna be weird, isn't it?"

"What is?"

"When I'm… I don't know, sixty or seventy, you'll still look like you do now."

I hadn't much thought about it. "I'm glad you're still planning to be around at sixty or seventy." I stroked his leg, savouring silence in place of things that didn't need to be said. Patricia would do her part for him, of that, I'd no doubt. But the outcome of this charade depended on Jorgas.

"How… how does this work?" he asked. "It's not a trial, exactly, right? Not a murder trial?"

"No. The killings themselves just gave someone the catalyst to put you through this."

"I thought the Quinkans were—"

"'These things only happen at the request of a third party. The Quinkans themselves are impartial."

"What third party?" he asked. "Who?"

"I think I know who, but knowing won't help you. They might not be trying to hurt you in any case, but me."

"You? Who are we talking about? Who the fuck's doing this?"

"Just focus on winning. Joboram pulls memories, feelings, knowledge… anything they can from you, me and Patricia, while this prosecutor watches. He's the one who petitioned the Quinkans in the first place. The main thing is, you must remember that you're worth fighting for. Stay humble. We're not denying your faults, but always, always come back to the truth. You made amends, you learned, you changed. That is not a crime or a sin, Jorgas. That is life, even if the stakes are higher for people like us."

"And after that, this Quinkan, or whatever, decides if I get to live? Fuck, I'm screwed."

"Don't make me slap sense into you," I said, taking his face in my hands again. "I need you to see what I see, not because of how I feel about you, but because of the man you are. You are worthy of this life, Jorgas. Stop doubting it."

He didn't say a word. He just brought his lips to mine and kissed me, slow and deep, savouring it before putting his arms around my shoulders. I held him until he relaxed, then eased back against the wall with him once more.

"Have you…" I hesitated, not sure if this was the time to bring it up. "Have you thought of contacting your mother?"

He stared at the brick wall opposite us. "What do you know about her?"

"Our paths happened to cross. She misses you."

"Funny, Iain told me the same thing."

"Do you think he was right?"

Jorgas shrugged, shifting his weight. "It doesn't matter, does it? Is she even my mum, anymore?"

I watched a small black cat drop from a ledge somewhere onto the lid of a dumpster, then into a box of recycling. "The great cosmic joke of Blood Shade immortality is that we die early in order to hide it. The moment the people I loved started seeing that I didn't age, I had to disappear. I'd say, if you don't carry that burden and she still loves you, then she's your mother for as long as you want her to be."

The metallic clang of the back door interrupted us. Kelvin stepped out, looking decidedly less gruff than normal.

"Patricia needs to see you," he said to Jorgas.

"Meeting of the war council?" I asked.

"Something like that."

Really? No snide 'pretty boy' at the end of that?

"I'll see you in a bit," Jorgas said, getting up and disappearing inside.

Kelvin leaned against the wall, sucking in the night air. His demeanour, his step, the way he held himself… He'd dropped the pretence. I was certain now.

"Your mannerisms are off," I said, looking Iain up and down in his newly acquired Kelvin suit. "And your ocker Aussie accent is dreadful."

"I'll take that as a compliment," he answered, humouring me. "I haven't had much time to practice. I'm pretty sure Patricia knows something's up, but so what? You need me."

"Dare I ask if this possession was consensual?"

"I'm sure Kelvin resents me for it, though given his usual disposition, it's hard to tell. I'm equally sure that like Brett before him, I am only helping to hold his body together in its current state. Consensual or not, I promise you, it's a mutually beneficial arrangement."

"Iain, I grow tired of these games."

"And I'm tired of being disincorporated, but here we are."

I had every reason to be furious, but he was right. "So? Where is your body and how do we get you back into it?"

"How about we focus on keeping Jorgas and Kelvin alive first, hmmm? The process you're talking about might have… complications."

"Indeed," I muttered. "A telepath soul-jumping from one body to another, propping up people with life-threatening conditions? I can't imagine how this can possibly go wrong."

"You know, you're strangely cute when you're sarcastic?"

"Please don't flirt with me, wearing that face. It's weird."

"It'd be a lot weirder if I flirted with the person he's actually devoted to."

Whoever he meant, I wasn't going to humour him. "Don't tell me you're doing this solely for Kelvin's benefit. Damn it, why should I trust you? How can any of us trust you, after what you did to Brett?"

"What did I do? He's up and about, is he not? At least, to the best of our knowledge."

"No thanks to you!"

"I'm not the one who drained him dry, and I'm not the one who lost him."

"So? Help us find him now!"

"I've tried. Or do you think I don't still care about you?"

I wanted so much to scream at him. To hit him, even feed off him with raw, unhinged malice. But we needed him, and I resented that most of all.

"I also care about Jorgas," he continued, "just as you do. I need you to trust me."

"That," I said, trying not to sound accusative, "is not a commodity I have in abundance right now."

The clang of the door opening again interrupted us. Clay looked at me, grinning with sharp, jagged teeth. "You blokes ready?"

"Ready?" I asked. "We're doing this now? Right now?"

Clay tilted her head in a way that made me feel stupid. "Relax. It's not like your fella's got anything to hide."

Iain and I exchanged looks.

"Oh," Clay grinned. "This is going to be good."

*   *   *

The faint smell of stale beer gave Patricia's new digs a distinctly unjudicial vibe. Nonetheless, this was our courtroom. Iain and I took two vacant seats next to Patricia and Jorgas. I say 'next to,' though the ring formed by the chairs must have been seven or eight feet across. I took Jorgas' refusal to look at me as a sign he'd devoted his energies to holding himself together. I snarled, cursing the whole farce.

Clay sat on the other side of Patricia, her arms crossed, looking bored with proceedings that had not yet started. Two vacant chairs remained. Did we win points if the prosecutor was late?

The lights of the bar dimmed with insufferable theatricality. At the same time, shadows began to stretch from behind walls, furniture and crevices, engulfing the place until darkness surrounded our circle.

I heard a door close somewhere in the uncanny gloom, followed by the steady tap of footsteps against wooden floorboards. I watched the empty seats with anticipation until the prosecutor stepped into the light and took his seat without looking in our direction.

Adrian fucking Tseng.

His face wore no smug, self-satisfied smirk of glee or triumph. It was like he'd come to do a job, no more or less significant than any other civic duty. Is that how he saw this charade?

I felt the temperature in the room drop a couple of degrees. Heard the slithering timbre of an unseen Joboram's voice as it broke through the darkness.

"The judicial tradition of the invaders has been invoked and accepted for this proceeding," they said, getting right to the point with tactful neutrality. "Advocates, you are prepared."

It seemed right to stand up. "Pardon me, your… your honour, may I clarify the nature of these proceedings for those of us new to them?"

The room fell silent. Even Clay shifted uncomfortably in her seat.

"Forgive me," I continued, doing my best to seem humble. "I simply wish to know if I will have the opportunity to speak on Jorgas'—"

"You are not required to speak." Joboram's voice was as calm and calculated as ever. "We are understood."

The look on Patricia's face dissuaded me from further inquiry. A circle of orange flame broke from the darkness. It evaporated just as quickly into smoke, leaving a scorched ring on the floorboards, bathed in light.

I frowned at the remaining empty chair.

"This is a Quinkan proceeding, heard under the laws of Country. All testimony, verbal or of heart, will be without trickery. Those who do not abide by these traditions are forfeit."

"Forfeit? Meaning what?" I saw Jorgas' shoulders tense, but I'd no room for ambiguity on this.

The voice in the darkness did not disappoint me. "The basis of this proceeding is candour and truth, Blood Shade. We are understood."

Yes. Yes, I think we were.

"Mister Tseng, before the shared binding begins, you have petitioned to make an opening statement. Proceed."

"Wait, he gets to speak?" I protested, quickly feeling every set of eyes in the room on me.

"It is the petitioner's right, Blood Shade."

Unbelievable.

The nonchalant manner in which Tseng rose from his seat, not looking at us, not looking at Jorgas or Patricia, or even Joboram as far as I could tell, unnerved me more. As if this arena were his domain, and we were all props in a circus where he was ringmaster.

"Joboram," If he was as clueless as I, he was doing a good job pretending otherwise. "The accused werewolf named Jorgas, known prior as William Myers the younger, son of William and Judith Myers, nee Hernandez, is known to have killed three Macquarie University students of minority age on Eora lands, known to the invaders as Lane Cove National Park, in early Autumn of last year. No arrest or conviction was made within the mundane judicial system, with the ferocity of the attacks being blamed upon an unknown animal, despite the incredulity of that hypothesis."

"Mister Tseng," the voice purred. "Mortal findings are irrelevant to this proceeding."

"I'm simply acknowledging that there is no current threat to the secrecy protecting us. Jorgas, and indeed, all of us, should know how lucky he is in that regard. Such near misses, however, offer insight into what we might expect of an individual moving forward. The killings in question prove Jorgas' capacity for violence."

"Capacity?" I asked, unable to resist getting to my feet. "This isn't a trial. It's character assassination!"

Joboram's voice purred in all its frigid neutrality. "The petitioner will finish."

"Like hell!"

"Joboram," Patricia said, standing up. "I must support Reylan's objection. Knowledge of this tragedy has pained Jorgas for as long as I've known him. But a 'capacity for violence' might be found within any of us, including Mister Tseng."

Tseng raised one eyebrow, as if to mock her. "Surely, Sister, there's a difference between you or I throwing a tantrum and a Flesh Master losing control of the lethal weapon contained inside him."

Joboram had as little patience for this posturing as I. "This is about the capacity and intention of one individual. If you cannot confine your opening statement to relevant points, Mister Tseng, you will yield the circle."

"Forgive me. I would, however, like to explore one other evening in Jorgas' past that I believe is very much indicative of his 'capacity and intention.'"

We all stood as black mist filled the circle. At last, it rolled back to unveil the wet bitumen of an alley slick with rain, the grimy surface of a dumpster, the dim light of a back street that could have been behind any number of bars, clubs, or shops in the city. Yet, I knew this place. I'd watched a man die here. I'd met Jorgas here.

I whispered to Iain. "I thought he was making a statement, not—"

He hushed me as my doppelganger emerged from the shadows behind… Rory. The rendering of my one-time companion was every inch the Nordic muscle boy I remembered, down to the icy blue eyes and the dimples that softened the square lines of his face. But his expression was far from the cocky, athletic man I'd led from the club that night. He swallowed, shaking as my facsimile took hold of his arm.

"Why are you nervous?" My double asked, smirk growing wide.

Rory shot furtive glances around the alley. "I thought we were going back to your place?"

"Are you scared?" My double's grin bordered on evil. "There's nobody here. It'll be hot."

"Let's head back, eh? Have another drink?"

I shook my head at the charade. This hadn't happened, at least, not the way we were watching it. It had been Rory's idea to have sex in the alley, before I'd sensed something wrong in the night air.

"This just doesn't feel... I should get back," Rory continued.

Before my double could refute him again, an image of Jorgas stepped from the shadows, right where I remembered him emerging. "All right, fags. Your wallets, now!"

This part was accurate. I saw the real Jorgas wince as the slur stung the air.

"Woah, woah, woah, it's okay!" Rory protested. "Cool down, mate! You can have them, all right?"

My double looked from mugger to companion with a detachment I most certainly had not felt in that moment. I remembered it clearly. I'd volunteered my wallet, just as Rory did now. I'd also told him to run. Instead, my double just stood there. *I* wanted to punch this version of me.

"I mean it!" the image of Jorgas continued. "I'm not fucking around, cunts. I'll fucking gut you!"

"Oh, fuck off!" snapped the real Jorgas. "I did not say that!"

"He's right," I said again. "Why is this fool even allowed to testify? We were both there! Use our memories if you want the truth."

"Enough!" roared Joboram.

The scene froze. The temperature in the room dropped again, this time to near freezing. The only sensation breaking the cold was that of a warm, sharp blade against my throat. Clay gripped its handle, her expression void of the cavalier cruelty I would have expected. Perhaps even Clay knew the limits of Joboram's patience.

"Do not test your immortality in this circle, Blood Shade," said Joboram.

Hell! I'd promised not to lie, and I'd be damned if I let Tseng so brazenly flaunt the same agreement.

"I was there, Joboram," I said, keeping my voice as calm as my predicament allowed. "This is not the way things happened."

"If Mister Tseng's memory were a deception, we would know it."

"It's not a memory, it's hearsay," I answered. "He wasn't there."

"I've watched this night over, and over, hoping I had it wrong," Tseng answered, with a resignation I wouldn't have expected from someone defending a lie. "Hoping that Rory wasn't dead, or that he'd—"

"Look," I tried to lower my voice again. "I am truly sorry for what happened to your partner, but if you want a faithful recreation of what really happened that night, take it from me. Isn't that the whole point of this? Evidence drawn from memory? Tseng, I witnessed the entire thing. Let Joboram see the truth firsthand."

"We will allow Mister Tseng to finish his statement," said Patricia.

I'd expected to be shut down, but not by her. "You know this is inaccurate!"

"Do I?" she asked, her expression not without sympathy or worry. "I wasn't there either, Reylan. I can only testify based on what I know of Jorgas first-hand."

"And what about me?" I asked. "I know him better than any of you. What of his own memories?"

"These, the binding will show," Joboram said. "Unless you wish to forfeit now?"

Jorgas stared at me, while Patricia slowly shook her head.

I fumed in my silence until at last, Clay withdrew her blade from my throat. The temperature in the room returned to normal.

"Mister Tseng," Joboram purred. "Continue."

"*Rashomon*," I muttered with disgust.

Iain leaned to whisper in my ear. "You're starting to understand."

Not thirty seconds later, my odious double abandoned Rory to a rapidly transforming werewolf, whose teeth sank into the recreation's neck before long, wicked claws ripped open his stomach. Jorgas' wolf form licked its chops with wicked glee. I looked over at Tseng, who, seemed to watch the horrific lie with genuine sadness. He believed it. Every frame of this grisly movie was, for him, his partner's fate. But he hadn't been there.

"I still don't understand how speculation and hearsay can be called testimony," I muttered to Iain. Formality be damned, at this point.

His response was a whisper. "Just wait."

We watched Jorgas shrink into human form, still covered in Rory's blood. The figure licked it from his fingers as the hair vanished from them, his expression one of undisguised relish. It was more than the real Jorgas could take.

"Oh, this is bullshit!" he startled us, turning on Tseng. "Who the fuck are you, anyway?"

"Someone whose home you destroyed," the man answered, every bit as calm as Joboram.

"Someone who wasn't there," I reminded him.

"He's lying! It wasn't like this! You're fucking lying! I'll kill—" Jorgas stopped himself, but the threat was plain. Clay tilted her head, seeming for the first time interested in the proceeding. Tseng, for his part, offered no reaction at all, while I turned to look at Iain.

"That's true," Tseng continued, all but dismissing the outburst. "I was not at this killing as it happened. But as a sorcerer of some talent—"

"Here we go," I muttered, apparently just loud enough to get another look from Patricia.

"—these events have replayed in my mind's eye with absolute clarity since the night I visited the scene. Again, and again, I have witnessed what we just saw. I assure you, Joboram, and you, Reylan, down to the last drop of Rory's blood, I know these events to be real."

"Bulls—" Jorgas silenced himself as Patricia rose to speak.

"A sorcerer of some talent? Mister Tseng, that's the first thing you've told this hearing that I do believe. Yet, I've never heard of you, at least not outside of your political career, which, I must say, is its own marvel."

"Flattery, sister?" Tseng answered. "I'm touched."

"Hardly. An openly Trans Chinese-Australian man from a once modest family, now one of the richest in the city, well-liked and trusted by both the Asian and queer communities, to the tune of being the frontrunner for a seat at Town Hall? Mister Tseng, your 'talents' speak for themselves. To what exactly can we attribute such rapid progress?"

"Adrian's not the one on trial here."

I recognised the voice immediately, long before the familiar bob cut cast its shadow across Tseng's recreation. Deborah stood at his side, her face impassive, glaring at Patricia in a way that made it seem like she was trying hard not to look at me.

"It took me a while to figure it out. The night you and Ross talked about a werewolf attack. How freaked out you were the first time he came into Valia's." Deborah nodded at Jorgas. "If I'd known—"

"You would have tried something stupid and probably ended up dead." Gentle affection belied Tseng's words.

"Do you really think I'd put you in danger?" I asked her.

"Maybe not," she admitted. "Never brought him in again though, did you? and you left out the bit about you sleeping with him."

Jorgas piped up, temper bristling beneath a now calm veneer. "*He* is sitting right here if you've got anything you want to say. Yes? No? Nothing else? This is all bullshit!"

"Jorgas, please," Patricia murmured.

"No, you know what? I've had it." Jorgas' voice was low, even as he clenched his fists, body shaking with rage. "Joboram, right? I want to hear it from you, in your words. What do you want from me? The truth? I killed those kids. Is that what you want? I did, and I am so fucking sorry for that! So sorry, I wanted to fucking die. Do you get that? Ask Reylan. He was ready to kill me himself. I wanted it!"

This much was true.

"But this?" Jorgas continued, pointing to the ruined facsimile of Rory's body and his own bloodied double. "This didn't happen!"

"It did happen," Tseng answered.

"Not like this!" Jorgas barked again, this time at his accuser. "You think I enjoyed it? Like some sicko serial killer? I lost control. You want me to say sorry? I am! I'd undo it right now if I could."

"On that note," I said. "I'm a little surprised, Mister Tseng, that as a sorcerer of no small skill, you haven't pursued such options yourself."

"I'm not a Necromancer. Even if I was, what I could restore would bear little resemblance to the man I loved."

"Ah, see, that much I do know. I was there when your partner died. Jorgas was not. I was the one who saw the extent of his wounds. I heard his cries, and in an act of mercy, not malice, I broke his neck, then stayed with him until he died. So, if you want to exact a toll for your anguish, charge me."

Tseng glared at me, seemingly lost for words. Jorgas stared as well. Perhaps I should have shared this information with him sooner to alleviate some of his guilt. I'm terrible at feelings. But I was not on trial here.

Joboram at last broke their silence. "What we seek from you, wolf, is hope. Your past is only a part of what we must consider. Our greatest concern is with your future on our lands. We are understood."

Jorgas nodded, retaking his seat.

"Mister Tseng, your statement is concluded." Joboram said.

"Yes," the sorcerer answered, visibly reeling as he resumed his seat with Deborah beside him. "I believe we're done, for now."

"Joboram," Patricia said, getting to her feet. "If you will excuse us a moment, I need to talk to Reylan."

"Be brief," Joboram acquiesced.

Patricia took me by the arm and whisked me past Iain, who seemed just as confused as I. Leading me to the small office where the fallen corkboard still lay on the floor, she shut the door and looked at me in a way I didn't like one bit. "We have a problem."

"Only one now?" I asked.

She didn't bite. "No sorcerer could have prepared that little light and stunt show alone. You know what that means, don't you?"

"That Tseng's coven helped him?" I asked. "And this surprises you?"

"Not at all. But a sorcerer—an Entropist—can manipulate the threads of time and fate. If Tseng is half as good as he seems, he can show us whatever he wants in that room."

"It's still his testimony against ours. As soon as Joboram touches Jorgas, they'll know that."

Patricia gave a vehement shake of her head. "That little display had one purpose, to rattle Jorgas and make him question himself. If, every time a key event from the past comes up, with Tseng in there with us…."

"You're saying Tseng can doctor Jorgas' memories? That's absurd! I thought the whole point of this circus was that Joboram could see through lies? What about Tseng's lies?"

"What lies? Tseng himself believed every frame of what he just showed us."

"That doesn't mean he can make us believe it!"

Patricia swallowed, looking at the floor. "I'm honestly not sure about that."

A loud knock interrupted our conversation. The door swung open to reveal an impatient Clay.

"You two ready yet?"

Patricia nodded, hiding the doubt that had coloured our conversation.

As I took my seat next to Iain, I spawned an idea. I didn't love it, but we'd little choice.

"Why do I get the sense this is about to get particularly interesting?" Iain asked, gently glowering.

"I need a rather large favour," I said, opening my thoughts to him.

He shifted in his seat, an odd smile breaking over Kelvin's face as he unpacked my plan. "You're right. That's a big one."

Maybe I was desperate. But a Mentalist would surely be our best defence from psychic attacks.

"Reylan," he said, "there's one more thing—"

"Good lord," I muttered. "What now?"

"Sister Bakker," Joboram said. "You will begin."

Patricia stood up and straightened the lapels of her suit. A swirl of dark grey mist caught the room's dim light. An opening formed, the mist framing the darkest doorway I'd ever seen. It looked ready to absorb anyone who strayed near it, and I'd no reason to think it wouldn't.

I watched as Patricia approached the doorway, then was gone, as if she'd never stood in the room. Had I blinked? Skipped a second? Blacked out?

"Jorgas, you will proceed."

Jorgas turned to me, fairly trembling.

"Trust me." I'd no time to explain my last-ditch effort to thwart Tseng's sorcery. With a silent swallow, Jorgas followed Patricia into the mist. He too was gone before he appeared to touch the threshold.

Deborah gave Tseng's arm a touch of reassurance as he rose from his seat, watching us. Iain wrapped Kelvin's wrinkled but strong hand around mine and squeezed it.

I steeled myself and stepped toward the mist, which promptly faded, leaving only the dark form of Joboram in its wake.

"Is there a problem?" Tseng asked.

"The Blood Shade's actions have proven him. A scourge on the Land was ended today, the one the Blood Shades call Beauvrie. In his destruction, Reylan has shown himself worthy. This will be considered as Jorgas and Bakker undertake the binding."

"What?" Tseng and I cried out almost in unison.

"You're joking!" Tseng stammered with rage. "So, he gets a pass?"

"You're saying I'm to just sit here and wait?" I asked.

"Maybe," Iain whispered, "we should just take the win?"

"But Jorgas—"

'One more thing?' He'd known. Iain had known what killing Beauvrie would mean to the Quinkans. More than just saving me, he'd as good as rigged this.

Tseng's face was petulant, his scheme unmasked for all to see. "Beauvrie should have killed him!"

"Oh, yes." I took out the eight-sided coin and flipped it back to Tseng. "You can have your little homing device back. And Tseng? Stay the fuck out of my dreams."

"Blood Shade," Joboram's voice could have torn through flesh and bone. "You will leave us to continue."

Fuck it.

"Not if Tseng's still going in there." I waited for Joboram to protest. They did not. "I'm not letting Jorgas do this alone."

"You do understand what you're saying?" asked Iain.

"I can't leave him," I sounded weak. I couldn't voice my fear about Tseng interfering, but I thought it, squeezing Iain's wrist, hoping he'd get the message. If he could just find his way into the ritual, protect our memories from Tseng…

The things I do for you… he answered telepathically.

"It is your right," Joboram said at last.

The mists swirled again and the doorway reappeared. I hoped I knew what the hell I was doing.

CHAPTER FOURTEEN

My gut tightened as I neared the barrier, like my insides had compacted into one small rock. As I crossed into the darkness, it felt as if the damn thing exploded, singeing me head to toe in an instant before wrapping me in sweet, cool relief. I opened my eyes to greet blinding whiteness, then shut them immediately and dropped to my knees, trying instead to focus on breathing. After a few seconds, I opened my eyes once more, focusing on a dark spot in the polished woodgrain floor. I staggered to my feet, drawing my gaze up to—

Gargh!

I jumped back as the gaping skeletal jaws of a prehistoric lizard greeted me. I looked the thing up and down, from its enormous snout, past its ludicrous tiny forearms to the three claws that equipped its feet. Satisfied that it was millions of years dead, I turned to survey the darkened hall. The soaring frame of the predator's long-necked cousin dominated the room, skull at one end to tip of a bony tail at the other. In the corner, a trio of small predators equipped with vicious sickles on their feet poised ready to strike another horned prehistoric lizard.

I hadn't expected a trip to the museum.

"How do you feel?" At least Iain had made good on his promise to follow me.

"Like that thing just walked over me," I said, pointing to the long-necked skeleton.

"Yeah, I'm told the entry is rough. Glad I don't have to make it, physically, I mean."

Turning, I was astonished to see the real Iain, with jet black hair, piercing bright eyes and a devilish smile, handsome as sin, standing behind me. "You're back! I mean, you're you!"

He nodded, admiring the exhibits of the darkened hall. "For now, at least."

"You're not going to explain that, I suppose?"

"Explain, explain, explain," he muttered. "Why, as a species, are we so hung up on explaining when we could be exploring?"

"I'm not sure our best scientific minds would agree," I said, "and I'm not your species."

"Touché." He grinned, eyes brighter than ever as he surveyed the central attraction. "Do you know what draws us most, as children, to dinosaurs? Were you a dinosaur kid?"

"Seriously, Iain?"

"Not much dinosaur fever going around Denmark in the mid-nineteenth century, I suppose."

I shook my head, in no mood for another Grieg diversion. "Why are we here?"

To my non-surprise, he ignored me. "I was a dinosaur kid. Fascinated, in fact. All those different species and exotic, scientific names. All the variations that should have been so similar but were so different if you knew what you were looking at. Iguanodon was my favourite. Odd choice, I know, until you remember how it came by its identity. One spike. A single pointed piece of bone. One could hardly expect even the best minds of Victoria's age to know it was the creature's thumb. So, with scientific zeal, they cast the bony protrusion in its most logical role."

"Iain, all this would be fascinating were we not—"

"A horn, see? Not unlike some lizard species. One clue around which to assemble the whole story. Why not presume it bears some resemblance to what you could already see with your own eyes? Now, of course, we have whole skeletons to complete the puzzle. Nice things, skeletons."

"Yes," I muttered. "I'm aware of your fondness for the grinning visages of the dead."

"Nice for what they preserve, I mean. A record of a time and a creature, an identity and a life, unquestionable. Of course, people will find their questions. Where there is curiosity there must always be questions, along with the potential for mistakes. But the solution, though one might miss it, is always absolute. It's present, right or wrong. I've always felt… well, known that as children, part of us craves that certainty, and dinosaurs, with their big, terrifying claws and teeth, millions of years distant, intersect it with the limitless potential of a child's imagination. A creature that both feeds our curiosity and strokes our egos as explorers. How rare is that?"

I grimaced, looking around the darkened hall at the grinning skulls of the creatures in question, at the shadows of ribs that stretched up walls. I was sure Iain had a point, I just wished he'd come to it. "What is Tseng looking for, in all of this?"

"What makes you think this is Tseng's doing?"

"Don't bullshit me. Quinkans or not, Rory's death was the first thing Tseng brought forth. That's clearly his main agenda."

"I'd expect no less. But as much as he can influence it, which is why you brought me here, Tseng can't game the system. Not in this space. Even outside, he could bring forth nothing without someone to complete the picture. That, dear friend, was you."

"Yes, as I told Tseng," I muttered. "I killed his partner. I had to."

"And you've been asking yourself if that decision was yours to make ever since. We know Tseng doubts your humanity. The question is, do you?" He led me to a set of double doors at the end of the dinosaur hall, gripped their handles and threw them open with theatrical flourish. "Welcome to the Museum of Reylan."

I followed him inside the darkened hall, immediately recognising the earthy smell of stewing root vegetables. It had been over one hundred and thirty years, but even an immortal being could only shed their origins so far. It so entranced me with its familiarity, though certainly not its aroma, that it took me a moment to notice other curiosities that dotted the room. The broken and twisted hull of a 50s car I'd wrapped around a tree on California's coastal highway. I despised driving. A handkerchief and communist manifesto left by a promising young Berlin actor, the discovery of which would lead to the premature termination of the man's career and for all I knew, much worse. I remembered the night we'd been raided, when I'd abandoned him in my haste to remain anonymous. A fancy belt that had belonged to another companion. A bloodied pair of shoes. A torn canvas with an unfinished painting. I couldn't place them all in memory, but each stirred the same feeling of unease. No, not unease… guilt.

At last, I came upon the bubbling brew, set on a large stove I remembered well. My sister fussed over it, limping just as I remembered, though I did not remember my mother like this. I'd not stayed to see her wither. I'd looked in on her once, and never again. Now, every reason why sat before me.

"What is that?" Iain asked, tilting his chin at the brew with disdain.

I shrugged, assuming it to be the only dish my sister had known how to make, not that we'd been spoiled for choice. "Potatoes and onions, I think. Perhaps a little pork. More likely fat."

"I can smell that. The finest Danish peasant cuisine, I take it? Not sure how that 'best restaurant in the world' thing happened."

"Mor?" I whispered, nearing my mother. I looked over at my sister. "Alvie?"

Alveda barely looked up from her work, and what little movement she did offer was directed at my mother.

"Alvie?" I said again before continuing in Danish. "Can you hear me?"

"That's hard to say." Either Iain could understand me or he was reading my thoughts again. "It's best to take what you see in this place as a rendering of truth rather than the truth itself."

I watched intently as Alveda spooned some of the brew into a wooden bowl my father had carved before his death and brought it to our mother. She wrapped her long, bony fingers around the bowl, holding it unsteadily in her lap. Alveda helped her keep it from spilling and spoke again, but I heard nothing. Any attempt at speech between us was mute.

Alveda waited a few seconds before dipping a spoon into the broth and lifting some of it to our mother's lips. I flinched as Mor spat it back at her, then watched Alveda take the bowl away, disappearing into the other room of our modest house. I waited for her to return, cleaned up and ready to try again, but she didn't.

"Mor?" This made no sense. My mother had never been a callous or unappreciative woman. I couldn't imagine age exacting such a toll, but when I'd seen her, that one time, the thoughts and fears that had filled my head… I'd staged my own death soon before my thirtieth birthday to obscure my lack of aging. She'd buried her husband, and I'd made her bury her son.

She stood up, crossed silently to the pot on the stove, lowered her hand, and before I could stop her, dipped it into the brew. She brought it up to her lips, slurping loudly and licking it from her fingers, red and blistered from the broth. She lowered her hand for another helping.

I pulled her away from the boiling pot. This time, I heard her. A loud scream, guttural and ageless, blasted through me. I felt as if the hardening that had seized me as I'd passed the barrier had exploded again, only faster, bigger this time. I released my mother, clutching my gut as I doubled over. A sizzling sound gripped my nerves as she lifted the pot from the stove and flung it onto the floor. I leapt to my feet just in time to avoid being scalded. My mother, now silent again, tore at her clothes, collecting them in ragged clumps to try and mop up the mess. Each new strip she tore was quickly soaked.

"Truth?" I reminded myself that I was watching an illusion. At least, I hoped so. "What truth are you showing me with this?"

"Me? I'm merely a spectator."

"But there's no more truth here than in a nightmare."

I turned my back on the image. "Where's Jorgas?"

"What's a nightmare, if not the fears we deny our waking selves? I wonder where those fears go when one can't dream? For all my knowledge of the mind, I've no idea."

"Iain!" I snapped. "We're here for Jorgas, not—"

"So, in the years after you abandoned your mother, you felt no guilt? No morbid fear of the fate to which you'd left her, or your sister? Perhaps she abandoned your mother too. The mind can be so fragile in those later years. It isn't easy to stick around."

"Would you have had me pop in for a visit? Scare her half to death with the face of the son who never aged? Better I never paid her another thought. That's all I've ever felt about it, if it's so bloody important to you."

He nodded, eyes never leaving me. "And yet, you brought them here."

I looked over the scene again, watching as the image of my mother crumpled in on itself, crumbling and fading into mist. "And if I did feel some remorse or regret? Have you no greater charge for me than being an unfeeling monster?"

"Unfeeling?" came a familiar voice that filled me at once with excitement and nauseating dread. "I wouldn't call you that, old man."

I turned to see Ross smiling at me, the sheen of his curly black hair reflecting a dim light whose source I couldn't find. His dark eyes shone just as bright, and his mouth tilted with that devil-may-care look that had drawn the lustful attention of so many humans.

"This charade ends, now." I tore my eyes away from the sweet illusion.

"You keep appealing to me as if I were in charge here. How many ways would you like me to say it? I'm here to protect your minds, as you asked. The pains and regrets you see are of your own making."

"He's telling the truth," Ross said, smile unwavering. "It's a bit out of character, to be honest."

"See?" Ian crossed his arms. "This one talks. Also, rude."

"Apparently, he does," I muttered. "I don't suppose you care to explain why?"

"I'm as intrigued as you."

"Not the word I was looking for."

"Are you both going to talk about me like I'm not here?" Ross asked. "Now who's rude?"

"You answer me, then." I fixed my gaze on this mockery of my late friend. "If you've something to tell me, out with it."

"Is that any way to talk to a friend?"

"You're not Ross."

The thing stepped forward, bringing itself fully into the light, revealing every exquisite and painful detail. The dimple on my friend's cheek, the tender, feminine curve of his throat, and that dark hair curled playfully over his ears. But more than anything, his smile, stinging me with sincere affection. My most loyal and noble friend.

"I'm here because you invited me," he said at last. "What is it you want to hear?"

Invited? I felt the first pangs of a headache.

Iain put a hand on my shoulder. "I suggest thinking less and feeling more."

I stared at the intruder for what felt like ages. How real was it? Would it feel like Ross? Would it have that same sweet smell of the delicate blood he so preferred? "Just give us a minute."

Iain didn't argue, withdrawing his hand and backing into the shadows until Ross and I stood alone.

I reached for him, tentative, as if my touch would break him, or at least, break the illusion. To see Ross made real in flesh once more? I didn't know if it was torture or a gift. Perhaps that was the purpose of this place.

Less thinking, Reylan. Less thinking.

I started as he grabbed my hand, breath catching as if this were the touch of a long-desired lover. His skin felt the same, on my hand and on my face as he caressed my cheek and brushed a lock of hair over my ear. Though our relationship had never been physically intimate, I'd craved his touch since he'd died. Craved it more than I'd let myself believe. A gentle kiss on my lips removed any doubt.

More feeling, Reylan. More feeling.

"Do you believe me now?"

"I don't know what to believe."

"You see what I am."

"Why are you here?"

"Why? How? Who? Is it so hard for you to admit that you need this?"

"Need what?"

"There's another one."

I pushed his hand away, not knowing whether to be angry or overjoyed. It was Ross, all right. Right down to the silly word games. "This isn't funny."

"Do you want me to go?"

I stared at him, barely noticing the outlines that had formed in the shadows. The others who'd died that night. "You know I don't."

He nodded, cupping the back of my neck with a warm hand and kissing me again on the lips. "Then I'll stay."

"Careful," Iain said from somewhere in the dark. "The last complication we need is a tear in your mind from wanting this to be real."

"I thought you said it was real."

"Do I feel real?" Ross' sweet breath warmed my nostrils.

"Don't lawyer me," Iain answered. "Just remember where you are and what we're doing."

"He's right," came another voice, prim, precise, and mildly irritated.

I tried to make out detail in the woman's face as she stepped from the darkness. "Elspeth?"

The prickly Shaper who'd given her life to destroy Sklav regarded me with her familiar, condescending glare. "You don't have a very good history with people like us, do you?"

"Oh, I can think of one exception…"

"Iain," I growled. "I told you to leave us alone."

"Can't lie, I'm a little jealous." A thick, veiny forearm snaked around my shoulders, accompanying the unseen voice of Matthias. I flinched as he kissed my neck behind the ear, not least because the rich, healthy scent of his blood, imbued with the crackling of magick, set off a rumble in my stomach.

"Seriously?" Elspeth asked her late cohort.

"Better late than never," Matthias answered with a shrug of his muscular shoulders.

"Am I intruding?" asked Ross.

"No," Matthias and I said simultaneously, I with a plea for help and he with undisguised lust.

Iain stepped from the shadows, clapping his hands with sarcastic lethargy. "Look, this is marvellously entertaining, but you are doing exactly what I told you not to do. One more time, we do not make friends with the ghosts, we ideally don't get stuck with them, and we absolutely do not fuck them. Is that clear?"

"Stuck with them?" I pushed Matthias off me and backed away, not taking my eye off the apparitions. "I don't even know why Elspeth and Matthias are here!"

"We died the same night your friend did," Elspeth reminded me.

"Again, with the talking like I'm not here," Ross muttered.

"And whose fault was that?" I snapped before getting hold of myself. "Don't think me ungrateful. We wouldn't have beaten Sklav without you, but it wasn't my idea to have you destroy him from the inside."

"Then, why are we here?"

I turned to Iain. "They were your employees, weren't they? Your moles in the Arcadia Trust?"

Elspeth's mouth flattened into a steely grimace. "Employees?"

"Moles?" Matthias raised an indignant eyebrow.

"Oh, this should be good," Ross said.

"They were… my apprentices. At least, Elspeth was."

"Yes, and I mentored Matthias." The female shaper straightened her glasses and began to circle me. "No Shaper can reach their full potential without studying under the tutelage of a neighbouring quarter."

Matthias pushed his shoulders back, setting off another rumble in my stomach. Damn it. I hadn't been this interested in him while he'd been alive.

Elspeth continued, ignoring him. "You're familiar of course with the four quarters of magickal practice, as I explained them to you, correct? We Shamans, the children of Isis, draw from what is known and fated, manipulating life and the flow of the natural world. Necromancers are our opposite quarter, exploring what is unknown, yet willed—"

"Raising the dead?"

"That's reductive. More accurately, the children of Osiris alter the layers between realms."

"The children of who?"

"Try not to get distracted by the mythology. The important part is, they traverse the realms, including our world, the land of the dead, the Patron's realm… and the consequences of mistakes can be dire. I've known relatively few Necromancers in my time, and I can't say that bothers me. Mentalists, like your ex-boyfriend—"

Ross' eyes widened. "Boyf… I'm sorry, what?"

"Continue," I muttered, ignoring him.

"I'm going to pretend that wasn't hurtful," Iain mumbled.

"—are all about what's known, and willed. They study the mind, but beyond mere observation, they apply clairvoyance and telepathy, even controlling another against their will. But fortitude of mind and will is paramount."

"Reylan," Iain took hold of my arm before he could finish. "I'd be delighted to tell you more about my expertise later, however—"

"Finally, Entropists, like Matthias and your friend Mister Tseng, are skilled manipulators of luck, fortune, and the passage of time. What is unknown and fated. The children of Nephthys."

"Always the one nobody's heard of," Matthias added.

"Yes, I got that," I said, trying to hurry her up. "Therefore, Matthias is Iain's opposite and couldn't study underneath him. Look, where is this going? I came here to find Jorgas. Not to get distracted by ghosts teaching Magick 101 with electives in Egyptology."

"See?" Ross said. "He doesn't want to hear it. And aren't you betraying some serious House of Magick confidence right now?"

"He needs to hear it," answered Elspeth.

"And now he's heard it," Ross interrupted again. "So, getting back to me, old man."

"Your friend's passing was tragic, but of his own volition," Elspeth snapped. "Not a bad death, if you ask me."

"A noble sacrifice," Matthias agreed. "Imagine his family's reaction, had he been there to face them with you."

"Hey, this isn't about my guilt!" Ross replied.

"Iain," I called. "This is getting out of hand."

"Out of hand?"

"I don't have time to listen to three illusions squabbling like old women. Do something!"

"They're not just illusions. They're here for a reason."

The three figures began talking at me all at once, words indiscernible.

"What reason?" I yelled over the cacophony. "Some puzzle or riddle I have to solve? The true meaning of Christmas? I need them to fuck off!"

"I don't know. I told you—"

"To think less and feel more? Yes, what I feel is annoyed! Where is Jorgas?"

"He's… I can't… Reylan, you need to—" A loud yelp of pain cut short his explanation.

"What's wrong? Iain?"

"You need to get rid of them! You need to work this out before I lose you both!"

"Lose us both?"

"You and Jorgas!" he got out, fighting through gasps for words again. "The place is trying to distract you."

I turned to Matthias, then Elspeth, and finally Ross, each of their faces a sadistic, angular mockery of the person I'd once known as it chewed on words like a cow chewing cud. Nausea hit me as I watched Iain fall to his knees.

"What are you doing?" I yelled at him over the din.

He turned his face to me, visibly exhausted. "Keeping you both sane."

Whatever that meant, he was losing the battle.

"Go help Jorgas," I said with finality. "I'll manage."

He didn't stall with stupid questions like 'are you sure?' He was just gone. So too was the scrambled ranting from the trio of apparitions. Instead, they stared at me in silence, any pretence of congeniality gone. I hoped letting Iain focus his energies on Jorgas was worth it.

"What are you, then?" I asked, turning my gaze on each of them, one at a time. "Answer me."

"We are exactly as we appear, old friend." Ross answered.

"No," I said firmly. "These people are dead."

"Yes, because of you."

I turned to face Elspeth, who'd levelled the accusation with such flat nonchalance, I wanted to dismiss it as another sick joke. I'd a feeling that with Iain's 'protection' gone, such jokes were not in the offing. "That's not true and you know it."

"Do you?" Matthias asked.

"Yes!" I was not about to fall for mind games, even as they circled me counter-clockwise like the Weird Sisters. "You said as much yourselves. Elspeth, Matthias, Ross… each gave themselves of their own free will."

"You may tell yourself that," Ross answered, breaking the circle to approach me. "You may believe it. Iain may even believe it, at least so far as he needs to in order to silence that tiny corner of your mind—"

"Be quiet," I said.

The image smiled, as if my sudden rebuke amused him.

I could no longer see Elspeth or Matthias, but Ross? Ross, I knew, and this was not him. If this was my madness, then I would set its terms. "I've felt a great many things about that night. Anger, confusion, frustration, pain, immeasurable loss… over, and over, and over, again, and for what? Yes, there is shame, and anger. What could I have done? Should the sacrifice have been mine? Would Ross still be alive if… if… if… and to what purpose? And what difference, dare I ask, does it make to you? Whatever you are, because you are not Ross."

"Which begs the question, who is he?" The Ross-like figure tilted his head at the apparition that emerged from the shadows behind him, its visage the ghostly remnants of a handsome boy, neck ebbing a slow stream of blood. "Or him?" To his left, another man emerged, this one bearded, his shirt, a relic of the 50s, drenched with blood. "Or do you remember that first unfortunate—"

"What is your point? What do you expect? An apology?" I turned to see the throng had grown to at least two dozen men and a sprinkling of women, all sporting graphic puncture wounds, and all quite… dead. I flinched as one grabbed my shoulder. I turned to see a youth in mid-nineteenth century dress join the growing assembly. His face, I recognised immediately.

Anker. Hard as you might try, you never forget the innocents you kill.

Each apparition's body soon collapsed into white dust, which drifted away on an unseen, unfelt wind. In its place remained only the head of each figure, floating above a small knot of entrails. Then, they rushed at me.

I turned and ran, hoping foolishly that I didn't trip or fall in the dark. But there came no obstacles. It was as if darkness itself had solidified without walls, ceiling or floor. A black morass absorbed each step as every movement became more and more difficult. I eventually felt my body suspended in inky blackness, enveloping my limbs until it at last spread across my stomach and chest like a suffocating unseen hug. I could still breathe, though sound refused me when I tried to cry out. I don't know how I recognised it, but the dust left by the apparitions stung like sand on my face. No… it was piercing, burrowing into the pores of my skin like a million insects. I watched lines form on my arm like a charcoal tattoo. They coalesced into faces, eyes and crying mouths wide with expressions I remembered all too clearly. The exquisite joy of climax that could only come from the bite. That sudden recognition of a fear long left in childhood. Ecstasy. Desire. Terror. They moment they'd surrendered to a vampire, and thought they were going to die.

Whispers filled my ears. Some called my name, some simply sighed with pleasure. Some choked as the sting of my fangs pierced them while others whimpered a short, feeble plea. 'Stop.' 'Wait.' 'What are you doing?' Exactly what you longed for, sweet human thing. Don't pretend to reject me now. I promise to return you to your ignorant life once I've had my fill.

I remembered each time I'd been unable to fulfill that promise.

The sweet shudder gripped my body as the blood nourished me a dark climax known only to my own kind. A delicate, ghostly hand, dotted with fine black hair slid over my shoulder and inside my shirt, the smooth flesh of its palm pressing against my chest as soft lips brushed my neck. I didn't resist, recognising the intruder by the familiar scent I'd longed for since the night of his death. As he pressed against me, I didn't care that he was an illusion. Or was he, in this museum of lovely ghosts?

"Is this what you wanted?" Ross whispered in my ear, stroking my neck with the back of his free hand and kissing my cheek.

Without thinking, I let my head fall back on his shoulder. It was bare now, like the rest of him. I sighed with pleasure as he laid a row of soft kisses down my face and neck, pulling my collar ever so slightly as he stroked my chest. The sweetness of fresh blood filled me from head to toe, making every nerve vibrate against the soft velvet of my unseen prison. Any attempt at movement inched me deeper into Ross' embrace. He pricked his finger on one of his fangs, and held it to my lips. That most shameful of vices, to feed on our own kind.

"Stop it!" I tried to reject him, but his grip was firm. Denied leverage by the darkness, there was no breaking free. "This isn't funny!"

I shuddered as he pulled back my chin and forced the bloody finger inside. Two more guided it in, leaving me unable to move. The voices of my past companions grew louder and louder…

Not all of my companions. Just Anker. Phillippe. Mason. Jamie. All innocent men. I recognised each of their final cries before Ross' hand muffled my own. I thrashed against him as his fangs sank into my throat, the ecstasy of the shared bite taking hold as we fed from each other. Was this what I'd craved all along? The real reason I'd rescued this beautiful Blood Shade boy I'd called friend, who now wrapped me in sweet violence from the grave?

Ross' fingers penetrated my mouth, gagging me as they bled to the back of my throat. I forced it down, ignoring the pain and wicked pleasure. Then, one more cry brought back the memory of another boy's body crumpling in my arms.

Simon, the werewolf. My fifth victim, but not my last. That honour belonged to someone much closer.

I watched a ripple in the darkness form into a man. Tall, once handsome, but now so gaunt I barely recognised Brett. He licked bloodied tears from my face, whimpering as Ross denied him so much as a fresh drop. His bony white fingers grasped at me, tearing my shirt until he reached my flesh. I tried to cry out again as Brett scratched and bit at my chest and arms with blunt human teeth, at last claiming his prize. I could no longer tell which parts of me bled and which did not. Every inch of my flesh was caught in its own torment.

Between them, they denied any movement, save one. If I'd been cast as the monster, then the monster, I would play.

I bit down hard, drawing more of Ross' sweet blood over my tongue and down my throat. Brett bit harder into my skin, emboldened by my attack. In that moment, all that mattered was blood.

"There you are, old man," Ross whispered, his voice noticeably weaker. "There you are."

I drank until we each tumbled into weightless shadow.

*   *   *

I couldn't make out the precise moment my feet touched solid ground. The darkness remained, though at least I was free to move. But where? I crouched and touched the surface on which I stood. It was wet, like spilled water on the floor, but thicker and warmer. Not blood; that scent, I knew. I could smell it now, not from the floor, but from two distinct, very familiar figures.

Jorgas' solid chest heaved as he rested unclothed in Iain's arms. His eyes were closed, thick arms and legs resting in the liquid while Iain, equally bare, stroked his shoulders, neck and chest, periodically kissing him with a tenderness that for some reason unnerved me.

"Iain?"

He raised a finger to his lips in a shush motion, then beckoned me over. Jorgas stirred in his arms, then resettled. "You made it. I was worried you'd lose your grip on sanity. It's what this place does."

"I'm touched," I muttered. "What's happening to Jorgas?"

"He's confronting his past, just as you did."

"And you're naked with him, why?"

"For Jorgas to feel what he must without surrendering to madness, he needs to feel safe."

"With you wrapped around him?"

"It's the safest he's ever felt."

I bristled, not knowing nor caring if Iain could see me in the dark.

"Jealousy doesn't become you. Besides, you needn't take it personally. In all the world, I'm the one who made him feel safest, while you're the one who most excited him and gave him purpose. A fulfilled soul must have both. Right now, he's empathising with his victims as wholly as one can. If you found yourself being torn asunder by a werewolf with no way to stop it, which of the two sensations would you find most useful? Safety, or excitement?"

The 'logic' of this still came out twisted as a Picasso. "I'm not about to just stand here and watch."

"Are you at last proposing our first threesome?"

"Iain! His life is in your hands!"

"His life, his mind, and his entire being, in fact, just as you asked of me." He gave me an odd stare. "Join us."

"Your little 'threesome' joke wasn't funny the first time."

He offered his hand, smiling in lieu of any more words.

Unsure what else to do, I began taking off my shirt.

"That won't be necessary. Just take my hand."

I at last saw the glaze that covered Jorgas' eyes, like some swirling, mystical cataracts. In any other time or place, I'd have worried. But Iain knew far more about this than I. Perhaps my eyes looked the same. I took Iain's hand and nuzzled myself against his shoulder, holding Jorgas' motionless body to my chest. I kissed his hair, its oily scent comforting me. Iain gently lifted my face and kissed me, a taste so sweet, I barely heard the distant screams.

CHAPTER FIFTEEN

One of sunset's simplest pleasures had always been watching that sliver of light on my wall disappear, welcoming the UV-averse among us back into the world.

It's a pleasure not all of my kind could share, particularly those who'd gone centuries or millennia without daylight. But for me, on those evenings when I awoke before dark, this one little ritual grounded me in its own way, reconnecting me to a world beyond nightly feeding, like the boy who slept beside me.

I waited for the light to fade, enjoying the gentle sound of Jorgas' breath as he snoozed against my chest. Trying to not wake him, I eased away, smiling as he rolled over and hogged the sheets. He could have them. As far as I was concerned, he could sleep all night.

"Hey," Brett greeted me as I entered the kitchen and slipped a t-shirt over my head. He twisted the espresso maker closed and put it on the stove. "Too early for eggs?"

"Eggs? It's just gone dark."

My Mannequin grinned at me, then fetched a plate down from the cupboard. "I always thought the 'dinner for breakfast' thing was weird."

"As opposed to 'breakfast for dinner?' I thought you were always a creature of the night."

My inability to remember the simple, mortal chore of grocery shopping had, among many other things, made Brett's skills as live-in help invaluable. He also wasn't unpleasant company, and he could cook, not that I personally drew much benefit from it.

"Jorgas likes them fried and a bit runny, right?"

"I think so." I frowned at the two lonely strips of bacon in the pan as Brett cracked two eggs next to them. "You're not eating?"

"Deb's waiting. We'll grab something at the show."

"Burgers? Hot dogs and chips?" I asked with disgust. "Why don't you ask her in? It won't take a minute to cook something."

"You mean, it won't take me a minute to cook something," he smiled. "Like eggs on toast?"

I skewered him with a look.

Brett grinned with satisfaction. "She just texted. The car's at the end of the street."

"I'll call you another one."

"Dude, it's cool. Besides, I forget who's opening, but Deb says we don't want to miss their set."

I watched Brett set the eggs to warm, then reach for his keys and wallet. I'd never known him to be so impatient. "You'd still better have something before you go."

"Umm…"

I paused, my wrist halfway to my mouth, fangs ready to puncture my skin. "When did you last feed?"

"You know, I'm actually good for now."

"You're sure? I don't remember feeding you yesterday."

Brett's phone gave a sharp, musical chirp. "She's out front," he said, checking it before sliding it back into his jeans pocket. "Honestly, I'm fine. Oh, you do know how to—"

"Young man, I am almost 160 years old—"

"—and you've never cooked a day in your life. Two minutes for those eggs, okay? No more."

I smiled, watching him leave. "Enjoy the sho—"

He closed the door swiftly behind him. Impatient, indeed.

Returning to the kitchen, I watched the eggs slowly whiten in the pan, at last shutting them off when they approximated something I'd seen Jorgas eat. Now, coffee was on the stovetop... Toast? Hell, I wasn't about to wake Jorgas up before he was good and ready, even if it meant taking him out for... actually that sounded much better. Dinner somewhere, followed by the bars, where I might even find some nourishment myself.

I collapsed into my couch, enjoying the early evening stillness. On such a night, I could normally hear Dorotha shuffling about upstairs, but not tonight. Tonight, I was alone with my thoughts, interrupted only by the odd snore from my bedroom. Wondering where Demetrius had got to, I tried calling him.

The snoring sharpened into one loud, long gurgle I soon realised was the espresso pot. I turned it off and poured the dark contents into Jorgas' favourite mug, the one covered in a bright collage of London's tourist attractions. Strange that it was clean. Brett's handiwork again, no doubt. I reached into the fridge for milk, only to find a small jar of fresh cream. Sure, why not? Truly, my Mannequin had thought of everything. Everything, that was, except his own needs. Why hadn't he fed? I was sure I hadn't... What had I done last night?

I watched the swirl of cream turn the inky blackness a colour I thought looked appetising. I'd never get used to the smell, but as long as Jorgas liked it...

A startled cry accompanied whimpering and several shouts that snapped me out of my domesticity. But by the time I reached the bedroom, Jorgas was pulling up the covers and rolling over, still fast asleep. I considered waking him. But for what? Perhaps I was just exhausted. I flopped down on the couch and tried calling Demetrius again. It took a moment, but I remembered, Dorotha had been looking after him at the care facility where… were they still there?

I hadn't fed Brett last night. He should have been starving. And he couldn't cook to save his life!

"Iain?" Now, I was sure. "Show yourself."

A pair of bony white hands squeezed my shoulders.

"Well, that's disappointing," came Iain's voice behind me. "I thought you'd get at least one night in before you realised."

"What do you think you're doing? The truth!"

"Fine. In order to pass this trial, Jorgas needs to know who he is. He needs to know his place in the world, a place where he can feel welcome, even… well…."

"Loved?" I asked.

"Your word. Not mine."

"And I suppose the authenticity of that place, or lack of it, doesn't matter?"

He slapped me hard across the cheek. "Did that feel authentic?"

I let the urge to grab him by the throat and hurl him across the room pass.

"I know. You're confused."

"Don't be patronising. Outraged, is more like it! Jorgas is in bed, fast asleep!"

"And if you had to relive multiple violent killings, wouldn't you find it easier within the safe confines of a dream?"

"And once this trial is passed? Does he get a gold star? Can we all go back to our fucking lives?"

"Your life? You mean, what's left of it?" There was no malice in this question. Frustration, yes. Perhaps even a little sadness, but he wasn't mocking me. "Where does that leave Brett?"

"Brett is…" I stopped, remembering the happy, bright young man who'd made Jorgas breakfast. I pointed at the front door. "That's not Brett!"

"You're sure?"

"Brett doesn't cook! None of this is real, Iain!"

"Well pardon us for making some improvements! Do I have to explain every variable? Or should I just hit you again? I promise, the most tedious maths equation you can imagine has nothing on what it took to restore all of this."

I looked around at each detail of my living room. It looked, felt, smelt, and sounded exactly the same. "This is not my life."

"It's the life you would have had, if a certain organisation hadn't dragged you into its web. A certain Sister we both know."

"Really? And here I thought you were so well informed! Whatever you might think of Bakker, she's the only reason I've come to… to care about Jorgas."

The thought of owing her this made me wince, but could I deny it? Iain, it seemed, could.

"Are you sure? Of all the possibilities, of all the choices you've made, the paths not taken, you're sure there's none that could have led you away from the Arcadia Trust, to a place where you, Jorgas, and even Brett could live out… ugh, I despise the phrase 'your best lives.'"

"And just how did such a path come about?" I asked. "You said you knew it wouldn't hold, so whose genius master plan is this? 'Pardon us,' indeed?"

He pinched the bridge of his nose, looking sheepish, like I didn't already know the answer.

"Tseng?" I whispered with barely contained fury. "Iain, he wants us dead!"

He sat beside me on the couch, comfortably crossing one leg over the other. "Accept this one gift, and Tseng won't trouble you anymore."

"I see," I said without looking at him. "But you *are* working with him."

"No," he answered sharply. "I negotiated a compromise, with clear terms to keep you and Jorgas safe."

"A plea bargain, you mean? Commuting our sentence to life in a gilded cage?"

"If you like such crass terms, I'm the best lawyer you could have."

"Without asking me? Yes, marvellous."

"There's that defiance. It's one of the things I find most captivating—"

"This is a lousy time for flirtation," I said, looking him in the eye at last.

Whatever he saw in my gaze, it sucked the playfulness from his voice. "If you truly never want to see me again, I'll respect your choice. This was about giving you and Jorgas a happily ever after, not me."

"Ah, so it's a noble sacrifice now, is it? I've heard quite enough about those for one evening, and it doesn't suit you, Iain. Sacrifice? Tell me one decision you've made in your life that wasn't completely self-interested!"

"There haven't been many," he admitted. "Remind you of someone? Before Jorgas, your life consisted of what? Hitting the bars up for fresh meals? Silly, juvenile games with your fellow immortals, competing to see who could suck down more celebrity Type O? That wolf boy, who right now can almost taste mastery over his own demons, has brought out the best in both of us."

"Perish the thought I don't show you my good side," I muttered.

"There's that flippancy again. You can sneer all you like, but you're a good person, Reylan. Under all that predatory selfishness, for all the mistakes you've made—"

"My 'mistakes' are none of your business.

"Do you think I'd do this for just anyone? You're right of course. Hell, I may be the most selfish monster among us. Possibly in this country. Let me give you and Jorgas a chance to live in peace, knowing who you are. That's all I'm offering. Whatever you choose to do with it, I'll not interfere, and neither will Tseng."

"A gift, then?" I muttered, unable to resist an incredulous smile. I stood up, taking in another view of the room. "That's what this is? A change of fate? Except fate is Tseng's specialty, is it not? Serendipity? Entropy? Paths not taken?"

"Remember the mathematical equation from hell I warned you about? The blackboard is coming down as we speak. You won't understand. I'm not patronising you, it's just a fact."

"I'm quite sure I won't. But I've learned enough about Shaper divisions to know this isn't your power at work. If this path is not just in our minds, if it's as real as you say, then it's not in my head. It's not some shared dream. This is physical. And if we are all who we appear to be, not some… homunculi or promethean doppelgangers—"

"Easy there, it's a spell, not Scrabble."

"—it has to be Tseng. This is his power, not yours. Not Deborah's. This is about Tseng, and a path without Bakker."

He stood up, sincere once more. "Perhaps even a path on which the House of Magick never used Jorgas to open the Wound in their removal of the Scimitars? Oh, I make no apologies for the results. We're all safer for the Scimitar of Light's end."

There was the cold agent of the House I knew was inside him.

"I'm just sorry it took the imprisonment of that boy. And the rest? You, gone for months while we rescued him? Brett, left without his master? What happened to me?"

"Your legacy," I reminded him.

He gave a slight swallow, which I took to be as close to contrition as he would get. "Not all of us have chosen to isolate ourselves from the bigger picture."

"The bigger picture?" I almost laughed. "Is that what you call doing the Houses' bidding regardless of who gets hurt?"

"Now, hold on just a damn moment. Let's not pretend you've ever cared about who got in your way."

"My 'way' rarely hurt anyone beyond leaving a few mortals light-headed on their walk home or wounding some idiot's pride. But you? Aiding and abetting kidnapping? Lying to me? And now, helping Tseng?"

He took his time answering me, never flinching. "This place was my idea, shaped by Tseng's entropic skill. Deborah's talent for the natural sciences filled in the blanks. A fully realised path of least resistance."

"Did you not think that Jorgas and I should have some say in the matter?"

"You do understand the alternative? You killed Tseng's partner. Tseng doesn't care about the hows, whys, and whereofs! Fortunately, like I said, I'm best lawyer you could have."

"Meaning you manipulated Tseng too?"

He fixed me with a glare so hard I wondered if he was trying again to penetrate my mind. "If you can't thank me, will you at least recognise that there's nothing I wouldn't do for you two? I mean, really? You'd spit in the face of this heaven? After you returned to a life gone to hell?"

"A hell you caused."

"Yet, you refuse the amends."

"Because it's a lie!" I snatched up a book from the coffee table and threw it down on the couch with a satisfying thud. "A tactile, handsome lie is still a lie, Iain!"

"It's not a lie," he insisted, voice still measured and even. "It's a path not taken, at least, until now."

I took a moment to steady myself, sitting down again on the couch. "And how did you persuade Tseng to create that path?"

"Oh, it was simple, really. I rearranged his thoughts to take advantage of his insecurities and doubts, making him realise he'd been the bad guy all along. I mean, it scrambled his brainwaves and turned him into a drooling vegetable for four days, but—"

"Iain…" I growled.

"He's a politician, isn't he? An opportunist, yes, but also a pragmatist. Dare I say, an idealist? I showed him what it meant to be recognised by one of the Houses. If he chose to destroy Jorgas, it would not only harm his standing in the House of Magick, but risk angering the House of Blood. Tseng's smart enough to see what a grudge would cost him. And let's be reasonable, Reylan. You never wanted responsibility, or community. You're good when a crisis finds you, but given the choice, you're entirely self-interested. Tseng is a different sort. So is Deborah."

"Yes, about her—"

"Let me finish. Tseng, Deborah, even dear Sister Bakker? These are people who want and need to be part of something bigger. Who need to act and make a difference. You and Jorgas aren't those people. But you have paid your dues, and Tseng, however reluctantly, sees that."

"Oh?" I folded my arms, flicking my tongue over my top lip. "Well, I'm glad to have the approval of Mister Tseng. Something bigger? Make a difference? Any more motivational sophistry you'd like to toss out there? All I see is a talented politician with a grudge using magick to get his way! You'll understand if your collaboration does not fill me with confidence, especially in you!"

Iain looked around the room again, admiring the detail of its recreation. "Deborah trusts him."

"But can we trust Deborah?" The question plagued me. Deborah had always been the no nonsense sort, but now? Was she even the same person I'd left behind?

Iain folded his arms and leaned against the wall. "Please tell me you have something to drink."

"You tell me! It's your show."

When a sarcastic head tilt was his only response, I crossed to the hutch behind my dining room table and opened it to reveal a row of bottles in various states of depletion dating back to the 1990s. "Help yourself."

He did, pouring himself a double shot of bourbon and downing it swiftly without ice. I'd never understood the appeal.

"How much longer will Jorgas be out?"

"Out?"

"Asleep? Dreaming? You said it protects him during these trials."

"Ah, yes. The nightmares will be awful, but they'll allow him to go through what he needs to without going mad."

"So? How long will they last? Is there any chance of him waking before one ends? Or of one manifesting or causing us harm?"

"No," he said, pouring another shot. "He won't wake up until he's proven himself or... He'll be fine."

"Or what?" I asked, not liking his hesitation. "Iain?"

"Not to downplay what you just went through, but the deaths Jorgas caused are not distant memories, nor comrades who gave their lives, like yours were. He ripped them apart, tooth and claw. There is a very slim chance that the guilt of that..."

I didn't wait for him to come up with the words. "Iain? Get him out of there, now!"

"If he wakes up now, assuming he survives the trauma of being ripped between the sleeping and waking state during his trial, then this life? This home? Brett? It all goes away, and Tseng will have his pound of flesh. That's if Joboram doesn't take theirs first."

I steadied myself against the liquor cabinet, pouring myself a shot of gin. I knew I'd feel awful in a few hours, but in the second it took to burn my throat, I didn't care. Think, man! Think!

"Reylan, try to calm…" Iain wisely trailed off. "You've done your bit. Billy's a strong kid. Let him finish this."

Hardly a kid anymore! Was this a solution? To live in Tseng's dollhouse because Iain had pleaded on our behalf? What proof did I have that Tseng would keep his side of the bargain? Or Iain, for that matter? I'd had enough of others deciding our fate.

"I need to talk to Tseng," I said.

"I don't think that's a good idea."

"I think it's the only idea that makes sense right now. I assume that as the architect of this nonsense, he can't be hard to reach. I'd appreciate it if you brought him here, now."

"Reylan, if he decides to kill you, I won't be able to stop him."

"You won't be able to stop him?" I laughed. "I think without his coven, Mister Tseng will be quite outmatched."

"I'm afraid he won't be."

"Is that a fact?" I realised he wasn't joking. "Why? What have you done?"

He stood and faced me, completely unaccusatory with that same deadly seriousness. "Hit me."

"Don't be an idiot," I said. "I could kill you."

His fist slammed into my jaw. I stared at the Shaper for barely a second before rage overtook me. I balled my hands into fists which… stubbornly refused to move.

"Now, do you believe me?"

I stood, bewildered, swallowing emptiness in lieu of rubbing my jaw.

"He can hurt you. You can't hurt him. A steadfast condition of our compromise. I'm sorry."

"Sorry?" I demanded. "You mean to tell me I'm defenceless? Jorgas too, I expect! And you expect me settle for 'I'm sorry?'"

"With the enemies you make? Don't be ridiculous."

Now he was just abusing the fact that I couldn't hit him.

"You're defenceless against we three, and we three only. And since I hope you've no intention of harming Deborah, I also hope you'll see wisdom in leaving Tseng alone. I promise you he'll do the same. Tseng's path is too important to be bogged down by a grudge. But if he has access to you, in person, I can't guarantee anything. He might decide two defenceless birds in the hand are worth… You understand me, don't you?"

"Yes. That's why he and I need to talk."

"Yes," he admitted with a solemn nod. "I suppose you do."

Whether the room darkened, just for a second, or I'd actually closed my eyes, I couldn't say. I wasn't surprised to feel another dip in temperature, nor by the appearance of Tseng on my couch. His sharp, intelligent eyes pierced me with a malevolence restrained by curiosity. Despite his capacity for cruelty, the man was no common bully or thug. Nonetheless, he hated me.

"Well?" he asked. "What do you want?"

By all means, sit down, I thought. "Can I offer you a drink?"

He dismissed me with a snort. "Two years sober. Thanks."

"Congratulations."

Exactly how he managed to make his expression even more condescending, I couldn't say, but he did. Of course, as a skilled politician, he was also a consummate actor.

"I'm not asking you to like me, Mister Tseng."

"That will save us time. Call me Adrian if you want to save some more."

The invitation caught me off guard with its cordiality. "If you insist."

"Whatever will end this faster. We made you a fucking paradise. What else do you want?"

"Paradise?" I asked. "With no Patricia? No Kelvin? No consequences for what happened with the Scimitar of Light?"

"Exactly. What's your issue, vampire?"

I scowled, leaning against the wall with arms folded, my hospitality already exhausted. "You're very confident in this protective bubble of yours, aren't you?"

He tilted his head in faux thoughtfulness. Of course, said bubble was the only reason he still had his head.

"We're both intelligent people," I continued. "Why don't we start with a simple gesture of respect? I'll not misgender you, so don't mislabel me."

"A fatuous parallel. I don't hold up my gender identity as a license to decide the fates of others."

"That's how you think we see the world? As an arena to play as gods?"

"You're beings of tremendous power, on top of immortality. Even a werewolf—sorry, I believe the term is 'Flesh Master'—can't match you in its human form. I've learned to watch anyone who comes into a large amount of power very closely."

"Sound advice, though we're ageless, not immortal. If you wanted to kill me, Tseng—"

"You'd already be dead," he answered. "That would be just. But I'm no monster, and Iain, for reasons that bewilder me, cares for you."

I decided to table my questions about the nature of their relationship. "Respect, then, Mister Tseng?"

"Respect?" He nodded slowly. "As you wish… Blood Shade."

I sat opposite the couch Tseng occupied, making myself comfortable in my own false home. "Indulge my curiosity. When exactly did you stop expressly wishing for my death?"

"When I realised it wouldn't change a thing. Unfortunately, I'd already reached out to the Quinkans by that point, and they don't take kindly to takebacks or having their time wasted. So, we crafted a compromise for you, once your trial was complete. A home where you and Jorgas can live out your days out of our hair."

"We? Iain is part of your coven?" I'd had my suspicions, but…

Tseng grimaced thoughtfully. "Let's say he takes an interest in us."

The chair squeaked under my shifting weight. "And the Quinkans?"

"Your trial is at your own request. Idiotic, if you ask me, but you passed. Only Jorgas and Patricia remain."

"That simple, eh?" I felt used. How long have you been practicing?"

"Longer than Deborah. We've been friends for a long, long time. Interesting that she never mentioned you until…"

"Until?" I asked as the sentence hung unfinished. "You became her mentor?"

"Better it came from someone she already trusted, though Iain would probably have done just as well. She was always going to find one, of course. One of fate's wrinkles, the ability of Shapers to always find our own."

"If you're about to tell me you sparkle for each other—"

"It's more… primal than that."

I caught myself looking at his crotch. "Does everything in the House of Magick come down to sex?"

"I'm sorry, shall we delve into the great myth of all your kind being asexual?"

"It's no myth."

"Yet you've managed to take both a Flesh Master and a Shaper into your bed, deriving great satisfaction from both. Unless of course you're just some anomaly of supernatural biology."

"I've been called worse."

"By me, among others. So, why refuse the simple gift of being able to live that life?"

I smiled, suddenly curious. "Am I still talking to Mister Tseng?"

"Adrian," he reminded me.

"Adrian? Am I talking to you right now, or to Iain?"

"You think he's possessed me?"

I snorted under my breath. "He needs a body just now, and in my experience, Iain does like to be in charge. Be wary of that."

"If control freaks scared me, I wouldn't have entered politics."

I was almost starting to like him.

"To be honest, I think Iain was looking forward to seeing what came of this life. This path. Call it what you will. It appeals to him."

"And to you?"

"It keeps you out of my way."

"Your way?" I leaned forward, fingers pressed together. "To do what?"

This time, he smiled. "Nothing outlandish, catastrophic or dangerous. The House of Magick—"

"Ah, there it is," I muttered.

"The House of Magick," he repeated, unphased, "simply wants a clearer picture of what's going on in Sydney. A firmer hand, but not an overreaching one. You and Jorgas will be free to live the lives that suit you."

"Doing nothing to shake the 'gilded cage' theme here."

"You're telling me you'd refuse the opportunity of a life without Patricia Bakker and her so-called Arcadia Trust? Oh, it's a noble idea. Supernatural beings in cooperation, without the Houses? It even makes sense somewhere like Sydney, and it works, until there's a crisis. A lost, angry youth with unchecked power to tear people apart? A malevolent being that's entered our reality from another? The Scimitar of Light?"

"A threat the House of Magick deliberately brought to our doorstep with their genocidal little scheme."

"Genocidal?" he scoffed. "The Scimitar threat is no more. And what about the next time a Patron breaks into our world? Do you really think such events are so rare? You don't hear about them because the Houses minimise the fallout and loss. Perhaps Jorgas' father would still be alive if—"

"Nobody mourns that bastard, and if you think the Patron incursion caused his death, you're not as familiar with my history as you think."

"Oh, but I am. Ross, I believe was his name?"

"Now you listen here," I seethed, rising from my seat.

"Sit down or this discussion will be over, along with any memory you might have that it ever took place. I can't restore Ross to you, any more than I can restore Rory. Even the most skilled Necromancer…"

I gave him a moment to find the words but none came. Watching him, I couldn't tell if he didn't know, was afraid to explain, or just assumed I wouldn't understand.

"You do understand loss, though?" he said at last, looking up at me with a smile. "Probably better than I do. An extra… what is it? One hundred and thirty years? It'll do that to you, I'm sure. Your family, and how many other friends? Others can only wish for a Blood Shade's ability to handle grief. Or maybe you don't handle it. Maybe that's what makes the oldest among you so bitter and cruel."

"If you wish to test that stereotype, I can arrange some introductions."

"Tell me, do your kind believe in soul mates? Is that how you see Jorgas? Surely not. I mean, barring accidents, you'll presumably outlive him. Eventually, you'll have to process that loss too. Or is it better to not get so attached? What if he gets attached? Would you leave him with that illusion?"

"You're vomiting words now, Adrian. The voters might be used to it, but I don't have the time. What's your point?"

"My point is Rory! We were happy! Planning to grow old together! To enjoy all we could make out of life until it ended, naturally, neither one of us left alone for too long. You took that from us! You and Jorgas!"

"Correction, I took it from you. And were those possibilities in Rory's mind too, or just yours?"

"Don't even—"

"Because Rory seemed more focused on what he could do to me once we got back to my place. He didn't mention you at all."

"Please! That same night, I was lying hooded and anonymous in a sling at Club Darius while seventeen guys fucked me. We enjoyed our freedom, Blood Shade. What's your point?"

I smiled, honestly not mocking him. "Punishing us won't ease the anger you feel at yourself, Adrian. Your partner died while you were living a whorish fantasy? I can't imagine how—"

"Oh, here we go."

"—how that felt to someone so determined to be in control of their fate they abandoned everything to master it." I leaned forward, resisting the urge to resort to mental trickery as I captured his gaze. I wasn't the manipulator, but the manipulated, and I needed Adrian to see that he was too. "Because you weren't out at Club Darius, were you? I suspect it's a little darker than that."

"Blood Shade, I'm warning you—"

"You're a fascinating man, Adrian, born for the times, or so it seems. The left loves you because you're exactly the kind of clean-cut Trans overachiever of colour they can put forward to look 'woke' as I believe the kids now call it. The right loves you because you're a self-made success story, a child of immigrants fleeing the communist takeover, who represents everything that's non-threatening about both the queer and Asian communities."

"You're on track to find out just how 'non-threatening' I am right now."

"It takes shrewdness to sustain both narratives. Such a perfect balance. Such luck! Now, I've no doubt your abilities as a Shaper have aided you in this from time to time, but there must be some mundane skill at play too, no? A healthy dose of ambition? How long have you been practicing magick? Or to be more specific, exactly when did your meteoric rise in the polls begin?"

He shot me a look so bitter, I thought he was about to launch himself at me.

"Fickle thing, fate. It has a penchant for giving with one hand while taking away with the other."

This time, he did come at me, stopping inches from my face, nostrils flaring and neck muscles twitching with the ferocity of an enraged bull. But he did stop, finally relaxing as he stood up and straightened his shirt, his politician's composure regained. "Enjoy your gilded cage, Blood Shade. It's more than you deserve."

I let him pass me without looking back, waiting until he was within a few steps of my front door. "One minute, Adrian."

The contempt in his face couldn't hide his curiosity. "What?"

"Watch my memory of Rory's death, from start to finish. No facsimiles or distortions." I stood, offering both my hands. "Just the truth, unfiltered. Unless you're afraid of what you'll see?"

"Just pull a memory out of you, eh? Sorry. Not my arena."

"Get Iain's help if you must. You were able to reshape countless small decisions throughout my life, accounting for more variables than any regular human could ever—"

"Everything you see, everything you touch, hear, and experience? It all comes from you. This 'cage' is of your own making. I know it might come as a terrible shock, but I honestly couldn't give a fuck about what you want, Reylan. At Iain's behest, I'm offering you the chance to improve both our lives and leave me alone."

"I think Iain knows me better than that. As for you, you're quite capable of killing us, yet you haven't. You left that for Beauvrie, a trick almost as impressive as this little doll house, and when that didn't go to plan, it didn't seem to bother you too much. But you also don't want us out in the world, interfering with your budding Shaper career. A shrewd politician in every arena."

"You can spend eternity theorising about this for all I care."

"Knowing you'd still kill us both, given the chance?" I glanced down at the now intact coffee table between us and the sharp, jewel-encrusted dagger that lay upon it. It was like some lavish relic from a lost empire, definitely not of this place. "If not, explain where that came from?"

The absence of surprise on his face spoke volumes, but it didn't tell me what he planned to do with the weapon.

I leaned forward and slid the knife toward him. "You don't trust me, Mister Tseng. That gives me no option but to trust you."

"To do what?" he asked flatly. "Give you a nasty cut that would heal in seconds? Or has vamp… Blood Shade immortality gone downhill in recent years?"

"Am I correct in assuming that blade is made of silver, or at least coated in it?"

He shifted his weight uncomfortably.

"It's for Jorgas, isn't it?" I continued. "How much do you despise me, Adrian? How badly do you want to hurt me?"

"I don't know what you're trying to—"

"A full coven's concentrated magick was always going to defeat Jorgas and myself, eventually. But it was never concentrated. No matter how hard you raged, your power relied on Deborah and Iain, two people who would never wilfully do us harm. That meant you would have had to betray them at some point, or dance endlessly around Jorgas and myself, your resentment growing as they refused to enable your so-called justice. Oh, but doesn't rage feel good? Once you've tasted the validation of noble victimhood, being a 'survivor' against an evil foe, it's very hard to go back. That's the thing about martyrdom. You're not supposed to survive it. If it isn't burned up and consumed, all that righteous energy just transforms into an explosion of ego, violence or both. Well, Mister Tseng, your explosion is at hand. If it's revenge you crave, take it now, or leave us alone!"

Shifting with my thoughts, the setting around us had changed to my bedroom. Tseng looked down at the sleeping form of Jorgas, who turned over, flopping an arm over his head in that curious way he often did while sleeping. How many times had it soothed me, just watching him? Only I wasn't watching him now. I was watching Tseng, whose hand flexed around the knife's jewelled hilt. His throat tightened as he looked down at his vendetta, now offered on a proverbial plate.

I'd stop him, of course, if his better nature didn't prevail. My reflexes were faster in every sense—

A long gash split across Jorgas' throat before I saw Tseng move, a shock so sudden and complete, it was as if the blade had slit my own. Blood poured from the wound, running in thick rivulets down Jorgas' muscular chest into the sheets. Only now did my lover's eyes spring open, staring, helpless and unable to see the knife Tseng still clutched in his hand.

I was on Tseng almost as fast, grabbing him by the collar and throwing him hard across the room. The loud thud of him hitting the wall at the foot of my bed muffled his cry. Had his sudden attack on Jorgas revoked his precious barrier? Whatever. I hoped I'd broken every bone in the bastard's body, and if I hadn't, I'd finish the job as soon as I… did what?

Jorgas choked, staring helplessly at me as he continued to bleed. Without stopping to think, I lowered my lips to the wound, hoping I wasn't too late. Jorgas pushed me away with such force, I heard the sliding wardrobe door crack off its rails as I hit it. In human form, with a mortal wound? I couldn't believe it. Nor could I believe the figure in the bed was no longer Jorgas. He was still bleeding out. Still had a vicious gash across his throat. But he was now Giorgios. Forget the blasted dream. Forget the body I'd seen at Valia's. The Premature had thrown me away in his final throws, but he was now quite dead.

More astonished than I was Tseng. Gathering himself, he staggered forward, not taking his eyes off his victim. "But that's…I didn't…" He couldn't get the words out. "I don't understand. He wasn't a kid! You saw him!"

"Yes, Mister Tseng. I saw you slit my boyfriend's throat." I wanted to throw him across the room again, and worse.

"I didn't mean—"

"—to claim your powers?" came a calm, familiar voice from the doorway. "To fulfill the fate that was always yours?"

We turned to face Iain, now united in our confusion and outrage.

"You've been seeing this in your dreams for years, Adrian," Iain continued, perfectly composed. "I even shared part of one with Reylan, taking a few artistic liberties of course."

Well, fuck. Of course he had.

"It's confusing and opaque, I know. The particulars are always so in matters of the future. My Becoming was very different. Each quarter fulfills a new Shaper's potential in a different way. Sadly, as is the way of nature, it usually involves bloodshed, often not in the way you expect. But murder? No. Absolve your conscience of that now, Adrian. The Prematures knew what they were taking on when they agreed to safeguard Elspeth and Matthias' knowledge until new acolytes were ready. They knew how it would end."

Two deaths. Two immortal beings, Giorgios and Sophia. The price of Tseng and Deborah's powers.

"But I've been practicing for years!" Tseng stammered. "This didn't have to happen. You made me kill a child!"

"As opposed to killing my boyfriend?" I asked.

He at least had the decency to look ashamed.

"Nobody made you do anything, Adrian. See, as a master of fate and time, an Entropist's Becoming takes place after that first manifestation of power. It might take years, or even decades. Sometimes, it's on an Entropist's very death bed that they take a life. The hardest part is never knowing who the victim will be, or when. Entropy lies at the intersection of what is fated and what is unknown, after all. And in this place, so, so much is unknown. Nothing is quite as it appears. It makes sense that it would happen here."

"Which begs the question, Iain, who did you kill?" I asked, feeling like a bit player in a murder scene set in my own bedroom.

The hint of shame in Iain's smile added another illusion to the list. "Where others must draw blood, Mentalists draw from the mind."

Tseng seemed as appalled as I. "So…?"

"You didn't kill yours," I muttered. "You drove them mad."

"There are Shapers who take perverse delight in the price of our power. I'm not one of them, and if it eases your opinion of me, he wasn't a good man. I was a real priest once, and the confessional can offer such windows on a person's character." He turned to Tseng. "Your inability to forgive Reylan and Jorgas is what led you here, Adrian. It disappoints me, but then, I always knew it would. You're on the precipice of your full potential, but are you ready to move on? To leave them alone?"

The Entropist looked down at his victim, face still frozen in shock.

"Alone to do what?" I asked. "Where is Jorgas?"

"He'll return to you soon, and if you wish it, you can go on with your lives, unhindered. That is, Mister Tseng, if you've had enough of this little quest for vengeance?"

"You lied to me!" Tseng hissed. "Again and again, you lied!"

"Don't be embarrassed," I muttered. "He's very good at it."

Iain ignored me. "I helped you manifest what you needed to see. The lives of the men who obsessed you, in your hands to destroy. Now, you see the price of that obsession."

"A child," Tseng muttered again. "A kid!"

"Technically, he was much older than you," I pointed out. "And immortal."

"Not immortal enough."

"Nonetheless, you did wield the blade," said Iain. "In the end, a childlike immortal instead of a young man who regrets his mistakes? You tell me, who should give up life for life? At least Giorgios was willing. Take his gift with gratitude and leave Reylan and Jorgas alone. We have more important things to do."

His sudden invocation of 'we' made me shiver. I knew Deborah to have a conscience, and it seemed, for all his vengeful opportunism, so did Tseng. But if both were beholden to Iain?

"You." Tseng glared at him. "I should have killed you."

"Now, there's an inventive solution, with one significant flaw. I'm not actually here." With that, Iain was gone. He didn't fade, or round the corner and disappear, or anything else that would have made any kind of linear sense. He just wasn't in the room anymore.

A few seconds later, neither were we.

CHAPTER SIXTEEN

Hollywood would have us believe that illusions covering a whole environment vanish in a thick fog, be it grey like grim weather, pitch black if it wants to be particularly sinister, or bright pink or green if the director wants to show off. The disappearance of Tseng's faux house that Reylan built—or Iain's? I had no idea at this point, nor did I care—boasted no such effect. The light simply drained until I once more couldn't see a damn thing. I took a step forward, reached for the edge of a closet that was no longer there, bent down to touch a bed that had similarly vanished, and hoped to whatever bored god was available that there would be a way out.

"Reylan? Reylan?" The voice seemed close, yet my hand touched nothing as I swept it through the space. "Hello?"

"I'm here." The urge to violently end Tseng and his vendetta had passed. The power of a crisis shared. I took another step forward, then turned, like some ludicrous children's game where we were both blindfolded. Tseng's voice seemed to bounce around the space, impossible to follow. "Are you standing still?"

"I'm not fucking moving. I can't see my feet," he answered, the sting of Iain's manipulation still fresh in his voice. "Can you… I don't know, count back from ten or something?"

He wanted me to do what?

"Any particular language?"

"Cantonese."

"Oh, fuck off."

"Then don't be an arsehole! Just do it, slowly. Make sure you annunciate."

I swore, if he asked me to sing… "Ten, nine, eight, seven," Each number bounced around uselessly, just as Tseng's voice had. I got all the way to four, then jumped as Tseng latched onto my wrist. "How?"

"Even if I can't see the space, I can see movements in time. Sounds are easier to see because they're slower than light. I just tracked them back to you. The familiar pattern helped."

I nodded before remembering he couldn't see me. "In that case, perhaps you can explain where the hell we are and how we leave?"

"That, I don't know."

"Mister Tseng, think hard and quickly, before I reconsider letting what you just did slide."

"Okay, you know what?" Silence followed. Perhaps the futility of sniping at each other in the dark had landed for him. As for my own barb, I regretted nothing; call me petty. "Fine. I'll… figure something, I guess."

"That's reassuring."

"Bitch, I am literally working in the dark right now with nothing to go on!"

"Nothing? You told me that you pulled the strings of fate and the past to bring that recreation of my home into being. I'm no expert, but it seems heavy magick for someone who's been practicing for how long, exactly?"

"I told you, the others helped, a lot."

"Deborah? Iain?"

"I thought you wanted a way out of here, not a behind the scenes tour!"

"You must know how you built it. What remains of it? You said you can see time? Surely that includes its manipulations, particularly when they're yours. Describe it to me like I'm an idiot, because in your line of work, Mister Tseng, that's precisely what I am."

"They're like… fragments, I guess? Threads and pieces of time and causality that connect."

"And you find these, how? Please don't tell me you need to be able to see in order to manipulate them."

Silence.

"Adrian?"

"Let me concentrate! I've never had to do this in the dark. Before, I had an object of yours to bring the threads back to."

"As opposed to now having my very presence within arm's length?" I felt Tseng pull closer to me, reinforcing his grip on my arm. The mild pain gave way to curiosity as I watched a dim blue light form within his clenched fist. He'd kept it turned down towards the 'ground,' which seemed smart. Better sense told me this was one of those times to just let the wizard get on with it. At least I could see us both, however faintly.

"So far, so good," he said.

"Confidence, Mister Tseng?"

He moved his fingers with gentle dexterity, never releasing the cluster of energy in his hand but instead setting it free one strand at a time. Each wrapped around his fingers, crossed the palm of his hand, and curled around the wrist like a bright tattoo, finding its own geometry.

I wanted to encourage him, tell him he was doing fine, but I honestly had no clue. Strange, how my perspective on the man had changed so quickly in the last hour, but we'd both been manipulated here. I didn't even know if it was worth being mad at Iain. Even his shiftiest machinations were never without cause, and they'd saved my life multiple times. It was a hell of a way to secure co-dependence.

Tseng startled me with a gasp.

"What's wrong?" I asked.

"Just… hold on… there's a lot… Argh! Ow!"

"Okay, whatever this is, it's not working."

He groaned, clutching his shoulder. The threads weaved around his hand in their wild dance.

"Adrian, stop!"

"I have," he all but wheezed. "It's still… Ah! Okay, that really fucking hurts!"

I could at least see him now, though part of me wished I couldn't. Lines creased his youthful face. His hands seemed tough and calloused, the skin of his neck, thinner.

"Adrian? What's…" I'd been so fixed on his changing visage that I'd not paid attention to my own rumbling stomach. My heart had slowed and weakness fogged my limbs. All symptoms of hunger. But I shouldn't have needed blood for hours yet. "What the hell is going on?"

"I don't know. It didn't do—Fuck!"

Ignoring the churn in my belly, I watched Tseng's skin shrivel on his bones. He smelt different too. "Adrian, you're aging!"

"What?"

"It's in your blood. You smell like you're almost fifty."

"How's that possible?" he asked, panic rising in his increasingly raspy voice. "I'm twenty-eight!"

"You tell me!" My gut felt like it was pulling itself apart.

He watched the bright blue threads weave up his arm, then turned to me, eyes filled with terror as the crows' feet at their edges deepened. "Time."

"What?"

"All threads of fate are really just manifestations of time. To move them around you need to turn them into something tangible, whether it's matter or energy or… whatever's pelting us."

"You're telling me it's raining time?"

"More like a hail storm," he answered. "This shit does not run off a duck's back."

Great. Fucking time itself was spearing us and… I grabbed his illuminated wrist and held it close to my face. "Look at me!"

"Huh?"

"Do I look normal? The same as I did before?"

"Only more freaked-out? Yeah, basically."

I nodded. "Because I don't age."

He looked at his hand again. "But it's aging me?"

"And it's starving me," I answered.

"An acceleration of time in direct contact with a biological organism without a Shaman to negate the physical effects," he muttered. "Or a… Uh oh."

'Uh oh?' I was not in the mood for 'Uh oh.'

"It's not just my body. How's your head?"

"Jokes, Adrian?"

"Thoughts! Can you think?"

"You mean besides this screaming hunger? Yes, yes."

"I'm not! I'm… words are hard."

"What? Words?"

"Need words. Can't…" he trailed off, then rattled off a string of Chinese before that melted to a series of grunts and stammers, like an animal or a baby.

"Adrian?" This was bad. If the wizard who'd gotten us into this mess couldn't communicate, we were royally fucked. And as my insides clawed at themselves, the urge to grab and drain him near overpowered me.

Tseng gripped my sleeve, his tongue flopping out empty mews. He'd lost his mind. Of course, had the coven been here, Deborah could have protected his body, while Iain protected his mind. Without them...

The threads of time had curled their way almost to Tseng's shoulder. His face looked like parchment. He needed food too, or at least, water. And he'd need it sooner than I needed blood. But from where? How was I supposed to find it before he shrivelled to his death?

Space. Time. The intersection of magickal forces. That's what this place was. Mentalists, Entropists, Shamans, Necromancers... Fate intersected with death and the realms that lay beyond, didn't it? Tseng whimpered with pain. Was that the only way out of here? To do nothing and die in agony?

Fuck that. Intersections were not dead ends.

I held him tight, and bit deep into his throat. His body jolted with alarm before the inevitable rush of pleasure tainted his veins. His heart slowed to sync with mine, and his hands gripped hard at my back as he tried to pull my kiss deeper. If he knew I intended to drain him dry, he didn't show it. He just latched on, allowing the blood to leave his body until his head flopped back. His weight evaporated from my shoulder as he slipped into darkness, taking the light with him.

As the sharp pangs of time stopped, I stood there and caught my breath, alive, sated, and alone.

I called Tseng's name, but got no response. Perhaps this was a relief. I couldn't guarantee that my rash action had freed him from this place, but even if I'd killed him, being drained by a Blood Shade was a far more pleasant end than accelerated starvation.

The darkness felt familiar, though it wasn't the same one that had brought Ross and the two dead Shapers to me. It felt cooler, more akin to the darkness I'd found in Isobel's home, that had stretched and folded space in ways that had completely disorientated me.

I'd freed Tseng. Now, how was I going to free myself?

"Iain?" I called. This was no time to be proud. "No more bloody tests!"

"My goodness!" The voice behind me was Iain's, all right, but weak, every syllable a titanic struggle. All the same, he gave a laugh that chilled me. "Never accuse you of missing a bold play, eh?"

"Iain…" I said again through slow, steady breaths. "Where are you? Where is Jorgas?"

His guttural drawl drew nearer. "I would have thought that you'd be more interested to know where you are."

A fetid stench of death had seeped into the air. I flinched as a hand stroked my shoulder and slinked across my chest. I felt the thin, bony form of a man curl up behind me as the hand took hold of mine. Its sunken flesh stretched across bones that were little more than twigs, and blackened scars crisscrossed it all the way up the wrist. "Iain? What's going on? What did you do to Tseng? To me?"

He hushed me quiet, stroking the back of my hand with a bony finger. His breath wasn't the source of the foul odour. Instead, it was sweet and rich with that spice peculiar to a practiced Shaper. The scent I knew. "Before you turn around, I need you to be ready for what you'll see."

"You mean you're here?" I asked. "I thought your body was lost. You mean to tell me you're actually, physically here? Not some ghost or possession or illusion?"

"Yes. But things have changed since you saw me last. I need you to not… overreact."

I snorted. "You think me shallow?"

"What I think is there are things that dwell in this place that will find the lure of an immortal being in terror, even for an instant, irresistible. I'm not sure how partial they are to

Shapers, but I'd rather not find out. Now, promise me you'll hold it together."

"Fine. Can we please get this over with?" I turned as he released me, choking on a gasp despite Iain's warnings. I looked down at his misshapen limbs, broken in ways no human injury could explain. Joints bent backward, flesh singed to expose muscle, even bone, not least of which were the pieces of bone lashed together into the walking poles that held him upright. Each segment was curved like…

"Ribs." The single syllable seemed to pain him. "My own, in fact. I can't begin to describe to you how that felt. What the Patrons would do to satisfy their curiosity."

Words failed me. Horror? Repulsion? Sympathy? Outrage that this man I cared for had met such a fate?

He shrugged, anticipating me. "This is what happens if they catch you. Now, you know."

I wanted to take his hand. Hold him. Anything. "Iain, I… I—"

"No," he said, sharply. "You're not sorry for leaving me behind. I knew the risks, just as I knew who you'd choose if it came down to Jorgas or me. I can't resent that choice. But don't patronise me with apologies, please."

I half expected him to lash out with one of the broken rib-sticks and skewer me with it. "What can we do?"

"Do?" he asked. "You mean to get out of here?"

"I mean…" I couldn't help but look him over again, his once handsome face now a barren waste of scars. It wrinkled as he smirked at me.

"I'm touched. But these are no mortal injuries. They remade me. Into what, I'm not sure, but it's nothing a mortal hospital can fix."

"Deborah," I said. "She's a Shaman. A healer? I know she's green, but—"

"And she'd do everything she could in a heartbeat. I suppose I should apologise for keeping you in the dark, so to speak. Deborah and I have grown close since you've been away, though of course, she's not physically seen me, her true teacher and mentor. Her 'Angel of Magick.'" He let out a sudden, harsh laugh that seemed to pain him. "Serving *Phantom of the Opera* realness!"

I shook my head, not getting the joke, and caring less. "She must be able to do something!"

"I appreciate your faith in our abilities, but this wasn't done by mortal medicine or biology. This was the work of the uncanny. Only the uncanny can undo it."

I licked my lips, not liking his flat, knowing smile. "My blood?"

He nodded, humourlessly. "Quite a lot of it."

"What's 'quite a lot?'"

"You drained young Adrian dry to release him from this place, didn't you? He died in your arms. His heart did stop, did it not?"

True, my blood had powerful healing properties, but if Iain was saying what I thought he was…

A sound like the distant rustling of trees distracted me. Iain's rueful smile fell from his face.

"What is that?" I asked.

"Before I joined you, you and Adrian weren't particularly… loud, were you?"

"Loud?" The rustling seemed mere feet away. It had shifted position, now coming from behind Iain. No, it was behind us both. We were surrounded.

"We need to get out of here," said Iain.

"You think? Why do I let you put me in these…" I trailed off. Not the time. "How?"

"Trust me."

I blinked at him.

"Fine," he muttered. "Just, please hold still."

The bones that jutted from his body sprang to life like the striking fangs of a giant arachnid. He pushed off the two elongated ribs he'd used as walking sticks and raised them high, skewering me in the shoulder with one.

I screamed as I went down, pinned to whatever passed for 'the ground' in this place. The rustling seemed right on top of us, all around now. I could feel it on my skin, on my face, in my ears, and under my clothes. Iain, for his part, was upon me like a savage beast as he drank from my wounded shoulder.

"Iai—" Opening my mouth was a mistake. I slammed it shut, but the things were already inside. I could feel them burrowing their way to my gut, tearing fibrous tissue in a way I'd not felt since my initial transformation. Iain's monstrous form gorged itself on my blood, draining me as fast as it could. I watched one of the bony talons rise into the air, then spear my wrist as it came down. I screamed. I'd taken an awful risk, killing Tseng to set him free. Now, as Iain drank from me, I only hoped to join him.

CHAPTER SEVENTEEN

"Hey, hey! Chill man. It's okay. You're good. Take it easy!"

I looked down at the wrist Iain had pinned to the ground with is bony spur. In it was an IV, steadily feeding me blood from a beautiful, familiar young man relaxing in an armchair beside the table on which I'd been slabbed.

"Paul?" I managed to get out with no small amount of pain.

"Hey," he answered warmly, standing up, carefully minding the IV. "You remember me?"

I did remember his kind eyes from the bar, the night Iain had taken me out in search of Luca, who'd disappeared among Sydney's men for rent. Besides offering useful information, Paul had sated my hunger that night, though I'd seen to it he'd forgotten that part. Dressed with the same anachronistic affectation, his grey shirt unbuttoned low, suspenders slung over his shoulders in lieu of a belt, he looked as handsome as I remembered.

I also remembered the room I was in. The parlour turned medical lab inside the Arcadia Trust, with its strange specimens in bottles, the sour, straw-like smell of dried herbs and plants in the air, and lingering above it all, the blood of the roguish beauty sitting beside me.

"Are you all right?" he asked.

I almost felt bad, grateful though I was to the city's sex workers for embracing remedial blood donation as a growing market niche. I wondered if he knew Leo. "Yes, Iai… You're Iain's friend."

Last I'd set foot in the Trust, it had seemed abandoned. But now? Apparently, when magickal gateways deigned to pop you out, geography was a secondary concern.

"So, you're feeling okay?" Paul continued. "I'm supposed to let them know, but I'm gonna say they heard. You've got a serious set of lungs on you."

Kelvin? Jorgas? I would take either at this point. "Please."

He nodded, taking out his phone and shooting off a text. "The guy also said not to leave this room for any reason. I think he locked the door. Whatever. It's his money."

Why did I get the sense this would end up being my money?

"Thank you," I gently squeezed the escort's wrist as he approached the bed.

"Just part of the job, man. Better you than Red Cross." He pocketed his phone, then threw a glance at the sheet covering the lower half of my naked body before smiling at me. "Unless you've got something else you need taken care of?"

His enterprising nature tracked with my memory. I rubbed his forearm with affection. "I think you've done more than enough."

"Suit yourself," he said, pushing his shoulders back in a way that splayed open his shirt, making a show of dark, trimmed chest hair that looked awkward on many men, but which suited Paul's incorrigible commitment to retro presentation.

A sharp knock at the door interrupted us.

"Come in," we both said at once. Paul gave me a meek smile and backed away from the table. Whoever, or whatever I'd expected to see, it couldn't have shocked more than the face I saw.

"Reylan," said Brett. "Are you okay?"

Was I okay? I doubted my senses, if not my sanity. His eyes were tired, shrouded by dark circles and drained of the curiosity that had once animated them. His arms hung thin at the sides of his blue t-shirt, and it looked like he'd not shaven for several days.

But he was alive.

"It's really you?"

His half-smile fell short of reassuring me, particularly when he opened the door to admit Deborah, who went to Paul's side and set about disconnecting the IV. She ignored me completely, beyond yanking the thing out of my arm.

"Ah!" I cried out. "Well, hello to you too!"

"Hold still next time," she muttered. "You've lost a lot of blood."

"Correction, I lost all…" I stopped myself. The mortal was still in the room. "Thank you, Paul."

"No worries, man. You're not the weirdest."

Was that a compliment, or an insult?

"Yes, thank you," Deborah said, putting a small plaster over his pinprick wound. "I'll walk you out. Stay close, please."

Despite his confused frown, Paul relented. I imagined no small fee had bought his blood, and his silence. Without looking at me, Deborah closed the door behind them.

Brett watched them go with dark eyes, full of grateful affection until he turned to look at me. His thin face creased with concern. "You're really okay?"

"All considered," I muttered, sitting up and regretting it as the dizziness hit me.

"Woah, easy," he said, catching me, then pulling me into a hug. "It's good to see you."

I buried my nose in his neck and clasped his bony shoulders, doubting even this moment, with my arms full of him. I'd watched him die. I'd killed him myself. My fingers brushed something hard and metallic, then something which yielded to them like bread pudding.

It shrieked. So did Brett.

Startled, I released him. "What the hell was that?"

"Sorry. I should have taken it easier. Still getting used to him, I guess."

"Him?"

Brett lifted his shirt. "This is Ash."

I stared at the fleshy, heart-sized creature looking back at me through a pair of misaligned eyes that appeared supplemented by a mechanism just above them. It had a mouth, but no limbs or neck to speak of. No feet, hands, or method of propulsion that I could make out either, which was just as well, since the idea of it leaving the chrome box now embedded in Brett's side horrified me beyond comprehension.

"Ash?" I asked. "You named it?"

"Yeah, after Bruce Campbell in Evil—"

"Brett, that is *not* the part of this I need qualified!" I assumed it was safe to yell, since the thing didn't seem to have ears.

"Yeah, okay, okay! I get it! He's… Ugh, look I don't know."

"You don't know how a…" Goblin? Gargoyle? I didn't even know what to call the thing! "You don't know how it came to be grafted inside your torso?"

"I don't remember much of anything. She said I would when I was ready."

"She?" I demanded. "Deborah?"

"No. Look, all I know is that he's keeping me alive."

"Who is 'she,' then? What's going on? You were insane!"

"Gee, thanks."

"Brett, listen to me. When I came back, you were a shell of yourself. The only thing keeping you alive and in your own head was Iain. He possessed you, until I… I told him to leave you alone."

He let his shirt fall back over the thing, and stared at me. "I waited for you, you know? I thought you were going to bring Peter and the others back."

Nothing about the part where I'd killed him? My mouth felt dry. Was it too late to take Paul up on his offer, albeit in a less lascivious way than suggested?

"I thought you were dead," Brett murmured, almost to himself. "Five months, man. Five months!"

"I know. For us, it was only minutes. I didn't mean to leave you, Brett. Please know that."

"And then I died? What the fuck?"

I reached for his hand, then stopped, unsure if he wanted to be touched. "I'm afraid that was me."

His sunken eyes widened.

"When Iain left your body, there were unforeseen effects. You attacked us, Jorgas and me. Brett, I'm so sorry."

"Attacked you? Wait, Jorgas is back too?" Brett leaned against a side table, staring at the floor. "Where is he now?"

"I don't know." Truthfully, I'd been hoping Brett knew. "Brett, I can't tell you how sorry—"

"Yeah, well, we're not gonna spend the rest of our lives apologising, are we?" He sniffed, folding his arms and looking at me, determined and resigned. "It's fucked. It's all been fucked. There's no part of this that isn't completely and utterly fucked. But I'm fine, thanks to this little guy in my side."

"No offence, but you don't look fine."

"Yeah?" he laughed through a snort. "For someone who's come back from the dead?"

"And… and that thing?" I asked.

"Some weird, bio-techno, supernatural combo in a box. I don't know. Nobody asked me before sticking him in., but he's keeping me alive."

"Barely. You need a drink," I lifted my wrist to my mouth, unsure how much I could share. But I couldn't leave him in such a state.

He reached out and stopped me. "That's not gonna do much for me anymore."

"Pardon?"

"That's what she said, anyway."

"Look, who is 'she?'" I asked. "If not Deborah, then who?"

Brett shook his head. "Try to sleep. You'll be safe here until she comes. It's good to see you."

"Safe?" Questions plagued me. What the hell had possessed him to return to the Trust? "Brett? Brett!"

My once faithful servant had already shut the door. A lock clunked into place behind him.

"Brett?" I called again, righting myself carefully and moving to follow him. I rattled the knob, but it was locked tight. "Brett, open this door! What's going on? What have you done?"

I wanted to trust him, but an awful thought beset me. He'd been quite upfront about the creature in his side keeping him alive. What if it had also been speaking for him? Lying to me, or even in complete control of the empty vessel that was Brett's dead body? The idea was morbid and awful, but…

I centred my thoughts. I would have answers, but first? Locked room. I set about finding something with which to undo it. How was there nothing, not a damn thing in this room with the strength and shape needed to pick a simple lock? I couldn't even find the IV, which I assumed Deborah had taken with her.

Deborah. Brett. These were my friends. Why was I locked in? Or was something else locked out?

Hell! Opening jars and bottles of fluid, I gagged as smells of death, decay and chemicals escaped into the air. Surely, one of them had to be corrosive. I pulled the sheet away from the examining table and poured a little from several bottles onto it, taking care to keep them apart. The liquids stained the cloth, but nothing would eat through. This was madness. Without labels to go on, I could spend hours trying to find something that could melt or ruin the lock. Yet they'd surely hear me if I broke it open with brute force.

I squinted, still trying to ignore the odours from the bottles. It wasn't my imagination. The room was getting darker, shrouding itself. I recognised the sensation.

"Joboram?" I whispered. "Joboram, is that you?"

Blood Shade. We've little time.

It was the same voice, only instead of being audible, it seemed to enter my consciousness, more like a frigid chill than Iain's warm telepathy. I shook my head, not willing to be dragged back to the hellish arena of the Quinkan's 'test.'

Your trial is ended. Let us talk.

I could sense Joboram's blunt impatience, but I wouldn't miss this chance to ask about Jorgas. "What about the others?"

Your lover, too, has passed. The one you call Bakker, however…

I waited for them to continue. In the short time I'd known Joboram, they'd shown no hesitancy when it came to words. "You… you don't know?"

A faint light now illuminated a spot where Patricia sat cross-legged, looking perfectly zen in her neat, cream suit.

She reveals nothing.

How was that possible?

No memories. No regrets. I cannot find shadow within her.

A nun, after all? I didn't voice the joke aloud. Apparently, I didn't need to.

All humans have shadows, Blood Shade.

"Are you saying she's not human?"

It is of no consequence to us. Without shadow, we have no concern. But it is the boy who matters to you.

The image of Patricia faded into darkness.

"I thought you said Jorgas passed."

He did. But the shadow did not release him. This too, is of little consequence. He is at peace with the Land, and so, at peace with us.

"Little consequence?" I hissed. "Where is he, then?"

When an invader slips from shadow, it has been known for them to reappear with another, one with a stronger, more personal connection to them.

"All right," I muttered, trying to keep calm. "And where would that be? I still don't understand this 'shadow' business. What do you mean by a 'more personal connection?'"

Memories. Stories. Regrets. Burdens. The things you face in shadow. Jorgas passed his trial. That means forgiving self. But if another shadow from his past bears a grudge? Jorgas is not of the People. With no anchor to the Land, it is possible that another shadow pulled him from us.

"You're telling me this now?"

That now familiar fierce chill engulfed my flesh from top to toe. *You do not appreciate the danger you are in, Blood Shade. Your lover as well, if he is with another spirit, such as the one that lurks here.*

"What do you mean, 'lurks here?'"

I had hoped to find clues. Why does Bakker cast no shadow? What force exposed her bodyguard to the mortal eye? What happened to Jorgas? This house sits on a place of great power within the Land. These questions have consequence. The first of them remains unanswered. But there is a shadow here, in this house, raging with rare fury. Until it is quelled, you, Jorgas, and anyone else in or connected to this house are in great danger.

"You're telling me the Arcadia Trust is haunted?"

You waste time asking things you already know. First, you must get out of this room.

"Okay, that, I know," I said, unable to help my tone. "Unless you can pick a lock?"

You think as a corporeal. You submitted to me once, Blood Shade. It will not harm you to do so again.

I wasn't sure if 'consent' was a concept Joboram valued or understood, but without hesitation, their presence wrapped around me like cold mud, then entered my body all at once. Or I entered them, for there was no longer any distinction between us. My vision startled me, as I now took in an overwhelming, panoramic view of the room through thousands on thousands of eyes, each one a fragment that was at once both Joboram and myself. 'Disorienting' was not the word. I'd been taken apart. I no longer knew where I was, where I was heading, or even what I was.

Close your eyes. Unless you want to go mad?

Thanks again for the latent warning. Even with my eyes closed, sickness swept through my disembodied gut, until I felt myself… whole! I'd not precisely felt it happen. I only knew I was solid and on the other side of the door, squatting in the Arcadia Trust's hallway.

I took my time standing up, touching as much of my body as I could reach, just to make sure it was all there. I felt normal. No sickness, no cold intrusion of a Quinkan or any other being. Just me, pale but fed, standing in my underwear, listening to whispers in the near silence. It wasn't until I drew closer that I could make them out.

Osiris, Osiris, Osiris, Osiris….

Osiris? God of the dead? Lover of Isis? I'd met enough supernatural beings in my time not to dismiss such ancient deities, even if the surrounding legends were fiction. Some claimed they were an aspect of the Patrons, which wasn't an encounter I wished to repeat. Perhaps I was getting ahead of myself. Perhaps Brett had locked me in to protect me from the angry ghost to which Joboram had alluded. If the Quinkan had been lying or setting me up, I surely would have known. We'd practically shared a body, after all.

And now, soft chants invoked a god of the dead revered by Necromancers. Fun!

I didn't need Iain's abilities to recognise the chanters. Tseng, Deborah, and who else? And dear gods, what was that smell? Like a mix of stale blood, mould, and rotting flesh.

Even to my un-Shaperly mind, invoking an ancient lord of the dead in a house already possessed by an angry spirit seemed a terrible, terrible idea. Unless, of course, they were exorcising it. Ugh! Was I supposed to interfere or not? I still knew next to nothing about Shaper ritual and lore. A mental visit from Iain would have been oddly welcome just now.

I crept into the shadows, casting just a little Blood Shade charm to obscure myself from view. They'd only see me if they looked right at me, and the chances of that seemed remote with their attention fixed upon the black sarcophagus, which sat at the centre of an eight-pointed star carved into the floor of the Arcadia Trust's ballroom. Such a versatile space! I'd mention it to Patricia if she ever decided to sell.

The star matched the one I'd seen in my dream, at Valia's, and at Isobel's house. But there was a difference, this time. The sarcophagus sat at the star's centre between the three white-robed figures, whose chants of Osiris were now all too clear. With the loud sound of an opening door, in came Brett, pushing some poor, naked bastard with a bag over his head and rope around his wrists into the circle. I tried to make out details of the man's body. Athletic chest, trimmed body hair…

My stomach sank. Paul.

The chants of Osiris stopped as soon as the hooded man crossed the edge of the star and approached the sarcophagus, calm as a hurricane's eye. At last, one of the hooded figures used a vicious-looking knife to cut the bonds from his wrists, then placed the knife in his hand. No! I wouldn't let this happen again, not to Paul, an innocent whose blood had saved my own.

But I also couldn't risk seizing one of the figures and draining them dry. Especially not Deborah, whatever monster she'd become. I'd have to be delicate, crafty as a cat. Keeping to the shadows, I crept closer to the nearest of them, ready to pounce.

Brett slammed into my side with the force of a rugby player and sent me sprawling to the floor. I stared at him in disbelief, coughing a spittle of blood as he pinned me down with a force that should have been impossible. "I told you to stay put, man."

I fought helplessly against him as unseen forces hoisted Paul into the air. His limbs broke and twisted in the same grisly dance I'd seen at Isobel's. With one broken arm, he raised the blade and began to slash at his body, bleeding into the grooves on the floor until he at last drew the blade across his throat. It was over. His twisted and shredded body collapsed next to the sarcophagus, which absorbed its blood through the carving's channels, then grew hotter, just as it had before. How much blood did this thing need? What was inside? Nothing good, if Iain could be believed. This time, I suspected he could.

Again, the sarcophagus gave off its strange heat, but while the foul smell that had engulfed my senses as I'd approached the room grew stronger, the heat itself was not unpleasant this time, more like a warm fire on a winter's day than merciless sunlight. I pushed against Brett once more, though I knew it was too late for Paul. Tseng and Deborah, who stood closest to us, pulled back their hoods. Their wonder matched my own as they watched the thing absorb its grim sacrifice.

"Will you hold still?" Brett muttered in my ear. "We're not gonna hurt you."

"Brett," came a voice from the other side of the circle. "It's done."

I knew that voice. I knew that voice very well.

Brett eased off me and helped me to my feet with a grip far stronger than it should have been. He looked away with shame when I shook him off with an angry glare. Tseng and Deborah withdrew to the edges of the room, allowing the third figure to approach me. When she pushed back her hood, I could no longer feign surprise.

"You owe me one hell of an explanation," I muttered.

"Don't agitate yourself, darling." Isobel tilted her head, thoughtfully. "It'll all be clear in a moment."

A wave of cold swept through the room, breaking the pleasant warmth as it rushed toward the sarcophagus. It was gone just as quickly, making way for a dry, suffocating heat that stung my eyelids and choked my throat. The air in the room tasted like the ashes of death. Burnt and stale, they sent Brett into a coughing fit as I tried to see what was happening to the accursed box. Tseng ducked as the lights, already dimmed at the room's perimeter, shattered all at once, like the thing had absorbed their energy. Cold, light, and blood in, heat and gods knew what else out.

Which gods? Osiris? Nephthys? Isis? Isobel herself?

I'd long known my friend and long ago protégé to be a student of dark arts, but this? In league with Deborah and Tseng? Perhaps they were her apostles, but if so, where did Iain fall into this? I remembered the evil I'd felt, touching that box. Why the fuck was I just standing here?

Brett took hold of my shoulders and squeezed, while Deborah looked at me and shook her head. The gestures weren't cruel, mocking, or imperious, but they stopped me in my tracks while Isobel advanced on the sarcophagus with eerie confidence. She splayed her body over it like a mourning widow. I jumped, hearing the faint searing of flesh.

Then, it began to liquefy under her touch. The thing was melting into the grooves of the floor, mingling with Paul's blood until it filled all eight points of the carving. Then, as the box reached a size no bigger than a cat, the bloody, black goo withdrew into it. As it did, the thing started to grow again. Now holding it in her hand, Isobel watched, eyes bright with fascination as the mass began to lighten, to grey, then brown, then tan, a flush of ruddy pink as it sprouted four clunky extremities. Each of us watched these grow hands, feet, and digits, while the rest of the thing stretched into the humanoid figure of a man, just under six foot from head to toe, naked in the arms of my friend as the spell coaxed a healthy crop of dark hair to cover his pale head and pepper the gooseflesh on the back of his naked legs. His body shivered and twitched as it took form, slim hips contracting as he pulled into a foetal position and clutched his head, howling into now fleshy palms. He could hide his face, but not his form, a form I'd taken in my arms and knew well.

Iain rolled over, his head in Isobel's lap, at last resembling the man I knew. His bare chest rose and fell with an uneasy rhythm, as if breathing itself were now alien to him. Perhaps it was. If it was a question of muscle memory, the 'muscles' he now possessed had only moments before been an accursed black monolith. But they were his. Every detail was the Iain I remembered, right down to the enormous dragon tattoo that covered his back. His hair, eyes, dimples, musculature, body hair, down to the dark thatch that framed his flaccid cock, were all unmistakeable. The whole ghastly process had played out like an experimental film Isobel and I had seen in Los Angeles in the 60s after feeding on two LSD-hazed hippies, only this had been real, and it had exacted a terrible cost.

"Satisfied?" Isobel asked in the now silent room.

"Like hell." I strode towards Paul's dead body and whipped the bag off his head to reveal an older face marked by coarse stubble and scars, a far cry from Paul's fine features.

"You remember Mister Donnelly?" Isobel asked.

The thug I'd knocked out at her home, now the final donor of Iain's resurrection.

Deborah and Tseng at last crossed the circle and went to Isobel's side. Iain smiled, face full of gratitude as he clasped their hands. If he could speak yet, he wasn't making the effort.

"When did you start working black magic with local covens?" I asked.

"There's no need to be unkind." Isobel smiled, patient and knowing. "No coven can reach its full potential if its men outnumber its women. Without me, there would be no coven."

"Indeed?" came a voice behind us. Patricia stepped into the room with Kelvin at her side. "Then you're the one we need to destroy."

That was when hell broke loose.

CHAPTER EIGHTEEN

A cry startled me, sharp, guttural, and familiar. I turned to see Brett nursing a deep cut on his forearm. Before I could ask, an unseen force ripped four long gashes through his shirt, leaving tracks of blood in its wake. Brett tried to lurch away, only to cop another invisible blow to his shoulder which knocked him to the floor.

Deborah rushed to his side, trying to shield both of them as the floor next to her erupted in splinters. A solid dent appeared in the wall. A nearby light fixture shattered, and the piano stool upended itself, forcing Tseng to duck again as it narrowly missed his head.

"Stop this!" Patricia advanced on Isobel with righteous fury. But my old friend seemed as surprised by the violent eruptions as any of us, flinching as Patricia took an unseen hit to the jaw and was thrown hard across the room where she lay still.

Kelvin tore Isobel away from Iain and cast her into the far wall, where her head cracked with a sickening thud. He rushed to Patricia, just as Tseng did to Isobel, which left Iain unprotected in the centre of the room as more ruptures broke through the floor. Donnelly's limp body copped another shredding, bleeding across the exploding floorboards.

Something caught the looming chandelier in the room's centre, sending a spray of broken crystal and bulb glass over Iain's prone form. I dove on him, trying to shield his body from the worst of it, even as fragments of glass cut my back and neck.

"Out!" I yelled, taking Iain under the arms and pulling him close. "Everyone out, now! Hurry!"

No-one argued until Kelvin had slammed the door behind us. "The library!" he said.

"What?" Deborah asked. "Fuck that, we need to get out!"

"It's still light out," he snarled. "The library's the best place the vampires can go, now move!"

We did, resting only once we were inside, where Kelvin, who'd again brought up the rear, bolted the door. Only the laboured breaths of the injured disturbed the sudden silence. Had the mayhem in the ballroom stopped, or were we insulated from it?

"Wards," Tseng muttered. "There are wards on this room."

"No shit," Kelvin muttered. "You think I'm talking out my arse? I don't know if they'll hold, but they're the best chance we've got."

"Not while she's here." Bakker got to her feet, shrugging Kelvin off her and staring daggers at Isobel. "What have you done this time? What are you trying to do to us? To this house?"

"Patricia," Isobel dismissed Tseng with a nod as she stood up. "This isn't like you."

"Isn't it?" the former nun snapped. "For three years, now, I've tolerated your experiments and vague explanations, your bloody constant evasiveness!"

"If I thought it was a danger to you—"

"A danger? Like the one currently tearing apart the ball room? You picked a lousy time to infantilise me, Isobel,"

Bakker snarled. "For the last time, what the hell were you doing in there?"

"Me," Iain murmured, forcing himself to sit up before resting his head on my shoulder.

"Why not?" Kelvin muttered. "Everyone else has."

Isobel ignored him. "Iain was trapped in the Wound just like the others. By the time we found him, there wasn't much left; not physically, anyway."

"The Wound? From which he and Reylan failed to return?" Patricia tossed me a shamed look that was clearly an afterthought.

Iain shook his head, every attempt at a syllable exhausting him until he rested his forehead against my cheek. A light squeeze of my hand was the only sign he'd not passed out.

"Patricia," Isobel said again, a growl creeping into her voice. "I'll try to answer your questions, but I'm not causing this. Please?"

I could see Patricia holding back a caustic remark as she examined the ruins of the Arcadia Trust's library. Ancient, invaluable books lay strewn across the room, their shelves collapsed, holes in the wall… Any wards here surely wouldn't protect us for long. Something had gotten through.

"We should go." Tseng moved to join Deborah and Brett.

"You'll stay," Patricia answered sharply. "We have no idea how bad this is going to get, and besides the question of your own safety, you're part of this foolishness, aren't you?"

"The foolish part was opening the Wound in the first place," Isobel retorted. "And when Reylan and Iain entered it? You have no idea what you let in here!"

"What *I* let in?"

"I'm trying to—"

"To what? Control it? Banish it?" asked Patricia. "Kelvin is dying! Tell me how we stop it!"

Isobel looked to the old man at Patricia's side, her eyes for the first time seeming rueful.

"Yep," he muttered. "It's me."

"I thought Joboram was helping with that," I reminded them.

"Joboram has fucked off," Kelvin muttered. "So did Clay. Something about Patricia not having a s—"

She silenced him with a stern look. But I knew exactly what Patricia 'didn't have.'

"Anyway, the deal's off. Isolationist Quinkan bullshit."

"They still call us 'invaders,'" Patricia pointed out. "Officially, they don't owe us anything."

Isobel shook her head, composing herself. "Deborah, I need you."

Patricia reluctantly made space for the two women as they each took one of Kelvin's aged and now trembling hands. It didn't take Isobel long to form a diagnosis.

"The Quinkans wouldn't have helped." she said with certainty. "He's infected with the same corruption that's in the building. Bottom line? We need to fix this house."

"I'm gonna guess *Renovation Rescue* won't cut it," Kelvin muttered.

"Look," Tseng snapped, "the ritual worked. We got Iain back. We're all alive."

"No thanks to you," I reminded him.

"What I'm saying," he growled, "is forget the house! If it's the problem then I say we leave. Burn it down. Destroy whatever's inside it."

"If you don't mind, I'll decide what happens to this house," Patricia said.

"Seriously?" Tseng scoffed. "My family's loaded. I'll buy you a new one."

"Even if that fixed this," said Isobel. "There's no guarantee the problem wouldn't just live on in Kelvin. It might even spread. Walking away isn't an option."

Why did I have the feeling I'd also lose Jorgas forever if that happened? Not an option, and if anyone could help me find him and end this, it would be Iain and Isobel.

But where to fucking start?

"You're telling us this was about resurrecting Iain?" I asked her, not buying it. "You could have done that anywhere. In fact, this isn't your first attempt, is it? I saw the markings on the floor at Valia's. I even touched the blasted sarcophagus at your house, and what I felt there was pure evil."

"It's not evil," Isobel repeated the word as if it bored her. "More like… will, in its rawest form. Yes, it took a few tries. We're lucky Iain's consciousness escaped. If he wasn't a Mentalist, we probably would have lost him for good."

"You kept his remains in that box?"

"Reylan, the box *was* Iain. The memory of him, his thoughts, his abilities, his consciousness… it's what you've been talking to since you returned. A melding of Iain and the Wound itself."

Does she always talk about the subjects of her spells like we aren't here?

I jumped.

"What was that?" Brett asked, now up and about. To my relief, he looked relatively healthy, either as a result of Deborah's Shaper abilities or 'Ash,' or both.

"Iain," I muttered. "In my head."

While you argue over my miraculous resurrection, this house is being torn apart. I know power when I feel it. Anger, too.

"Do you want to hurry up and translate?" Kelvin asked. "We're running out of time here!"

I know that scent, mind, and presence very well, and so do you.

"Jorgas?" I asked aloud. "You're telling me it's Jorgas?"

"What was that?" asked Patricia. "Jorgas is causing this?"

Something else is with him. I don't recognise it, but I can feel its rage. Like righteous fury.

"Righteous?" I asked. "What does that mean?"

"Reylan!" Patricia snapped.

I relayed the bare facts, along with other adjectives Iain had used.

"Joboram…"

"Joboram?" Patricia asked. "What about them?"

"Before they left, they told me there was something dangerous and malevolent here, like a haunting."

"A haunting?" Deborah turned to Isobel. "I thought you called it an infection?"

"There's little difference, and if it's affecting Kelvin's powers," Isobel said, "there's no reason to think it won't affect others. That means the Blood Shades, the Talysman—"

"The what?" I asked her.

"Ash," Brett said.

"Cyrill," Isobel corrected him.

"If I've got to take care of this little guy for the rest of my life, I'm not calling him Cyri—."

"Will you two focus?" barked Kelvin.

"I'll bet it affects Shaper powers too." I approached my old friend and former protégé. "Can we have a private word?"

"Private?" Patricia asked. "Nothing you want to share with the rest of us?"

I shook my head at her.

Patricia grimaced, but nobody fought me.

*   *   *

Isobel unlocked the small door at the back of the library and led me through. She switched on a dim lamp to reveal a modest but comfortable study that showed no signs of the chaos that had torn the library apart. Perhaps we were hiding in the wrong room.

"You're angry." She crossed to a small side table and opened its cupboard.

"Should I be? I wish you'd be more forthcoming!"

She placed two squat glasses on the table and procured a decanter of rich red liquid. It smelled like blood. "Synthetic, but it's decent."

While the short-lived vegan Blood Shade movement had failed to find traction, even being condemned by some as a dangerous unbalancing of the relationship between Blood Shades and humankind, synthetic blood had somehow managed to stay in circulation.

"I'm fine, thank you."

"Suit yourself. Apparently, they age this one in bourbon barrels, though I swear they mix in at least a pint of real booze."

"That good?"

She smiled, holding the glass she'd half-filled for herself before setting it down. "No, it's quite ghastly."

"Then why not hunt?" I asked.

"Too busy, I suppose."

"Indeed. The coven? Explain that, and don't tell me I wouldn't understand, because I need to."

She dropped into a plush chair behind an oddly low table with a chess board on it that I guessed had once been a desk for the Prematures. I would have followed her lead, but there was nowhere else to sit. This was an office for one, just the way Isobel liked it.

"It's not unknown for supernatural beings to manifest Shaper talents. You know that."

"Do you really trust your Shaper friends not to bring their House knocking? Do you trust Iain? Hell, I don't trust Iain!"

"I trust Iain to do what's right for Iain. That included keeping Brett alive until his Talysman was ready, for which you're welcome."

"So," I purred, beginning to understand and not much liking it. "You've become a Necromancer?"

"A cursed legacy. Honestly, I suppressed the talents as long as I could."

"And why not just be honest with me? You must have had some idea," I said. "About your family?"

"I don't know if I'm the product of a Blood Shade infiltrating a family of Shapers, or a Shaper who fell in love with a latent carrier of the Blood Shade gene," she continued. "But they made it clear that a daughter who manifested both talents was not wanted."

"What hurts is that you didn't tell me! Even after this grand journey of self-discovery, you thought your newfound talents didn't warrant at least a heads up to your mentor?"

"And risk the House of Blood finding out, most likely through Colin, who, as your mentor, would demand to be told? No, darling. Until I was ready, I couldn't risk that."

"Ready for what?" I asked. "Has the coven been your goal this entire time? That seems… forgive me, awfully small for you."

"I'll take that as a compliment," she muttered. "Why do you think I sought out Patricia in the first place? The Trust? The blending of Houses? I still support her goals, and to realise them, she needs a new coven of capable Shapers. The Prematures were never going to be enough."

"So, they willingly went to their deaths for it?"

"Funny thing, death." She pushed aside the glass of blood and gestured to the tidy, well stocked bookshelves, which preserved a sliver of the glorious order that had once been the wider library. "When a building is a nexus or terminus of power, it blurs the lines between the living and the dead, the corporeal and the disembodied, the sentient and the inanimate."

If she was about to break into freestyle verse…

"Iain was that box," she reiterated, "and Sophia and Georgios are this room."

I stared at her, haunted by the silence. "I watched Georgios die!"

"Giorgios died the second he accepted it was his fate. Adrian just fulfilled the contract. But look around. This room is the only part of the house the infection can't reach, because the Prematures are defending it with every bit of lore they ever learned. Every few days, a new book forms on that shelf. While the house is under siege, it's about all they can manage. They've certainly changed form, but in their own way, they're as alive as ever."

Questioning everything I'd ever heard about transfiguration, I took one of the books off the shelf. It had all the trimmings of one of the ancient volumes now strewn across the floor of the next room, but it was in pristine condition.

"Don't think this was easy for me to learn either. It's only possible because the Arcadia Trust sits on the terminus of a ley line. These go all over Australia, like they do anywhere else. Ancient creatures were said to walk them as pathways, carving the world into being as they went."

"Which is what brought the Quinkans this far south?"

"I persuaded them. Until Adrian got it through his head to let the death of his partner go, he would never have left you alone."

"You sound very invested in him."

"Why shouldn't I be?" She opened the drawer of her desk and began placing a wooden model in each corner of the chess board. "I'm his mentor."

A seated woman. Another with outstretched wings like a hawk. A mummified king carrying a crook and flail, and a noble-looking hawk. Egyptian icons, no doubt connected to Shaper lore.

"The Patrons aren't the only ones who can rework life's very nature, and they despise us for it." Eyes full with anticipation, she crossed to the bookshelf at the far end of the room, unlocked a glass cabinet with a delicate-looking key and lifted a wooden box from it.

"I take it Osiris is the Patron you're referring to?" I pointed at the mummified king. I didn't need Shaper abilities to know she was about to put much more at stake than a board game. Something was very wrong about those figures too. "You called his name enough times in there. I half expected a visitation."

"Osiris, Isis, Nephthys, Horus. Four guardians of Egypt. Four quarters of magick. It's mostly pageantry, but the House of Magick does love its rituals and traditions."

"Don't they, just?" Iain's sudden presence startled me. He stood leaning against the doorway, dressed in a black t-shirt and navy sweatpants I recognised.

"Are those Kelvin's clothes?" I asked.

He folded his arms with smug satisfaction. "Mysticism and pageantry are powerful tools. Just ask the Catholic church." He sat down on the edge of the desk, looking down at the figures with obvious amusement before continuing. "I sent the others away for their own safety."

"Good idea." Isobel placed the box beside the chess board. "Reylan and I can't leave, but there's no point putting everyone at risk."

Iain nodded. "Then let's do this quickly."

"Hold on, hold on," I said, my unease returning. "What exactly are 'we' doing?"

"Going to get Jorgas, and find what's attacking this house." Urgency had returned to Iain's voice. "Or rather, you're going. You'll be safer with Isobel and I staying behind to protect your body and mind."

"With help from your divine Egyptian friends?" Here went nothing. "Tell me, which 'divine' are we talking about?"

Iain's even expression wavered long enough for me to spot alarm in his eyes, a rare lapse in composure that confirmed I was not chasing shadows.

"I'm no Egyptologist, but I've had plenty of time in my life to read. This little band of gods? Not quite the original lineup, is it?" I placed my fingertips on the hawk's head, and with apologies to Horus, flipped it off the edge of the board.

Isobel caught the figure with Blood Shade speed. "Careful, darling."

Iain kept his cool, but I knew the scent of human annoyance as it flushed beneath his skin. "We need to get started. If we miss our window, we will lose Jorgas, this time for good!"

"I understand that. I just need to know whose power you're invoking." I pointed to each of the figures in turn. "Isis, patron of Shamans. Nephthys, patron of Entropists. Osiris, patron of Necromancers… Who's missing, Iain?"

"It's just a legend," he muttered, "We're running out—"

"Who is the true patron of Mentalists, Iain?" I snapped. "Who are you invoking to bring Jorgas back?"

Iain exchanged a look with Isobel, before taking the figurine from her. He cupped it tightly in his hand, then placed it where it had been before. Where there had once been a falcon, there now stood a horned man, whose face stretched into a long, vicious snout. As Iain withdrew, the pattern on the board changed. Where once had stretched an eight-by-eight chess board, now lay their damned eight-pointed star.

I felt vindicated, though frankly, the star looked pissed. "Set. Egypt's devil, who murdered Osiris and scattered his remains through the Underworld."

Iain grasped my hand. "How much is Jorgas worth to you?"

"You mean, enough to embrace a chaos god's daemonic power?"

"It is my power, and I use it as I see fit." he answered. "Right now, I suggest we use it to save Jorgas, before he loses this fight, and we lose him!"

"Reylan?" Isobel asked, her gaze earnest. "It's your call…"

If it were anyone but Jorgas… "Fine. Let's call the devil." I'd never hated magick so much.

Isobel opened the box. Inside was a dark red lump the size of a wilted and shrivelled bell pepper, which she placed between the four icons in the centre of the star.

"Why do you have a pickled heart in a…"

Pickled be damned. The thing began to beat!

"How good *is* your Egyptian history, Reylan? Perhaps you've heard of King Akhenaten, best known for his failed attempt at converting Egypt to monotheism. The worship of Aten, the sun god." With great dexterity and care, Isobel lifted the beating lump of flesh from the board and held it out to me. "One bite. If this works, you'll be able to join Jorgas, wherever he is, and help him."

"And if it doesn't?" I asked.

The sudden anxiety on Iain's face was neither a typical nor comforting look. "It's the heart of a disgraced Pharaoh who tried to convert his nation to a sun cult. What do you think that's going to do to a Blood Shade?"

"So, if this fails, I die."

"Darling…" Isobel looked distressingly contrite. "This will kill you, whether it works or not."

CHAPTER NINETEEN

"I… Okay? Dead? Me?"

"Yes."

"Reylan, we don't like this any more—"

"Iain," I cautioned him. "I'm getting very tired of hearing how much you 'dislike' plans you seem perfectly willing to carry out. You'll both excuse me if I'm not keen on one that will result in my certain death."

"Iain and I will be watching over you. You'll only be dead for a minute, two at most."

"And I'm what? Supposed to find Jorgas, placate or defeat whatever he's facing and find a way to bring him back in these precious seconds, hoping this works and that your ancient devil doesn't fuck us all for shits and giggles? Forget it!"

"Reylan," Isobel took my chin in her fingers. "It's me."

"And me," Iain added, putting his hand on my shoulder that made the small room feel oddly claustrophobic. "We're going to bring you back safely, I promise."

I shook them both off and stared at the immaculate bookshelves. All the information the coven had shared and everything I'd seen of their motivations made it clear this was no House of Magick trap. This was coming from Isobel and

Iain, and damn it, yes! 'Trust' was not the right word, but I knew the two of them cared for me.

"I brought back Iain," Isobel pointed out.

"He wasn't dead," I reminded her.

"The Prematures?"

"You turned them into an office! I don't even know what to call that!"

"I also brought back Brett."

"Brett is a mortal man! Not to sound self-absorbed, but we're talking about disrupting an immortal existence. Mine! Never mind the bloody… god of chaos who may or may not be enabling the process!"

"It was Iain who helped me animate Brett long enough to get him here for his resurrection," Isobel added. "I know my shit, darling, and I'd really appreciate some faith from you right now."

Several crashes came from outside. Iain quickly shut the door to the office but we could still hear the noise, until a mighty bang struck the wall, briefly dimming the lights.

"Reylan," Isobel said again. "This is literally our only option."

Iain took my hand and squeezed it. "We've got you. Both of us."

Another crash. Another dimming of lights. Hell.

I closed my eyes, took the accused lump from Isobel, and bit into the blasphemous Pharaoh's heart.

*   *   *

I'd expected pain. A burning, perhaps, as the essence of a sun prophet, however false, destroyed my insides. But I felt none. Nor distress, fear, or even discomfort. The only change within the room had been the disappearance of Isobel, Iain, and the heart I'd held in my hand. I gingerly pushed open the

243

door to the library, only to find the orderly room I remembered, though it was freezing cold. Almost by reflex, I reached for one of the books, only for my hand to pass through the edge of its spine. The contact pricked my fingertips like electricity until I withdrew.

This was death, then? Even the loud crashes and mayhem that had shaken the house were gone. Nonetheless, I did not want my intrusion announced. I cursed the creaking door as I pushed it open, wondering why I hadn't passed through it or fallen through the floor.

Right. Think less. Feel more.

I entered the darkened hall, the sudden chill of it rippling my skin as I waited, tucked away in the shadows. It all felt so wrong. The dark, silent corridor, the unseasonal cold, the artificial neatness of the place. My attention flitted from shadow to shadow, watching for any signs of movement, unsure what to expect. For something to be thrown? Lights to flicker? Those were the symptoms of a haunting in the world of the living. They didn't apply here.

Instead, I heard the sounds of flesh striking flesh. I smelt fresh blood and sweat. I could hear voices too, over grunts and the frustrated roar of a young man.

Make that two. I could smell them both.

"Come on!" a gruff voice said. "Are you fuckin' fighting or dancing? Hit him!"

The hard thud of a fist hitting muscle came from the ball room. Then came a harder thud still, followed by an abrupt whimper that quickly turned into a snarl.

"Pathetic," the older voice continued. "Both of you!"

More blows followed, the kind that didn't land from simple sparring. If the man was training the two boys, it was to do serious…

My heart sank into my stomach. There was Jorgas, stripped to his shorts, his face bloodied, body bruised between his tattoos, hair stuck fast with sweat to his scalp and murder in his eyes, which remained locked on his thinner, taller opponent… Simon.

This couldn't be. Simon was dead and rotting in the ground. I'd drained him myself! Yet here he was, as beaten and bruised as Jorgas, bleeding from his cleanshaven jaw, his slim, wiry arms up in a defensive posture as he and Jorgas exchanged blows, neither getting the upper hand. Jorgas had power, but Simon had speed. And they both had rage.

Egging them on was Donnelly, which might have surprised me had I not been staring at a dead, closeted, rich Saint Barnabas brat werewolf trying to win a fist fight with my boyfriend. I edged closer, picking up the scent of Jorgas' blood, and Simon's. I could not smell Donnelly, however. He stood away from the two combatants, dressed in the same dark clothes he'd hoped would keep him hidden the night I'd fed on him at Isobel's. He spurred Jorgas and Simon on like it was a… dog fight? I couldn't believe that neither of them had shifted into wolfen form, which would have ended, if not the fight, then certainly Donnelly within minutes.

I clenched my fists, resisting the urge to go to Jorgas' aid as Simon landed a firm blow across his cheek. Jorgas recovered quickly and flipped his opponent's body. Simon screamed as Jorgas twisted a wiry arm up behind him, but quickly adapted, using the momentum to free himself then sweep his legs under Jorgas, who went down hard before rolling out of the way of another kick. Donnelly kept chiding them both.

I threw the door open and launched myself inside, grabbing Jorgas under the arms and pulling him away from Simon, who advanced on us, hateful, yellow eyes betraying the wolf he harboured. No thick hair had shrouded Simon's twinkish body, while Jorgas remained solidly human.

The claws Simon used to slash my face however, were not. I screeched as they drew blood, dropping Jorgas and backing up to the wall. Before I could move again, Donnelly was at my throat, head abruptly tilting like a broken, grinning carnival clown. His eyes were wide and inhuman, and his breath smelt like a charred corpse.

"They ain't done in yet," he growled in an inhuman perversion of an Irish accent that couldn't possibly have been Donnelly's real voice. Of course, I wasn't looking at the sacrificed human thug, or even his spirit. The full maw of razor teeth was another hint.

'Done in?' This had to be stopped now. Daemons that fed off anger and violence were common enough. It didn't surprise me that with the sheer volume of magick that had poured through the Trust, from the Wound to Iain's return, that a daemon or two had come along for the ride. They were opportunistic little fucks. Cocky, too, though not terribly bright.

"Mmmm," the thing continued. "You smell, feel, taste like dess—"

I bared my fangs. The thing's face dropped. For a moment, it bore the same terrified expression Donnelly had when I'd fed from him at the house. Only this time, I wrapped my arms around its head, and swiftly broke its neck. The creature fell to the floor, spasming several times as it flopped around, any pretence of humanity gone.

I looked up at the two Flesh Masters, their bodies streaked with blood. Jorgas grabbed hold of Simon and threw him against the wall. He landed with a loud bang that shook the room. It couldn't possibly have come from Simon's slim build, yet it would have broken the wall if...

So that was it! On this plane, they were just two young men, fighting like brutes. But in the physical world, the essences of two fully transformed werewolves were trying to tear one another apart, and they were taking the Trust with them.

"Jor—"

Bony fingers latched around my foot before I could finish. I looked down to see Paul's handsome face, trembling and streaked with tears as he clutched at me.

"P-please?" he said. "Don't leave me. You can't leave me here!"

I hated few things more than being taken for an idiot.

"Please?" the thing sobbed again. "Reyla—"

The invocation of my name only brought me extra satisfaction when I brought my foot down hard on the abomination's skull and crushed it. Now, it was dead.

"Jorgas?" I called.

Both wolfen men ignored me, hateful yellow eyes aglow.

"Jorgas?" I said again.

"This doesn't concern you," he growled as he and Simon circled each other.

"Oh, it might," Simon sneered. "When I rip his throat out."

Jorgas knocked Simon to the floor, punching him repeatedly across the face until Simon recovered enough to dig his claws into Jorgas' shoulder. My lover's scream shook the room, with more than the hint of a canine howl.

"Stop it!" I barked. Could I intimidate them? I'd kill Simon again if I had to, but was that even possible? He was still dead. Technically, so was I. Jorgas had felt solid enough when I grabbed him and pulled him away. But then, so did Simon when he grabbed my shoulders and tried to spin me around. I pushed him back with a force that sent him sliding along the wooden floor.

His eyes glowed above a scowl that craved my blood, but he didn't get up. Jorgas made another run at him, but I caught his arm and shook my head. I felt like I was holding back an attack dog from... Hell, that's exactly what I was doing; keeping two attack dogs from tearing each other apart. At last, Simon got up again and approached us, his chest heaving, wiry muscles flexing through his arms and abdomen, teeth bared like he was ready to spit every curse he could muster at both of us. Yet his one great weapon, the wolf, remained at bay.

"You can't shift," I said, knowing I was right. "Either of you."

Jorgas growled. "I don't need to shift to take down this fuckin—"

"What are you, bloody children?" I swore, if either of them called me 'Dad…' "This little spat ends now. It's tearing the Arcadia Trust, the *real* Trust apart."

"Let me end it, then," Jorgas answered. His muscles twitched under my grip, but I held firm.

It looked as if the daemon were still egging them on. Unless it was the infection Isobel had talked about. Perhaps the daemon had been just one more aspect of it, along with the building's ruin, and the loss of supernatural powers. An ugly gumbo that had rotted the Arcadia Trust from within.

"Try it, you dumb fuck!" Simon snarled.

Of course, in life, the boys' mutual loathing had been genuine. I didn't have time for it. One or two minutes, the Shapers had said. Now, I suspected that was generous.

"If you two don't stop, we're all dead," I said plainly. "You, me, Isobel, Iain, Kelvin, probably Brett—"

Jorgas shook his head. "You're not making any sense."

"I don't have time for it to make sense! I need you to trust me."

"Trust you?" Simon broke into a cruel laugh, rocking back and forth on his feet, thumbs hooked into his shorts. "That's funny. That's real funny."

"Simon, I need—"

"*You* need? Get fucked!"

Beyond his temper, Jorgas didn't worry me. But Simon needed to understand, and if he didn't… I had to assume my powers were evaporating too. Could I even hurt him, without supernatural speed or strength? Possibly without my immortality? He would need to see reason. I doubted an apology would do.

"You're right," I said. "You have no reason to trust me. I won't tell you I'm sorry, Simon. You almost killed someone very dear to me."

"Almost? Cute. You finished me off!"

"I didn't mean—"

"You murdered me! I didn't… I didn't fucking deserve that!"

"Except for being a rapist," Jorgas snarled.

Simon turned on him, face frozen with rage. "What the fuck did you say?"

"Sarah Bateman. Ring any bells, arsehole?"

"Jorgas," I cautioned. Christ, I'd forgotten about the very charge for which Simon and his friends had let Jorgas take the fall.

"Is that what you think? Seriously?"

"You told me that Ritchie made you—"

"Lie!" Simon protested. "That's all I fucking did, was lie! I covered for them, okay? I told the cops it was Billy, that's all! I don't even know who it was. Ritchie? Gage? I don't know! I even tried to take her out of there, but she wouldn't listen to me!"

"Did you tell her what your mate was gonna do?" Jorgas growled. "What you blamed on me?"

"Simon?" I asked. The question was fair.

"I didn't know!"

"You didn't know it was a terrible idea to let a drunk teenage girl go into a room of horny boys from rich families with no sense of accountability?" I asked, turning to Jorgas. "No offence."

"None taken," he sneered.

"They were my mates! I never thought any of them would—"

"So, you're at very least an accessory."

He turned on Jorgas. "Look, I fucking hate that it happened, okay? And that I dropped you in shit! But you already killed me. What the fuck else do you want? You didn't warn her either!"

"Oh, you did not just—"

"I said stop it!" I took the little supernatural force that remained in my voice as a win. "Regrets? Apologies? We're wasting time with things we cannot undo! Yes, Simon, I did kill you, and as pointless as it may seem, I am sorry. Because I didn't do it for Jorgas, I did it in anger, for revenge. I would take that back a thousand times if I could, and give you the same chance we gave Jorgas, but—"

"Jorgas?" he asked. "You mean Billy?"

"Is there a difference?"

Jorgas shifted his shoulders back, standing straighter. "Yeah, there is."

"There is," I agreed. "And it's one you should have been allowed to make too. But I was too driven by anger and revenge to let you. For that, Simon, I am truly sorry."

His wolfen eyes pierced me with fury, though they soon faded to the gentle brown of his human form. In the sudden silence, I could hear his heart beating, muscles stretching and contracting. My apology was too little, far too late. But it was something.

"Whatever, man," he said at last, turning his back and dropping into an armchair in the corner of the room.

I heard Jorgas' heartbeat slow. Confident that he wouldn't do anything rash, I approached Simon, but he wasn't having it.

"Oh, fuck off! I don't want either of you here!"

"Reylan," Jorgas muttered. "Let's go."

"Just a moment," I said, not taking my eyes off the angry dead boy. "Where is 'here,' Simon?"

He raised his arms, mockingly, looking around the room. "Purgatory, I guess? I don't fucking know." Right. Catholic. "It's not like there's anyone to ask!"

"And you've been here since you died?"

"Since you exsanguinated me," he muttered, seeming almost amused. "I always loved that word. Now, the one time I get to use it is in reference to my own fucking death."

"What do you remember?"

He rolled his eyes as if the question bored him. "Cold fog? Bright light? All the bullshit you hear about, and… I'm here."

"In the Arcadia Trust?"

"You mean this house? Only when I felt something in it blow up. Maybe five months ago?"

"Five months?" I asked, all but ready to solve the Wound-shaped puzzle.

"Like this big explosion of energy. I tried following it, thinking just maybe it could help me find a way back."

You didn't try going home?" I asked.

"Of course I did, first thing! That's when I knew for sure I was dead. Tried hanging at a few of my favourite places, just seeing if I could get someone to notice me. I'd knock cutlery off the table, rattle doorknobs and windows, stupid shit like that. It all just reminded me I was gone. I went to my own funeral. That was a weird day."

"You were there?" I asked.

"It's not like you would have seen me. But yeah, I saw and heard everything." He shot Jorgas a contemptuous look. "Nice speech. I can't believe anyone bought that bullshit."

"What bullshit?" Jorgas answered, coming closer. "Oh, when you told your little story to the cops, I realised what a piece of shit you were. But until then? I thought you were one of the good ones, Simon. I actually really liked you."

The dead boy shifted in his chair, as if this perplexed him. "Wait … *like* liked me?"

Jorgas harrumphed. "Don't flatter yourself. I got over it real quick."

"Why didn't you say something?"

Jorgas paused. "You're not fucking serious?"

"Oh, don't worry. I got over it too. You're a dick!"

"As fascinating and disturbing as this is," I interjected. "Simon, we need to leave. Whatever's going on in this place, it's destroying the house, our powers, and maybe our lives."

He slowly rose from the chair, crossed to the centre of the room, and started laughing. It was a mirthless, hollow sound.

"Simon, I know you don't have any reason to—"

He outstretched his arms like a ringmaster. "You think I want to stay here? Do you think I'd be here if I knew how to leave?"

Jorgas turned to me. "You don't have a plan to get back?"

In truth, I'd come hoping Isobel and Iain would handle that part, which seemed increasingly foolish with each passing second. Simon laughed again. Resisting the urge to punch him myself, I turned to Jorgas. "We have to communicate with the others, somehow."

"Riiiiiight. You got ideas?"

"Simon?" I asked.

"Communicate?" he wheezed through his vindictive glee. "What do you think I've been trying to do ever since I died?"

"But you did make your presence felt," I said. "Knocked things off tables? Made noises?"

"That didn't do shit!"

"Maybe not to people who don't believe in ghosts. But Iain and Isobel are actively trying to bring us back."

"You're sure about that?" Jorgas asked. "For all we know, another six months has passed since you left and they've given up!"

"I don't think so. They said I'd be dead a minute, maybe two, tops."

"Hold on, what?"

"Yeah, what?"

Both men stared at me. Here we were, coming back to that futile 'make sense' thing again.

"We're in the layer between the living and the dead, aren't we?" I asked. "How else do you suppose I got here?"

"Shit," Simon murmured. "You really love him, don't you?"

I swallowed, not ready to feel quite so called out by a man I'd killed. "Yes. I'm sorry I took away your chance to have that too."

Simon shook his head, giving way to a hint of the sweet boy I'd taken to my bed all those months ago. How ignorant we'd both been. "Fine," he said, looking up at last. "What do you need?"

If angels could sing… though if they weren't here by now, I had a feeling they weren't showing up.

"Anything you can do," I said. "Noises? Smells?"

"I can try."

"Flickering lights?"

"Tried that once. Apparently, you can still get a shock after you're dead. Who knew?"

"We can turn them on and off, surely? Throw books around? I'm just guessing. The library on our side is a mess."

"It's gotta make sense though, right?" Jorgas asked. "They have to be able to understand us."

"Well, Iain…" I stopped mid-sentence. I had no evidence that Iain would be able to read my thoughts in here. "Do either of you know morse code?"

"Are you for real?" Jorgas muttered. "We're werewolves, not fuckin' boy scouts!"

Simon shook his head in agreement.

I looked around the room. Was it my imagination, or was the place getting darker? Perhaps my eyes. Oh shit! My enhanced eyesight and hearing… "Options, guys, now!"

The three of us looked at each other helplessly, until Jorgas looked over my shoulder. "There!"

"What?" Simon asked.

"The piano. There's one on the living side too."

"Will that work?" I asked. "Will they hear it?"

"We can try."

"Wait, you play?" Simon asked.

"Oh, use your fuckin' brains!"

"Hey," I scolded. "We're all on one team here."

Jorgas continued. "My point is, we don't need to play to make some noise."

"Okay, great, if they hear us," Simon muttered. "But how do we communicate?"

I shook my head. "First, let's let them know we're here."

With the zeal of attention-starved toddlers, the three of us began whaling on the keys. Juvenile as it was, it was an improvement on having Jorgas and Simon whaling on each other.

"Hey!" Jorgas yelled over the din. "We're here! Can you hear us?"

"Save your breath," I said, continuing to pound at the centre of the keyboard. "For all the signs we got you two were tearing each other apart, we never heard your voices."

"How do we know this is doing anything, then?"

"Wait, stop," I said, putting a hand on Jorgas' wrist and backing away from the piano. The others followed my lead, watching the keys. Would this work both ways? Nothing. Silence.

Jorgas sighed. "We tried."

"Patience," I said, squeezing his hand. "Patience."

The three of us near leaped as the piano came alive with a spirited Rachmaninoff sequence, tapped out with technical perfection.

"Who's the show-off on your side?" Simon asked, a dry smile curling his lips.

Iain? It was probably Iain.

"All right, we have a voice. Now we need a language."

Simon shrugged. "Every note's a letter of the alphabet. We could use the piano like a Ouija board."

"A through G?" I asked. "Even if we assign letters to the ebony keys, that gives us a very limited vocabulary."

"Good thing we've got registers then, eh?" Jorgas said, sitting down at the now silent piano like he was about to give a command performance. "Intervals? Chords?"

"I thought you didn't play?" Simon asked.

"I took music in school. I remember the notes."

"He remembers everything," I added, unable to keep a hint of pride from my voice as Jorgas moved through a sequence of scales.

"Major sixth, minor fourth…" he muttered as he struck at keys. "Minor second… that's the *Jaws* one."

"Getting kind of niche now," said Simon.

"Jorgas, he's right. We don't need a whole vocabulary. Stick to the ivory keys, one note for one letter."

"Makes sense," he agreed. "If they know where middle C is, they'll get it."

"Someone just played us back a concerto," Simon reminded him. "I think we're good."

"Indeed," I said. "But we should still have a way to answer yes or no questions quickly."

Jorgas hammered down a chord on a high register of the piano, then one on a low register. "That do?"

"Good enough," I agreed. "Now, let's make sure we're all speaking the same language."

"On it," Jorgas said, striking a note near the middle and moving up the keys one at a time. After twenty-six notes, he paused, then started again, repeating the same notes.

"A," Simon said. "He's starting on A."

Jorgas played the sequence a couple more times, then let our rescuers play it back. He grinned, playing the chords at opposite ends of the keyboard again. They were repeated in kind. "I think we're cooking."

"What are you going to use for 'good-bye?'" asked Simon.

"I'm hoping 'good-bye' will be us landing back in the world of the living," I said.

Simon nodded. "And me?"

Simon's fate hadn't been top of mind. "You… need to move on, surely?"

"What? 'Go into the light?'" he snorted with derision. "You think I'll be welcome?"

"Simon…" I wasn't sure if he was shaming himself as a gay man, a werewolf, or an accessory to assault. Maybe it was just good old unabsolved Catholic guilt. Given all I'd seen so far, he was more likely to meet Anubis than Saint Peter, and that was a complication his theology did not need. "I don't know how to bring you back."

"Iain's a Shaper," said Jorgas. "He's gotta know somebody into… I don't know, necromancy or something?"

I shivered, still not quite parsing this revelation about Isobel. "Yes, I'm sure he does. All right."

"All right, what?" Simon asked.

"We'll do what we can."

"You promise?" Simon asked, grabbing my hand. In life, I'd never seen him look so sincere. Gone was the cocky, playful glint of flirtation, or the sneering superiority of a brat born to privilege. Instead, he stared at me with the gaze of a man terrified of being left alone. "Even if you can't, just do something. Something that isn't this."

It was the least I owed him. "I promise. Even so, we need to contact them first."

"Hold on." Jorgas turned and played five clear notes. S-I-M-O-N. He played it again.

"What are you doing?" Simon asked.

"They can't do anything if they don't know you're here," Jorgas said before playing again. S-I-M-O-N. H-E-R-E. Once more, then we waited.

"Do they even know who I am?" Simon asked.

Good point. If only Iain and Isobel were there…

S-H-I-T, came the response.

"I'm gonna say they do," Jorgas muttered, taking up the keys again. S-I-M-O-N. S-T-U-C-K.

W-A-I-T.

We spent a good minute doing just that. Simon looked nervous. What I hadn't and couldn't promise is that he'd like their 'solution' any more than his current state.

C-E-N-T-R-E. R-O-O-M.

What did that mean?

Jorgas looked at us, just as confused. W-H-A-T.

M-I-D-D-L-E.

Middle of the house? I didn't even know where that was. Isobel's new office? The hall?

H-O-U-S-E.

Jorgas tapped a high black key I assumed now stood for a question mark.

We jumped as the middle C came down several times with force, followed by B-O-D-Y.

"Body?" Simon asked. "What? Mine?"

"Can't be," Jorgas muttered, the model of sensitivity. "We say them bury you."

"Then it's got to be you," I said, hoping 'B-O-D-Y' referred to a living one.

The middle C banged again. What the hell?

"C?" Jorgas asked. "Sea? Fuck, I better not be underwater."

"I doubt that," I said, watching the key go down again. "C… C…"

"Middle C," Simon murmured. "Not just any C, middle C. Dead centre of the keyboard."

"Middle…" I muttered. Centre! "Help me."

I led them to the centre of the room, examining the floor. It hadn't occurred to me before, but the entire surface of it seemed remarkably well-maintained. I knew with Shapers in the house, no level of restoration was impossible, but the floor looked new, or possibly replaced.

I stomped on it to try and break one of the boards, but my strength had already yielded to human limits. Simon and Jorgas exchanged a look. We needed a crowbar, or—

CRACK!

Down came their fists with enough simultaneous force to splinter the wood. It left them both with bleeding hands, but more importantly, it gave us an opening. The boards may have been new, but they weren't thick. Together, we widened the gap large enough to see the promised B-O-D-Y about four feet down. Simon's form lay frozen, perfectly preserved with neither decomposition nor odour. It seemed impossible, but then, we were not in the realm of what was possible. Another trick in Isobel's toolbox? Whatever. Simon still had a body!

The shock drained from his face as the implication hit home. "That's… that's me! I mean it's still me! It looks…"

I wished I could offer him certainty. We also still needed to find Jorgas' physical form. In the meantime, I had to confirm this was no sweet illusion. "Wait here."

The wolves watched, wide-eyed as I lowered myself with great care into the strange hovel that held Simon's body. Still no smell. No odd chill or sense that I was intruding where I had no place. It was as if the body were still alive, save for the complete absence of breath and pulse. His features were as fine as I remembered, his skin soft, hands untouched by manual labour as I took one in mine.

"Everything okay?" Jorgas called.

Had the body been Simon at all? I couldn't tell. I slumped to my knees beside it. Someone above me cried out again. It wasn't an excited or happy cry. It was anguished and full of panic, like the kind one dismisses instantly as imagined. I felt the warmth of a body beside me. I smelled its scent, warm, solid, and familiar. Most of all, it was breathing.

Jorgas' body was not the one I'd expected, but it was the one I'd hoped for. Perhaps that made me a terrible person. Perhaps Simon's body was here too. I would not lose hope for him yet.

I slipped a hand around Jorgas' shoulder and gently shook him.

"Get off, I just got to sleep." He rolled over, scowling at me, his eyes closed. How I wanted to laugh, even as he raised an arm to flop it over his head, only for his hand to graze the floorboards. "What the fuck?"

"We're under the ballroom, I think." I tried to get Simon's scent, but found nothing beyond Jorgas.

"Under?"

Good question, to which I knew we'd get no answer. "What's the last thing you remember?"

He lay still and silent, the question hanging in the air. "Simon," he said at last. "He was crying, screaming, almost."

This was not the answer I'd hoped for.

"As soon as you touched his body, the guy freaked. I went to grab you, but..."

"But what?"

"Nothing," he said. "I woke up here. Nothing else."

And Simon? There was only one way to find out. I began hammering at the boards above us.

"What are you doing?"

"I'm sorry, are we planning a romantic tumble under Bakker's floor first?" The idea tempted me in its perversity, but no. "Help me!"

It didn't take us long to draw the attention of the others, who pulled up the floorboards with ease and soon had us free. Iain took us both in a big hug that raised Patricia's eyebrow, but nothing was said about it. More hugs followed, from Brett and even Deborah. Tseng's face remained frozen in its disdain.

"Where's Kelvin?" I asked.

"I'm here, pretty boy."

I turned to face the voice directly. Now, I could see him, but no sooner had I tilted my head than he seemed to fade again.

"It'll take time for our powers to return," Isobel explained. "But they're improving. The infection, whatever it was, seems to be fading. You scared the hell out of us when you disappeared."

"Disappeared?" I asked.

"Like the house consumed… Anyway, I'm glad you're here. Good thinking with the piano, though you're lucky Deborah and Adrian came back. Neither Iain or myself have a musical bone in our bodies."

"Who was playing, then?" Jorgas asked, his eyes landing on Adrian.

The man shot back daggers. "Oh, the Asian? Sure. Cute."

"I did not say that!" Jorgas snapped back.

"More like the Entropist," Iain said with a smile. "They're usually the musicians among us. Some of them make it pretty big, like Bow… anyway, if Adrian hadn't come back, I don't think we could have opened the crack for you."

"You can thank me by never mentioning it again," Adrian muttered.

"You have my word," I said.

So, they'd come back voluntarily? Perhaps I'd underestimated the bond between the Shapers. "What about Simon?"

"Who?" Brett asked.

"What about that little shit?" Kelvin chimed in. "He's dead!"

"He's stuck there. He helped us. We need to help him." I turned to Isobel. "You're not sensing him at all?"

She shook her head. "What are you proposing?"

"I don't know, exactly. I saw his body there. It was intact, like it was waiting for him to occupy it again."

"Were did you see it?"

I turned and looked at the empty hole in the floor, then felt a hand on my shoulder.

"Reylan," came Patricia's voice, "he's long gone."

"But I saw him! He's here. His spirit is here. His body? I touched it!"

"Want us to dig him up and prove it, pretty boy?"

I'd liked Kelvin a lot better when he was visible and scared for his life.

"Reylan, you were at the funeral." Jorgas, this time, as if he hadn't seen the frozen body, same as I had. Or perhaps he hadn't. Isobel had made it perfectly clear to trust nothing in that place.

"Okay," I said, trying to believe them. "Then we find him another body."

"Why?" Kelvin asked.

"And whose body do you suggest?" asked Isobel.

Deborah shook her head. "Guys? Getting beyond fucking creepy now."

"Yeah," Brett agreed. "I'm out."

"Me too." Tseng followed them as they left the room.

"A fresh corpse?" I asked. "One that won't be missed?"

"Or recognised, I suppose?" Patricia asked. "How long do you propose we spend finding a suitable candidate? Or do you plan to keep Simon prisoner even in physical form to avoid people seeing a dead man?"

"He can go anywhere in the world," I snapped. "I… we have to! We're responsible. We killed him."

"No, pretty boy. You killed him."

"Kelvin, I swear to every god—"

"Reylan?" Iain at last broke his silence with an authority that suggested he'd crept ever so slightly into our heads to make sure his point landed. But he didn't say anything when I turned to him. He just shook his head, his face grim.

Jorgas took my arm. "Why do you care so much? Fine, we'd help him if we could, but—"

"He's still here," I said. "You understand that, don't you?"

"You're saying he's the infection?" Isobel asked. "He can't be. It's already healing. If he's still here—"

"The infection was a wrath daemon and it's dead. Simon's still in this house. We have to do *something* for him."

"Something," Patricia agreed, pushing aside a board from the ruined floor. "All right. We will do something. Look around, Reylan. You'll understand if I have more urgent priorities?"

What sort of promise was that? One no less valuable than the one I'd made to Simon, it seemed. I'd failed him. I'd failed Luca. I'd failed Colin. In a way, I'd even failed Brett. But Simon? Simon I'd failed twice.

"It's dark," came Brett's voice from somewhere behind us. I barely heard it.

"Come on," said Jorgas, squeezing my hand. "Let's go home."

CHAPTER TWENTY

A week passed before I was summoned back to the Arcadia Trust.

Jorgas and I had settled into something of the normal life I'd hoped for when we'd returned from the Wound. There were no more tricks. No bloody coffee or ghastly illusions. Dorotha made excuses to drop food off twice during the week, and neither of us complained. We slept, Jorgas ate, we made love, we watched television and went out to a play. We hit the bars a few times, enjoying the heightened energy and in my case fresh flavours of a pre-Mardi Gras Oxford Street. My taste buds travelled the world. A South African, a Canadian, a couple from Serbia, a Brazilian… each sent on their way with a blissful smile, having ticked 'threesome (or moresome) with two Aussie boys' off their list of must-do local attractions. Jorgas hadn't complained either.

Brett paid us several visits, mostly to pick up his clothes, though he stayed for a drink each time. Deborah joined him on one occasion and had seemed unusually quiet. It reminded me how little I knew about her. Now she was a full-fledged Shaper, I expected I'd know even less. Neither of them had discussed the Trust and we hadn't asked. Her Shaper studies were going well. Iain and Isobel were fine, and Brett was adapting to his new life at the Trust, sustained by a cybernetic parasite rather than my blood.

This was freedom, then?

Not once did I feel badly for Simon. Not once did I feel anything about Simon. Was that worse? A companion whose name I'd long forgotten had once told me guilt was not a sexy restraint. I agreed, which did nothing to shed it.

My invitation to the Trust came from an unlikely guest.

"Tseng," I said, standing in my front door like someone trying to fend off evangelical preachers. "This is unexpected."

"For me too," the man answered. "Can we talk?"

Hell. I offered him a seat and a glass of whiskey, which he accepted.

"I thought you were sober?" I asked, handing it to him.

"After all this?" He sipped it gratefully. "Just one though."

"I wasn't offering a top-up," I muttered, settling into the armchair opposite the couch.

Demetrius jumped up on my lap, hissing once at my visitor before he settled.

Tseng's gaze roamed my living room. "We got it pretty spot-on, didn't we?"

"Close," I admitted. "You had me fooled for… oh, let's be generous, ten minutes?"

He nodded, sipping more of his drink. "Iain calls failure the only honest teacher."

"He's not wrong." It did strike me as rather odd that Iain hadn't come to see us, or even popped in telepathically. Perhaps he was giving us our space, which seemed unusually considerate. Did it matter? Jorgas was my priority right now.

"Seriously?" Jorgas asked, spying Tseng from the kitchen.

The Shaper shifted awkwardly in his chair. "Billy, will you join us?"

Jorgas crossed to the sideboard where the glass of whiskey I'd poured for him remained. He picked it up and retreated without a word to the room that had been Brett's. A closing door and the muted sounds of a video game followed.

"I guess I deserve that."

"Right as you are, you'll forgive me if I never want to hear about what anyone 'deserves' ever again."

"I know. Perhaps it was arr… No, it was arrogant, I know."

"Mister Tseng, why are you here?"

He frowned, ignoring my question. "I was so sure. When Isobel said there was an angry spirit in the house. That it had beef with you and Jorgas, I was sure it was him! Then, if the Quinkans wouldn't punish you, I thought at least we could…"

I looked away as he angrily wiped away nascent tears. Demetrius, it seemed, was happy to stare at him for me. Little arsehole. "I'm sorry it wasn't who you were hoping for."

He wiped his face and forced a smile. "We tried contacting him a couple of times. No dice. Apparently, that's supposed to mean they're at peace and have moved on. Nice, eh? He's 'moved on.' I swear, I'm mentored by a Necromancer and it doesn't occur to him to say goodbye."

We both laughed at that, despite ourselves.

"You know Jorgas didn't mean him harm," I said. "And I made his end as quick and peaceful as I could."

He held up a hand to silence me. "Unfortunately, that's another sore spot. I can't even stay angry about it."

Time to let that one go. "So, is Isobel is your mentor, or is Iain?"

He shrugged. "Column A, column B, in as much as they're anyone's. Iain keeps things at arm's length for safety. Opposite quarter and all that. Isobel's just…"

"Distant by nature?" I nodded, slowly. "Do you know how long we've known each other?"

"I don't suppose if I asked you anything about her, you'd tell me?"

"You assume it would be true? I didn't know she was a Necromancer until a week ago."

"Then maybe you don't know her as well as you think?"

I gave him a look that suggested this was true of anyone, but didn't voice the platitude aloud.

"There's another reason I'm here," he said at last, draining his whiskey. "Patricia wants to see you, tonight."

"Tonight?" The summons didn't surprise me. Its urgency probably shouldn't have, either, nor the fact that she already had Tseng so well-trained. "Very well."

I tapped on the closed door and let Jorgas know I was going out. He didn't respond, but it seemed polite.

"There's no rush."

"You're done with your drink, aren't you?" I asked. "No offence, Mister Tseng. I think we've spent enough time in each other's company for now."

He took out his phone and summoned a car. The ride was mostly silent, despite the driver's best attempt to ask us our plans for Mardi Gras.

"We're not a couple," Tseng said, gruffly ending the well-meant interrogation.

I couldn't help it. I was starting to like him.

*   *   *

Tseng left me waiting in the hall, which was fine by me. I hadn't expected Patricia to see me right away. It gave me a chance to look over the place, which in just one week had been restored to its former glory and then some. I was about to take a self-guided tour when the scent of Iain crept in behind me. He greeted me with a warm hug and kissed my cheek and neck. "I hear they had to fetch you?"

"A curious choice for an envoy," I murmured.

"Adrian's processing things. Poor guy just had his whole worldview turned upside down. I suppose you heard his campaign's done?"

"I don't much pay attention to news." Not that this particular piece surprised me.

"Shapers wielding power in mundane politics? Oof. We're trying not to draw attention, since we're likely to have the House breathing down our necks soon as it is." He looked me over with undisguised fondness. "I'm glad you decided to come back. Any news about Simon?"

"No," I answered, gently bristling at the question.

He put his arms over my shoulders, pulling me closer. "You can't save them all. You understand that, don't you?"

"Please," I said, pushing him off. "I don't know what you're talking about."

He let me step away before stopping me. "Jorgas? Brett? You mentored Isobel into one of the most fascinating and talented Blood Shades I know, and I hear nothing but good things about Ross. Give yourself some credit, will you? You claim you don't care, Reylan, but this is who you are. You're good at it."

I thought about Ross. About Colin, Luca, Peter, and Suzette… about Elspeth and Matthias, and the Prematures, who were now what? Furniture? Light fixtures? Bookshelves? Absurd. "Not half as good as you seem to think."

"So that's it, then?" he asked, following me. "No more Arcadia Trust? Back to your life? A new boy-slash-blood bag every night? What about Jorgas? Is that enough for him?"

"I didn't say any of that."

"Good. Before you do, I want you to consider what's at your disposal now. Isobel? Deborah? Adrian?" he stepped closer, until his lips brushed mine.

"You?" I asked.

He smiled with that same seductive warmth, free of any agenda. Of course, with Iain, I knew better. "I hope you'll want me, regardless."

Fuck it. I did. As I pulled him tighter against me, I wanted nothing more. This man whose strange loyalty had saved my ageless existence more times than I cared to think about. Who'd helped me rescue Jorgas at the cost of his own mortal body. And for all the doubts I could have, of his methods and his morals, this was a man, who for me, had gone—

"To Hell, and back," he said, smiling. "And I would again, though preferably not, if it's all the same to you."

"Will you—"

"I didn't, I swear!" He laughed, raising hands to protest his innocence. "It was in your body language. On your face. I'm touched, though I'd appreciate it if you didn't tell Patricia that."

I grinned, taking his hands in mine. "You have my word."

"Speaking of, gents," a gruff voice said from somewhere behind me.

"Kelvin," I said, turning to see an apparently empty hallway. "You're looking well."

"Oh hah, bloody… Yeah, feeling pretty good too, thanks."

"Kelvin and Brett did a lot of the restorative work on the house," Iain explained, narrowing his gaze at the spot where Kelvin stood. "Despite strict doctor's orders to rest and recover."

"Which you, my newly resurrected friend, followed to the letter, I suppose?" I chided.

"Of course! I wouldn't ruin these with manual labour." He brushed my cheek with lily-soft fingertips, then leaned close to my ear. "Not until they've had a chance to do other things."

"Do you guys want a room or what?" Kelvin interrupted again. "Patricia's ready for you, when you're done."

Tempting as it was, I had a feeling such an excuse for tardiness wouldn't go down well.

The head of the Arcadia Trust sat behind her desk, determined eyes set on an electronic tablet. As I shut the door behind me, she glanced up and smiled. Actually smiled. I wondered if Patricia wasn't the one in need of rest and recovery.

"You're very chipper tonight, Sister." I sat down in one of the two plush chairs she'd set in front of the desk. A Pride Flag hung behind her. I nodded at it and raised an eyebrow.

"Hmm?" she glanced behind her. "Oh! Well, why not? It's Mardi Gras. That is, unless…"

"Pride daemons?" I asked, smiling. "Not a thing."

"Good to know. How's Jorgas?"

"Fine," I answered. "Enjoying the rest, I think."

Right. Because four all-nighters during Mardi Gras week at Blaze, Fantasy, Third Rail, and Waves, where Jorgas had complained relentlessly about the 'oldies' music, had been so restful. On the contrary, it had probably been just the distraction he needed. The fact that he hadn't shared with me what he'd seen during the Quinkans' trial, or wanted to discuss Simon at all concerned me slightly, but this was Jorgas. He would talk when he was ready.

"I'm glad to hear it."

"The place looks great." I said, leaning closer, though I knew full well that if the spirits in the house wanted to hear us, they would. "Which leads me to wonder, where's Simon?"

"Ah, yes." She put down the tablet and removed her glasses. There was exhaustion in those eyes, but of the kind that came from satisfaction, not defeat. "Simon? Anything you'd like to add?"

The display on the tablet changed to one short word in large text. *Thanks.*

"Is this a joke?" I muttered.

"Not at all. It was quite easy to keep communication going once we had a basic code. The piano got a bit cumbersome after a few days, so the Shapers devised a way to link him with this notepad directly."

"You put him in a computer?" I asked, alarmed.

"No. Simon is as you left him, unfortunately. The only way we can move him into a living being is if a person has freshly died. They also need to be roughly Simon's age and size. Mister Tseng put the odds of finding such a donor at… well, we'd have to kill someone, which Simon won't allow."

This didn't surprise me. He wasn't a bad kid, but I'd known that even as I'd drained the last of his blood.

"I made him another offer. This house might look great, but the Wound left its supernal scars. We needed someone to keep watch for anything else that might try to come through from another side. And if we do ever need to speak to the dead, having one of their own on our side can only help."

"On your side?" I asked. "How about letting him pass on?"

"That's the first thing I asked. He doesn't want it. He's afraid, and he needs to feel useful."

The more I sat considering this, the more it made sense. Simon had lived a life of parties, gossip, money, designer drugs and gods knew what. Now, he had a purpose, however lonely. Iain was right. I couldn't save them all.

"That's not why I asked you here." Patricia put her glasses back on, picking up the tablet. "I just received an encrypted email from a Blood Shade named… Loïc?"

"We're acquainted," I muttered. "Why is the House of Blood contacting you? And encrypted, how?"

"A fusion of magick and technology. Adrian made short work of it, with a little help from Giorgios. It's quite handy having the Prematures' consciousness and knowledge be part of the architecture."

That was still, and would forever remain, utterly bizarre to me.

"Behind the encryption was this." She turned the tablet to show me grainy black and white security footage of an alley one could have found in any city in Europe. Before I could ask for an explanation, she paused it, enlarging the face of a young man looking right at the camera. He was dressed in a dark jacket, a baseball cap pulled low over his eyes. But I knew those eyes. I knew the scar on his neck where his throat had been cut.

"Luca?" I fairly breathed. "Where?"

"We don't know, and this the only footage."

"Even if the Patrons released him, it'd be in some god-awful Mutilated form."

"Not necessarily. There are records of Mutilated with beauty beyond imagining, depending on the Patron who kept them."

"But he looks exactly as he did when he was human."

"Or he can control how he looks." She picked up a small, stiff white envelope with a freshly broken wax seal and handed it to me. "And he meant for us to see him."

I took the envelope with care. Inside was a drink coaster decorated with a playfully erotic, yet strangely familiar image of a woman sipping champagne out of another woman's... I *had* seen the image before, many decades ago. I traced the overdrawn lips and eyelashes with my finger, the memory of sharp cocktails, cigarette smoke and sweaty, oversexed Germans of every gender returning to me with absolute clarity.

"Berlin." I turned the coaster over.

When you're ready. C.

My former mentor preferred to keep things old school.

Patricia nodded slowly, unsurprised. "How soon can you leave?"

Ugh. I hated flying.

Another knock struck the door. Iain swept into the room, still smiling from ear to ear as he flopped down into the seat next to mine. "You told him then?"

"I did," Patricia said, standing up and crossing to the front of her desk, where she perched on its edge in front of us. "Quite the revelation."

"You think?" I asked. "How did they wind up in Berlin?"

Patricia put the pad aside and cupped her hands. "The Wound spat you out with a time displacement. God knows where they ended up when they escaped, or how many of them made it."

"But we are hopeful," Iain added. "Provided this doesn't fall into House of Magick hands. I don't think my old comrades will be too keen on suffering a former Scimitar or his friends to live."

"I'd say not," I muttered.

"Especially not now we have a four-pointed coven," Iain continued, looking at me with utmost seriousness. "Being part of one is by far that fastest way to increase one's powers."

"And perhaps the most dangerous." Patricia shook her head and put her glasses back on. "It also increases a coven's hubris, inverse to its sense of morality."

"So, more skill equals Shapers gone bad?" I asked. "That's not very reassuring."

"We just have to be extra careful," Iain continued. "But imagine what the Trust could do. You could stop worrying about the Houses altogether."

"I haven't volunteered to play any part in this!" I protested. "The Houses only tolerate the Trust because we're so far away. Now, you're putting a literal target on your backs with this… "

Iain put a hand on mine. "We're taking every precaution we can. No four-way spells. At least, not yet."

"And do you know for sure what effect this may have on Isobel, or Deborah, not to mention you, Iain? You're gifted, not immortal!"

"Think of it as a deterrent, something to keep the Houses at arm's length so Deborah and Adrian can develop their skills and Isobel can become… whatever she's becoming."

"As in a big stick to wield if the House ever decides to punish your treachery," I clarified.

"Is it treachery to follow one's heart? In the end, Patricia and I share the same goal. Co-operation between species. This way, the Arcadia Trust will be a voice to be solicited and bargained with, rather than scorned or eradicated."

I couldn't deny his argument, but… "Patricia? It's your organisation. What are your thoughts?"

"My thoughts?" she asked. "I am certainly tired of being underestimated."

A flash of silver caught the light for less than a second as a tan blur whipped across Iain's throat. My mouth fell open in horror as blood began to run from the deep gash. I lifted my wrist and punctured it, but before I could set the life-giving blood flowing, Patricia gave Iain three short stabs in the neck, ripping the last out with a brutality that sent a spray of blood across her desk. Iain gave her one last look, eyes frozen wide, then turned to me. His soft fingers brushed my hand, and he was still.

Patricia cleaned the letter opener on a white handkerchief, then put it on the table. I couldn't move, as if some force compelled me to be still instead of launching myself at her throat with unbridled rage. She got up, rounded her desk and took her seat.

"*Why?*" I made no effort to conceal the monster that fed on humanity as I screamed the word. It burned behind my eyes, longing for release, more than it had the night Patricia Bakker had first brought me to this godforsaken house against my will and taunted me with her cavalier arrogance. The walls shook. Paintings, lamps, and curtain rods rattled, along with any object that wasn't nailed down. I wanted to spray her arterial filth right across her blasted flag. There were no words. She would feel the wrath of the monster who'd witnessed her crime.

"You know why," she answered with cold detachment. "I need people who have my confidence."

"Like Tseng? Does he have your confidence?" I laughed bitterly, tearing a gash down the arm of the chair and wishing it was her wrist.

"Tseng is still finding his place in the supernatural world. Iain was all too aware of his, and has exploited it with great dexterity."

"To our advantage!"

"To your advantage, Reylan, when it suited him. Oh yes, Mister Greig was very charismatic, and a looker too. He even charmed his way into Jorgas' bed, and yours. Well, none of it was real! Iain Greig wouldn't have saved his own grandmother if it didn't suit his agenda."

How I wanted to flip the desk onto her, to pin her there and tear the flesh from her face one strip at a time like Beauvrie. But Iain had just died. Iain had… just died.

"I'm getting Isobel."

"There's no need."

"One more word," I seethed. "And she'll be resurrecting two, if I leave you in enough pieces to—"

"Be quiet!" The force of her command surpassed my own rage, setting the room's fixtures ringing again and ruffling the furls of the flag as it forced me to comply.

I could feel the blood flush through my neck, a hot rage demanding release. But my body refused the urge to lash out and strike her, just as it had in the facsimile of my house.

"You knew a very different Iain Grieg than I." Patricia looked at me with deadpan clarity, then extended a hand. "You can take my word for it, or see for yourself."

"See what?"

"What I saw when I was teaching, in the eyes of a ten-year-old boy, the memory of which returned with complete certainty as soon as I saw the man."

"Oh, this is sick!" I hissed. "Now you're blaming a child?"

"Or, you can go back to your life with memories unsullied by the truth."

Damn her 'truth.' I gripped the extended hand.

A powerful sting gripped my nerves so quickly, it left behind a bitter cold that seemed to swallow the sun in its entirety and drain the night of its warmth. I saw the streets around me, just as if I were hunting in the humid night. One after another, I watched the evil I'd felt in that dark box consume each soul it touched with no distinction between good or evil. One man burned up, screaming where he stood. Another's head and body crumpled in his clothes like sand. A woman began violently vomiting into the street until filth gave way to fetid blood and she collapsed, desiccated. A rough-looking young man whose skin had begun to blister and peel off his bones rubbed at it, screaming until he at last took out a knife to slit his own throat rather than endure the pain. One by one, they screamed and suffered, as gusts of fetid air danced to human screams. Yet, I knew they weren't dying. I knew the smell and taste of mortal death. This was something else. It was not their bodies dying, but their souls.

I released Patricia's hand with a start and leapt to my feet, waiting for some reassurance that what I'd seen had been a trick, conjured to justify the murder of my friend. But for all the tools in Patricia's war chest, she was not prone to deception.

She plucked a tissue from a small box at the corner of her desk, removed her glasses and started cleaning them. "I take no pleasure in sharing this with you. But as you can see, the political implications are not my only worry where a four-pointed coven is concerned."

"But Isobel…"

"Brought him back because she knew his powers would strengthen the coven. She also knew what he meant to you. So, until the last, I tried to dismiss the terrible promise I'd seen in that child's eyes. But I kept seeing it, each time we spoke. He'd make any excuse for a meeting, all while trying in vain to get in here." She replaced her glasses and tapped the side of her head. "It must have been driving him mad, not being able to read me. That posed a risk I could not take."

I gripped the back of the chair I'd been sitting in as she leaned closer.

"You touched the box," she continued. "You felt the truth of him, just as I have."

'The truth of him' was lying in a chair, neck ruined and bloody. Eyes once filled with intrigue and mischief now stared at me with cold, dead indifference.

"Go to Berlin," Bakker said, the sudden directive snapping me back into the room. "We'll preserve the body, if you'd like to make any last arrangements for him."

It was a cursory, even laughable attempt to smooth our relationship. But I was not in the mood for laughing.

"Please, Reylan, I'm very tired." She gestured to the door.

Refusing to look her in the eye, I left the body of my most complicated lover for the last time.

CHAPTER TWENTY-ONE

I shut the front door quietly and let the gloomy silence settle around me. I could have argued or fought with Patricia, but to what end? For a man who, deep down, I trusted as little as she did?

A man who'd kept Brett alive in his time of greatest need.

A man who'd abandoned him to madness to prove a point.

One who'd saved my life more than once.

One in a pact with a devil who would put all our lives in danger with his proposed super-coven.

One I'd watched die, moments after he'd embraced me.

Jorgas was already in bed, a dark lump under the covers. I stripped off my clothes and joined him. Much as I wanted to hold him close, it seemed cruel to wake him just to push my body against his in the summer heat.

I rolled over and tried to quiet my thoughts. Gentle hands brushed my back, followed by an arm that snaked around my hips, and a body whose presence calmed my rapidly beating heart.

"You don't believe those things she said about me, do you?" Iain whispered.

I pushed back against his cool skin as sleep took me.

"No," I said, "and I never will."

Also in *The Arcadia Trust* series:

THE BEAST WITHOUT

Reylan is everything a Sydney vampire aspires to be: wealthy, handsome and independent, carefully feeding off companions plucked from the gay bars of Oxford Street.

When one of those companions is killed by Jorgas, a hot-headed young werewolf prowling his streets, Reylan reluctantly puts his cherished lifestyle of blood and boys on hold to help a mysterious alliance of supernatural beings track down the beast. It can't be that hard…not when Jorgas keeps coming after him.

But there's more to this werewolf than a body count and a bad attitude. As their relationship grows deeper and more twisted, Reylan tastes Jorgas's blood, reawakening desires the vampire had thought long dead. And what evolves between them may be far more dangerous than some rival predator in the dark…

THE ORCHARD OF FLESH

Reylan's last assignment for The Arcadia Trust brought a rebellious human servant under his roof, and a volatile werewolf lover named Jorgas into his bed, leaving the self-reliant Blood Shade—known to the outside world as vampires—in no hurry to risk his immortality for them again.

But when a new terror starts disappearing humans from a bad part of town, Reylan must do everything in his power to keep Sydney's supernatural factions from the brink of war. Having an ambitious, meddlesome human in the mix is only going to make things worse…especially when that human is Jorgas's father.

Reylan will need all his determination and cunning to keep the peace under his roof, between the night's power brokers, and in his lover's troubled heart.

SINS OF THE SON

Abandoned by his werewolf lover, the only thing Reylan wants is to return to his vampire life of blood and beautiful boys. It's a solid plan, until his first meal as a single man tries to kill him.

Hoping to free his young would-be assassin from the religious zealots that sent him, Reylan enlists the help of Iain Grieg, a charismatic priest with unsettling knowledge of the night's secrets.

Surrounded by conflicting agendas and an army fuelled by hate, Reylan fights to secure his future, if he can only trust the mysterious priest and bury the ghosts of the past.

Also by Christian Baines:

MY CAT'S GUIDE TO ONLINE DATING

A hook-up gone bad can be purrder.

Fresh from a breakup, deeply closeted freshman Zach jumps at the chance to housesit his family home and enjoy a long, horny summer free of both his ex and his religious parents. But when an old enemy turned hot hookup falls to his death, Zach turns to the only true friend he's ever known—his cat, Grace Jones.

With the dead man's phone and a knack for texting, she promises Zach help, for a price that will satisfy both their appetites. Does it matter if Grace Jones' powers draw on something far more ancient and sinister than a cell phone?

"Get laid, Zachary. Get laid."

Each new hook-up brings Zach darkly humorous discoveries about life, love, sex, and his own desires. But Zach knows it's only a matter of time before someone discovers his secret. Can he rely on his feline protector, or is he trapped in a hungry devil's bargain?

PUPPET BOY

A school in turmoil over its senior play, a sly career as a teenage gigolo, an unpredictable girlfriend with damage of her own, and a dangerous housebreaker tied up downstairs. Any of these would make a great plot for budding filmmaker Eric's first movie. Unfortunately, they're his real life. When Julien, a handsome wannabe actor, transfers to Eric's class, he's a distraction, a rival, and one complication too many. Yet

Eric can't stop thinking about him. Helped by Eric's girlfriend, Mary, they embark on a project that dangerously crosses the line between filmmaking and reality. As the boys become close, Eric soon wants to cross other lines entirely. Does Julien feel the same way, or is Eric being used on the gleefully twisted path to fame?

SKIN

Kyle, a young newcomer to New Orleans, is haunted by the memory of his first lover, brutally murdered just outside the French Quarter.

Marc, a young Quarter hustler, is haunted by an eccentric spirit that shares his dreams, and by the handsome but vicious lover who shares his bed.

When the barrier between these men comes down, it will prove thinner than the veil between the living and the dead…or between justice and revenge.